Inside the Locked Box

———

INSIDE *the* LOCKED BOX

a novel

Ruth E. Weiner

INSIDE THE
LOCKED BOX

———

PART ONE

Agnes

Daddy throws a duffel and a backpack onto my bed—bags I've never seen.

"Clothes and food in the backpack. Letter blocks in the duffel, just the big ones that I carved." He jabs a bony finger at me.

"Now, Agnes. No questions. Just do it."

No questions? Seriously? I swallow hard and push back. "Where are we going? Why so fast? And is Ivy going too? She hasn't been home in three days. She doesn't care if I'm alive or dead."

Ivy is the worst excuse for a mother on the planet. I can't even call her Mother. It's Ivy. Always Ivy.

"What's going on, Daddy?"

"Nothing you need to worry about."

I cross my arms. "I'm fourteen. Old enough to know when something's wrong. So tell me."

"You're not going to like it."

I don't like a lot of things, but I wait. I'm good at waiting.

Finally he snaps, "Vixen is hell-bent on vengeance. She thinks Ivy is honing in on her territory." His snaggletooth clicks like a time bomb. "Vixen's out to get her."

My throat goes dry. "You mean like murder? Like in *Killing Mr. Griffin* or *Carrie*?"

His face darkens and the scar between his eyebrows gets red and blotchy. "This is real life, Agnes. Not one of your books. Here's the truth: Ivy finds runaway kids. She gives them to Squid. And Squid...finds uses for them."

Wait. What? "So Vixen wants the kids for Squid, and Ivy's in her way?"

"That about sums it up."

The names terrify me—Vixen, Squid. "Can't Ivy just... disappear? Then maybe you and I can stay here, together?"

Daddy leans in. I can taste the beer and cigarettes on his breath. "Listen, Agnes. We're in big trouble. So pack your gear and stop arguing."

We? "It's Ivy who's the troublemaker. Why do you and I have to leave?"

Daddy raises an eyebrow, his lips tightening like he's about to chew me out. Instead, he stomps to the back of the attic, pries up the floorboards, and hauls out the silver suitcase. I've seen it before—after a drug buy, or when he's settling up with Squid. His hands shake as he thrusts it at me.

"Hold on to this. Let no one take it." He points to my scarf. "And cover those birthmarks on your neck. Promise me, Agnes."

I don't want to promise. I don't want the duffel, or the suitcase, or the scarf. With Vixen roaming the streets of Hull, hunting for Ivy, I'd rather stay put. But he says we're going. I have no choice but to obey.

My hands move like they don't belong to me, but my eyes drift to my books—*Little Women*, *The Outsiders*, *The Joy Luck Club*, *Flowers in the Attic*, my dictionary, my thesaurus, my atlas. My daily escapes.

"Forget the books. They're too heavy."

My books howl in protest. Every word, every letter cries out.

Daddy doesn't understand that leaving means abandoning my entire world.

I'm used to my attic room, the holes in the floorboards I skip over, the webs in the eaves that look like lace, the patched ceiling like a checkerboard. Even though I'm shut in here most of the time, waiting for the latch to unlock, the space is mine.

The alphabet runs across walls, beams, corners—letters of every size and color. I trace them with my finger, slow, like greeting old friends. The walls seem to breathe warmer when I do.

"Agnes!" he wails. "We gotta get out of here before Vixen finds us."

V-I-X-E-N. The letters rip free from the word, twisting in the air like they've grown teeth. The V lunges first, drilling into me—knocking the wind out of me. I slam my mind off to the other letters or I'll suffocate. Vixen isn't just an insane banshee monster; she's hell bent on devouring Daddy and me.

I saw her once through the floorboards—spiked white hair and black lips. She was screeching and plucking out the hairs in Daddy's eyelashes and carving a line between his eyebrows until blood dripped down his face. He said he'd cut himself shaving. Did he think I was blind?

Daddy drops onto my bed like a broken-down clown—puffy eyes, turned down lips, his snaggletooth jutting. "Listen carefully, Agnes. I've never kidnapped kids. I swear. This is all on Ivy. But she's my wife and your mother and we have to protect her."

Protect her? From Vixen and Squid, and Sergeant Stone too? I saw that butt-faced cop press a gun into Ivy's stomach. I was hiding in the bushes when Ivy came out of the basement carrying a girl — Suzanne, she called her. She was wrapped in a blanket, her blonde hair spilling out one side and her toes sticking up on the other. Daddy said Stone was taking her to a doctor.

I wanted to believe him. I did. I wasn't blind. I just didn't want to see. My stomach churns just remembering.

And the night at the docks—Stone lifting a different girl onto Squid's boat. Jazmin. I was there, out of sight. Ivy passed out in the van while I crept off and watched. I thought I saw my father too, but he swore he was never there.

Was he telling the truth?

"So where's Ivy now and does she know what we're doing?"

"Ivy will catch up with us."

I don't care about Ivy. She's nothing like the mothers I read about. Ma Ingalls would've fought a bear for her girls. Heidi's mom carried her up a mountain. Ivy can't lift her head off the couch.

"I'll explain it all after we're out of here," Daddy says, his voice softening for just a second. "I have a few loose ends to clean up before we head for the horizon. Stay put!"

Head for the horizon? All I see from my portal window is water and sky. We won't survive out there.

Barreling down the ladder, Daddy doesn't stop to lock the door.

I finish packing, then sit. The letters W–I–Z–Z grow before my eyes and blot everything else out. W–I–Z–Z. Wizz—that's what everyone calls my father.

When he's Daddy, his letters balloon out, round and playful, like puppies tumbling over each other. Like he's full of good. Like he loves me.

But when he's Wizz, the Z's take over. They zig and zag so fast they cut him up, yanking him around like he's on strings. I can't catch him. I can't hold him still. The Z's won't let me.

So now I'm here with my duffel and my backpack and the silver suitcase...waiting. I'm always waiting. That's what I do. Daddy's a carpenter, a whittler. He made me miniature blocks when I was six and taught me how to put my letters together to form words. That got me reading and that's how the time passes. And there's a lot of it when Wizz forgets me and Ivy can't be bothered.

When I turned seven, he bought me paints and I covered the walls with letters in all shapes and sizes. Daddy didn't mind bringing me more supplies so that now as I look around, there's hardly a bare space.

I listen for house sounds. My father is scrambling around in the kitchen, probably packing food. No one has shopped in weeks, so I'm figuring there's only crackers and peanut butter, maybe a few sodas. Mostly there's beer and vodka. I've tasted both and they make my mouth sour. Maybe that's why Daddy smells like my socks. They don't get washed either.

Then I hear footsteps on the front porch. I go to my portal to see who's there and catch a glimpse of black—a coat? boots? shadows in the dim light?

The door bangs shut. "Where is she, Wizz?" screeches a voice filled with poisonous thorns.

It's Vixen! Here, in the house. Right this minute.

I want to scream Daddy, LEAVE! Get out while you can. I'll be all right. She doesn't know I'm alive. But I've been warned over and over and over again, never ever make a sound when people are in the house. So I smash my lips together.

Then I hear my father stomp toward the woman.

"I don't know where Ivy is," he says. "Beats me."

"Gladly," Vixen cackles—then I hear a heavy thud.

"Get off me, you psycho!" my father yells.

What's going on? Daddy, are you hurt? What can I do? His words pound through my head: *Stay put.*

I move closer to the ladder to hear better.

There's shuffling. A struggle. Grunts. Feet scraping.

Then the front door slams open again. "Fuckheads. I'm home."

It's Ivy. I need to warn her, but I know not to make a sound. I pray she turns around. Leaves. Runs. Vixen is here to kill you.

"You! Bitch!" Vixen screeches—sharp, high-pitched and not human. "Your time is up."

A chair scrapes. Something crashes against a wall and the house shudders.

"Ivy!" Daddy cries out.

A scuffle. Heavy, brutal sounds. A scream—Daddy's—shoots up through the floorboards.

No—no, no, no. Daddy. I'm coming downstairs. I'll save you. I'll even save Ivy.

"You killed her, you lunatic!" Daddy's voice breaks like glass.

My mother is dead? How can that be? I've wished for that, prayed for it, begged for it a hundred times. No way. She's too mean to be dead. It can't be true.

Vixen's voice slices the air—sudden and sharp, like an S. "You're next, Wizz. Your bitch wife steals my kids, but you steal my money. Where's the stash? I hear it's in the walls."

"There's nothing here," he chokes out.

I hear another thud and moaning.

No. No. No. This isn't happening.

Stay calm.

C-A-L-M. I whisper it like a spell and the letters float up around me. Like a hug, like shoulders to lean on. They let me breathe and then breathe again.

"There are secrets here," Vixen hisses. "I feel them. I will find them."

Then the house explodes. Glass shatters. Wood splits. Walls crack like knuckles.

I crawl into a corner and press my hands over my ears.

Footsteps are on the stairs. Vixen's on the second floor.

Whack.

Whack.

Whack.

If she finds me, she'll bring me to Squid. He'll steal me away and I'll vanish like Suzanne and Jazmin.

The sound moves into the back room. She's near my ladder! My latch is unlocked. She'll come up here and kill me like she killed Ivy. Or she'll give me to Squid and I'll be his slave, even if

I'm not young and blond and pretty. I curl into a ball, like an O, hoping its armor will keep me safe.

Then there's more noise on the deck. The front door bangs open. A gravelly voice roars, "Why didn't you wait? What a goddamn mess."

It's Sergeant Stone. His voice is like rusted metal. My skin crawls.

I hear Vixen on the stairs, moving away from the closet, away from the ladder. I hold my breath. Am I safe?

"Looky, looky, who's finally here. About time," Vixen hisses.

Then I hear whispering. Sharp and quick. I can't catch the words.

"I'll write this up as a murder-suicide," Stone says loud and clear.

My blood turns cold.

Vixen laughs. A sick, wet sound. "That piece of shit is still alive."

Daddy's still breathing. I can still save him. My heart jumps and then drops—what if going downstairs kills us both?

"Wrap Wizz in the tarp. Make sure he can breathe," she says. "I need answers from the fucker."

What answers? About the stash? About the kidnappings? What else will she do to him?

Dragging sounds. Grunts. Thudding feet. On the deck. On the stairs.

I run to the portal, but it's too dark to see anything. I strain my ears, but all I hear are the ocean's waves, no footsteps, no hissing, no Daddy.

Then—

Silence throughout the house.

Not peace. Not calm.

A silence so big it hurts.

I wait. Frozen. Listening.

A car starts. Drives off.

Still—I wait.

The quiet presses down on me like a lid.

Something cracks open inside me.

Ivy might be dead, but Daddy's still alive.

I glance around the attic. My painted letters. My beloved books. The stars blinking through the portal window. What once felt safe now feels like a trap.

I hear Daddy's words, again. *Head for the horizon.* Can I really run? Knowing they're out there? Where would I go? F Street has been violated. Just look at the letter—half its head is cut off. But all the streets in this town are named for letters; that has to mean something. Maybe A Street—my special letter—holds answers? I'm not dumb. I pay attention. I know how to survive. I've lived in this space for ten long years practically by myself. I can do this. I have to.

I grab the backpack, the duffel, and the silver suitcase. I climb down the ladder. Every step creaks like a scream.

At the bottom, I freeze. It's insanely quiet. Too quiet.

I hear footsteps. Slow. Creeping.

I crouch low and make myself invisible. Then I hear a voice I know. It's Gregg.

"Agnes?"

Gregg is here—my friend Gregg. He's on the landing. But why? Did my father send him? To rescue me?

"I'm here," I call softly. I reach up and latch the attic shut, locking away my painted walls, my alphabet, and my miniature blocks.

They cry out—"*Don't leave us.*"

I hear them. I feel them.

But I don't answer.

I'm not ready, but what choice do I have?

I leave my childhood behind.

Gregg

Gregg steps out of the shadows on the second floor landing.

"Gregg, something horrible happened," I whimper.

His eyes dart over his shoulder. "Thank God, Agnes. You're all right."

"It's awful," I cry. "Vixen killed Ivy and hurt my father."

"Shh, shh, Sweet Pea. You're not safe. We have to go—right now."

"But Daddy. He needs me. We have to go after them. Vixen and Sergeant Stone. They were here. They did this. They have to be stopped."

Gregg wraps an arm around my shoulder. I sink into him, comforted by the weight of his soft belly and wide chest. He sighs, and I take a deep breath, trying to calm the trembling in my body.

"We'll talk later," he says, low and fast, steering me down the stairs and through the kitchen.

From the corner of my eye, I get a quick look into the living room. The couch is slashed, its stuffing spilling all over the room. Blood stains the walls, the floor, the furniture.

"Don't look," Gregg says.

I let him guide me through the back door.

Outside, the world stretches dark and quiet, the ocean barely visible in the distance. How can the earth still spin? Just an hour ago, Daddy and I had a plan—to escape together. Now, everything's upside down.

At Gregg's van, I scramble into the passenger seat. My knees knock. My breath fogs the glass. I don't want to think. I just want to sit here and let Gregg help me.

The door slams. Tires squeal. We speed off, the marshes blur by, until Gregg pulls onto the side of the road. Hull is gone. The alphabet streets are gone. The place where I could find Daddy—and save him—is gone.

"Agnes," he says, turning toward me, his voice strained. "Are you okay?"

"My father made me promise not to come downstairs. There was nothing I could do to stop them."

My teeth chatter. I am so so cold.

"I did nothing but listen."

"It's not your fault," Gregg dabs my face with a balled-up tissue.

"Then why did this happen?"

"Because your parents took things that weren't theirs."

"Like what?" I ask, desperate for Gregg to tell me my father wasn't anything like Stone and Vixen.

"I don't know." Gregg shrugs. His chest jiggles with the movement.

I slump, every bone in my body rubbery and trembling. "There was a crash when Ivy fell. Then Daddy dropped. Sergeant Stone came in, yelling. Vixen said she had ways to make Daddy talk." I grip Gregg's sleeve. "He's still alive. Can we save him? Please?"

Gregg's face goes all blotchy. "I'll find Wizz. I swear. I'll fix this. I'll bring him back to you."

"Promise?"

"I promise."

Gregg pulls me into him. He pats my back, and strokes my hair.

"Shhh. Shhh. Those people? They'll kill you for a penny. Forget what you saw, what you heard." He cradles my face. "I'll keep you safe."

Can I believe him? He's been my friend. My teacher. My only connection to the outside. I hold the suitcase tight to my chest, like I'm hugging Daddy.

"What's in there?" Gregg flips on a dome light and reaches for the suitcase.

"No!" I jerk back, holding it closer. "It's mine!"

"Agnes, Sweetie. Maybe it has the answers we need."

Before I can stop him, he yanks it away.

"Let's have a little look." He pops the lock. Inside are bags of powder, pills, and crushed leaves. Gregg lines his palm with white powder and sniffs it hard.

"Gregg?" my voice wobbles. "What are you doing?"

He doesn't answer. His hands tear through the suitcase like he's digging for gold.

"What about the duffel?" he asks, not looking at me. "What's in it?"

"My letter blocks. My clothes."

Gregg lets out a sharp laugh. "Those dumb blocks. Seriously?"

His words hit hard. He knows how I treasure my blocks. I talk about them all the time. Daddy carved them for me. Each letter speaks to me. Each letter is my friend.

Gregg gives a quick glance at the duffel but doesn't bother with it. It isn't what he wants. I don't want him touching my blocks anyway or the suitcase, but it's too late for that.

He kills the light and throws the van into gear. "Rest now, Agnes. I'm taking you somewhere safe."

"Only if you give me back the suitcase. I promised Daddy I would keep it safe."

Gregg tosses it toward me and I draw it into my lap.

We speed along. Then the van jolts—the tires hit a dirt road.

The shocks rattle my bones and the horrors of the night come smashing back.

"Where are we? Where are you taking me?"

"World's End," he says. "A spit of land jutting into the sea where no one will look for you."

"Why do I have to hide?" I ask, my voice barely there.

"Because you know too much."

"But no one knows me. Only you."

"Agnes, Sweet Pea, that's the best part." He smiles, but it doesn't reach his eyes.

He's like the wolves in Jack London's books—eyes sharp, steady, almost friendly...but I can feel danger coiled underneath. When will he strike?

"I'll protect you until I can find out what happened tonight. Then we'll head for the horizon together."

Horizon. That's a Daddy word. He was always looking ahead—another high, another deal, another wood project. Maybe that's why he never treated me like I was right there in front of him. I was put away for safekeeping, to be taken out later. When I asked about leaving the attic, he'd get that faraway look, though maybe that was just the pot.

He and Gregg used to sit on the porch, talking and smoking. I'd listen from my portal window. Back and forth, like the tide. I caught bits: President Reagan. Contra Wars. Contraband. War on drugs. They'd laugh at that last one.

And now, Daddy's left me a suitcase full of drugs. Was that his next stop on the horizon?

Gregg flips on the interior light. The back of the van glows warm and strange—wooden shelves, fresh sawdust, a smell like someone's been building something special. It smells like Daddy after he's cleaned up and presentable. He built secrets too. All over the house. All over the yard.

"Did my father make this?"

Gregg nods. "Wizz was back there for days. I think he wanted to use my van as a get away vehicle."

"So you knew we were leaving?"

Even before I knew?

"I did, but I never predicted tonight." Gregg sighs, rubbing his face. "It's been a long day. Let's sort this out tomorrow."

He's right. I need to sleep and when I wake up this whole nightmare will be over.

I climb into the back. It smells like pizza and pickles. Weird and kind of gross. Does Gregg live in here?

He grunts, hauls himself out of the driver's seat, then squeezes into the back with me. I make room for him, but I shift my backpack and duffel behind me so he won't take them.

"The suitcase, Gregg." My voice is small, but steady. "My father said it was mine and I shouldn't let anyone else have it."

Gregg strokes my hair.

I pull away. My skin crawls. I don't like being touched. I'm not used to it, and Gregg's hands are more than I can handle.

Gregg leans against the front seats. "If Vixen wants what's in here, you're in danger. Besides, I'm here now, and Wizz would trust my judgment."

My father and Gregg *were* buddies. But Daddy set out rules for him and one was no touching. Ever. Gregg knows that. It's creepy when Gregg's hands find my face, and his fingers comb through my hair.

Then, like nothing's happened, Gregg reaches between the seats and brings out a bag of chips and a thermos. "Here, this will perk you up."

He hands me the bottle. It smells like peaches and plums. I take a sip. Sweet, like soda pop.

Gregg unwraps a brownie from a foil package. He takes a large bite. "Try some."

The brownie tastes bitter and earthy—maybe it has pot in

it?—but I'm hungry, so I keep chewing and drinking. After a few minutes, my head feels floaty, like it's not part of me anymore. I lie on my back, scissoring my arms and legs.

I look like an X, all spread out in this little box of a space. "I'm an X," I say proudly.

Gregg chuckles. "A what?"

"An X. You know, the letter X."

"If you're an X, what am I?" Gregg asks, popping a pill, and then two more.

"You're my G." I draw the letter in the air, looping it wide, and I laugh. The line in the middle wobbles. "It looks like it's sticking its tongue out at me."

Gregg's tongue darts out, sprinkled with brownie and potato chip crumbs. He licks my nose. "Yum."

I giggle, thinking how Daddy used to lick my nose and pretend to spit me out. It was safe then. But Gregg doing it makes my stomach flip. "I'm not very tasty," I say.

I snap my legs shut and become a Y. Arms out, legs together.

"What's going to happen to me?" I whisper, my voice small against the weight of him.

"I'll take care of you," he murmurs.

Gregg circles my body, his belly pressing gently against my back. I'm curled inside him, like a C, and he's protecting me. Maybe this day will end with some peace? Maybe I'll sleep and wake up and this will all be a dream.

Then I feel rubbing against my head. It's his nose sniffing my hair. It hasn't been washed in a week—I bet it smells sour. But he doesn't care. His nose keeps circling, like I'm some kind of fruit.

Is this a sex thing? Daddy always warned me about sex things. He said I had to stay pure for him. But this feels kinda good, kinda like I'm his pet. So maybe it's not sex.

Daddy read *Romeo and Juliet* to me and they had a sex thing. And we read Judy Blume together. Until I was twelve, Daddy would sometimes lie down with me at bedtime and I'd ask him questions, but he just shrugged and told me about a puzzle box he was building.

"Life's like a box, Agnes," he said. "Sometimes you have to look carefully, try different angles, and be patient before the answers come."

I think about that a lot, and the letters blow up in front of me. B-O-X, big as my attic room.

The B bumps against me, whispering a secret.

The O rolls over me. I get all flat and quiet.

Then the X swoops in, all angles, showing I can feel many things at once and still keep them apart.

All that floats through my head as I lie in the van with Gregg wrapped around me. He shifts, and I shift too. His arms come closer, holding me like I might float away. Maybe this is how a baby feels—safe and warm, tucked inside something bigger. Maybe nothing bad can find me here. No Vixens, no Ivys, no stabbing V's. No chaos sneaking in. Just quiet. Just stillness.

Then I feel something hard press against me. Is this part of Gregg's body? I inch away, not sure if this is a good thing or a bad thing. He doesn't seem to care what I think because his hold gets stronger.

"You're all I've ever wanted, Agnes. Wizz was going to take you away, but not now. Not now. Not now." He whispers it over and over again, like we're back in our private classroom on F Street and he wants me to memorize a refrain.

I feel him rub his body against mine. No, this doesn't feel good. Not at all. I try to move, but he holds me so tight, I feel like my bones are being crushed.

"Gregg, stop it. You're hurting me. Let go."

I squirm away, and I'm shouting at him now. "I don't like what you're doing!" But he pins my arms and clamps his hand over my mouth.

"Get away from me. Now! Please!" But the words come out muffled. I try biting his hand, but he's pushing and shoving his body into my backside. His breath is hot and angry in my ear. He grunts with every move.

"Stop! Just stop!" But he isn't listening.

Then something wet seeps through my jeans.

For a second, I think maybe he peed on me—but it feels worse than that, wrong, just plain wrong. I want to throw up. What did he do?

I lie silent, trying to figure out where my body ends. Trying to tell if I'm still whole. I shrink into myself, embarrassed, like I've done something wrong. I want to disappear, but my skin won't let me.

"Gregg?"

No answer.

"Gregg, I don't like this. Let go of me. I want to go home."

"You have no home, Agnes. I'm your home."

"No, no. That's not true. Daddy is still alive. Where he is, I'm still me. Still Agnes. Still his little girl. I need to find my father."

Like magic, moonlight zigzags through the slats in the back windows—sharp and jagged, like the Z's in Wizz. It's Daddy. Telling me something important. Like the back of the van isn't a place of pain. It's a place he created and it will keep me safe. But I'm suffocating here.

I can't move, because Gregg's arms surround me. Even though I want to get out of here, I'm so so tired and my head spins and all I see are the letters S-L-E-E-P—huge and glowing until they pull me under.

When I wake, it's still dark. I don't move. I listen. I wait for his breathing to slow so I can slip away. When he rolls to the side, I bolt for the back doors, but I'm not fast enough. His hand clamps around my leg.

"Let go of me. You're not the person I thought you were. I

trusted you. I believed you were my friend. What kind of person does this? I hate you."

His mouth droops so far down I think it might fall right into his chin. Focus, Agnes. Focus. I've escaped before—three times from the attic until Ivy dragged me back. I can do it again. Gregg's not my friend. Not anymore.

I slam my heel into his knee. His grip loosens—just enough for me to see a red V carved deep into his wrist. Vixen did that, I'm sure of it. Does that mean Gregg was part of Vixen's plan? Was he in on it? Panic rips through me like a tidal wave.

I look up to see Gregg's face turn gray and ashen. "Agnes, I'm sorry. I don't know what came over me. I'll make it up to you." His voice softens. "This isn't how it was supposed to be."

"Then let me go," I say, my heart pounding. "Please, Gregg."

His head droops. "I was just trying to get the stash. Wizz's stash."

I go still. "My father's stash? How do you know about that? I never told you."

"You did, Agnes," he says. "You just don't remember."

Then I do.

It happened months ago, after Vixen carved the V between Daddy's eyebrows. Ivy and my father weren't in the house. I sat on the stairs leading to the second floor and waited for them to come home. Gregg huffed in, lugging a greasy-smelling bag—fries, garlic, something sour. He stopped short when he saw me. "This is a first," he said, surprised to see me downstairs alone.

I ran to him. "Do you know an ugly white-haired woman who wears black lipstick and caws like a crow?"

"Slow down," Gregg said, leaning in like he was inhaling me.

"The witchy woman. Her name is Vixen," I blurted.

Gregg's jowls shook, hard, like the name created tremors.

"She hurt my father and told him to get Ivy under control. I'm afraid she's going to kill them."

"What did Wizz say?"

"He told me not to worry, that he has insurance."

"Like All State or Prudential? Did he say that to her?"

"No, to me! If I tell you, you have to promise to keep it secret."

"You can trust me," Gregg said, his eyes soft and soothing.

T–R–U–S–T. The T's twirled me around and I spun like a top. But Gregg was my friend, so the T's settled into a post that I could lean against.

"My father hides money and other stuff." I loved how Gregg was listening to me. His eyes had grown into giant O's.

"That's smart of him. Is it in a safe place?"

"He makes fake cabinets all over the house and puts stuff inside them." I opened one of the wooden doors above the sink and removed a panel. Behind it was a thin briefcase.

Gregg leaned against the counter with his elbows; his enormous rear stuck out into space, his backside wiggling like a dog. "Are there hiding places all over the house?"

I remember thinking I had said too much. I closed the cabinet and stopped talking. I didn't mention the suitcase that was hidden in the attic under the floorboards, or the closets inside closets, or the hidey-hole in the basement, or the structure Daddy was build-ing in the backyard.

"Don't worry, Agnes, my little Wafer. Nothing's going to happen to Wizz or his hidden money." He put his beefy arms around my shoulders. "I bet that's exactly what Wizz said."

I'd trusted Gregg then, but now my stomach seizes with his touch. He was involved. Somehow. Now I'm the one who has to pay.

Again, he reaches for the suitcase—for the drugs inside. It's like the bags are calling his name. He opens the suitcase slowly—like he's opening a treasure chest—and pulls out the powder.

I watch as Gregg leans in and snorts, loud and deep. He pulls back and blinks—slow and heavy. Like something just cracked inside his brain.

"Take the suitcase," I say quickly, my voice catching. "Take it all. I don't want it. It's yours."

I hope that calms him down.

But it doesn't.

Instead, his eyes go strange. His pupils enlarge, his mouth twitches. He starts to smile, but it's crooked, like something's mis-wired.

"It's mine," he says, his voice like mud. "All of it. Always was." He locks eyes with me, unblinking. "And you're mine, too."

No, no, no. I'm not. I never was. I want to spit at him, shove the words right down his throat, but my voice feels stuck somewhere between my ribs and my teeth.

Then his knee slams into my chest.

I fold over, choking for air. My ribs ache, my lungs scream. I try to scramble away, but his hand catches my ankle.

"Stop!" I try to say, but the word comes out as a gasp, like air leaking from a balloon.

He tugs a rope from a box.

Did he bring it for me? Did he plan this? How long has he been waiting? Weeks? Months? My mind races ahead of my body, throwing up useless questions like roadblocks when what I need is a door.

I shake my head, but he's too fast.

He covers my mouth with tape, pressing hard. My screams vanish into silence. I repeat the only thing that keeps me sane— the alphabet—backward, forward, again and again, silently in my mind. It's my lifeline.

My wrists burn where the rope rubs raw. I twist them anyway, harder, trying to slip free. My teeth gnash against the gag, frantic, animal-like, as if I could chew through it. My brain screams fight, fight, fight, but my body is pinned. I scream inside my throat, a sound no one will hear, a sound that feels like it's eating me from the inside out.

Then the van doors slam open and Gregg drags me outside.

Fog rises off the mossy floor of a wooded area. The sun peeks over the horizon. There's still an outside! There's a chance to escape.

I make my move. I duck under his arm, and ram the top of my head into his chin with all my strength. He staggers back, rubbing his jaw, breathing hard but already regaining his footing.

I don't wait to see what he'll do next. My eyes search for anything sharp, anything to save myself.

Scream! Run! Someone! Anyone! Help!

But the gag swallows all sound.

Gregg charges forward. His backhand cracks across my face, whipping my head to the side. My knees buckle, and I hit the dirt hard.

"You'll get used to me," he growls, his voice thundering through the woods. "You have no one else."

I lie still, dizzy from the impact. I wait for the next blow. But it doesn't come.

Instead, I hear his breath—ragged, like he's winded. Something shifts. The anger in his voice fades.

Why is he quieter now? What's happening? My brain can't keep up. First rage, now pity? It doesn't make sense. Nothing makes sense.

I try to focus, try to think past the fear gnawing at me. No one else. . .Is that true? Am I really alone here? I have to be strong. But everything in me just wants to curl up and disappear.

Stay calm. Breathe. I will be strong. He will not win.

Gregg drags me to a clearing and ties me to a tree. I struggle, thrashing, but the ropes hold fast.

"I don't want to hurt you, Agnes. I really don't. But you have to stay quiet. Just for a little while. Let me handle things in Hull—and when I come back, I'll make it right. You'll see."

All I see is a fat man who lied to me. Who hurt me. I'll find a way out. I will. I have to.

He disappears into the van, then returns with a bundle of poles and a green canvas. I watch, helpless, as he quickly sets up a tent. Then he grabs my backpack and duffel.

The blocks tumble out, chunky and wooden, thumping across the ground. The letters on the sides explode in color.

Gregg crouches, staring at them for a long moment, his expression unreadable. With a grunt, he kicks the blocks aside, clearly disgusted. Then he digs through the backpack with rough fingers, finding nothing worth his time. He tosses the bags aside like they're trash. A sneer crosses his face.

I feel my chest clench. Those blocks, my clothes, everything that had once felt like *mine*—to him, are just worthless. All that matters is the suitcase. The one thing I'm supposed to protect.

With a swift slash of his knife, he cuts the rope from the tree, but my wrists stay bound. He ties my ankles next. The pain burns through me. Then he tosses me into the tent like I weigh nothing. Like I *am* nothing.

I want to kick, to fight—but I'm frozen, my own breath choking me. The walls of the tent close in on me.

Outside, his shadow presses against the canvas. His voice comes through low and soft, almost tender. "I'll make this right, Agnes. You'll see. I'll take care of everything. We'll leave together. Just you and me."

The air inside the tent thickens, stale and heavy. My breath comes fast and shallow.

No! No! No!

I force myself to focus. Slow. Steady. Breathe, Agnes. Breathe.

The ropes slice into my wrists, burning, pulling me back to

the moment. I can't let myself think beyond that. I can't let myself think at all.

But the silence presses in around me. I'm alone, trapped. He's gone, and all I have is this darkness.

There's no way out.

No one's coming to save me.

I squeeze my eyes shut, forcing myself to focus on now, to shove last night into a locked box. But thinking won't save me. I'm stuck in this tent. Helpless. Just like always. And that's my truth, isn't it?

Agnes is weak.

Agnes is afraid of bats and rain and spiders and everything that sneaks into the attic. Agnes plugs her ears whenever Vixen and Stone and Squid's names are mentioned.

Agnes stands up to no one.

No more.

I need my letters and my blocks. I need them NOW!

I need their strength, their power.

I will become ANGEL.

I'll soar like the A. I'll tower above everybody else.

I'll rise up again, like the N after a brutal defeat.

I'll be forthright and direct, like the G that cuts through lies with its sword.

I'll branch out like the E, finding roads and routes and lanes to explore.

I'll run barefoot on the sand like the L, my neck bare, with no scarves to hide my purple stains.

And when Gregg comes back, I'll rise like the A in Angel and get my revenge. But I'll be smart about it. He'll untie me first. He'll carry me outside. Then I'll punch him, and kick him, and scratch him—anything to show him I'm strong and powerful and capable. And then I'll run. I'll find help. I'll tell them everything.

Angel will survive.

If I live long enough to try.

THREE

Clare

Then I hear it—a soft tearing sound, canvas ripping.

My breath catches.

The wind? Please be the wind. Maybe it's trying to save me.

The sound is followed by a voice, dry and crackly like twigs snapping underfoot. "I'm here to help you."

My heart bangs against my ribs; I can't move. Is it Vixen pretending to be someone else? Did Gregg send her to kill me? I try to scream, but the tape steals my words. My legs are tied so firmly I can't even curl into a ball. I sit, exposed, waiting.

A knife slices through the canvas, its edge flashing in the faint light. I breathe fast. Too fast. The blade widens the hole until a face appears—wrinkled, eyes sharp and focused, framed by thin wisps of white hair. "Don't be scared," the ancient woman says. "I'm getting you out. You can stab me with this knife later if you think I deserve it."

She steps inside, her movements quick and deliberate. Her hands, knotted with veins, reach for my face. I flinch.

"It's okay," she murmurs, peeling the tape from my mouth.

I suck in a ragged breath. "Who are you?" I gasp. "Why are you doing this? Where did you come from?"

Tears spill down my cheeks.

"Shh," she says, sharper now. "No time for crying. I live nearby. We need to move before the fat man comes back. I saw what he did to you. Bad business."

Is she really here to save me? Am I imagining this? Or is this a trick?

Crouching, Clare saws through the ropes. The fibers snap apart, and my legs collapse, useless and burning. I try to wiggle my toes, but nothing happens.

"Set your wrists here," she says, pointing to a nearby rock outside of the tent.

Her voice doesn't leave room to argue. I hang back. She's small, her shoulders hunched, her legs bent like the bow of a ship. I could run if I have to.

"Now," she says.

I place my wrists on the rock. The blade slices through the ropes in one clean motion. My arms drop into my lap, tingling as circulation returns.

"Breathe," the woman says, almost gently. "You'll feel them soon enough."

She stuffs the cut ropes into her pockets and slides the knife into a sheath at her belt. "Let's vamoose."

Vamoose? The V! A stabbing, sinking, dangerous letter.

"I'm Clare," she says, extending her hand.

"How do you spell your name?" I blurt.

She raises an eyebrow but humors me. "C–L–A–R–E."

The letters click into place—caring, strong, always looking forward. Not like Gregg's.

"And you?" she asks.

"Angel." The name rolls off my tongue. Agnes lies there, in the tent. Buried alive.

Clare nods. "Angel, grab what you need. We're leaving."

I scramble to my feet as pins and needles stab my legs. I grab my backpack and duffel, scooping up the blocks Gregg scattered like garbage. My blocks. My friends. "Child, hurry." Clare's red rubber boots flash as she heads up the slope. "The tide's coming in, and that porker could be back any second."

I follow, my chest tightening with every step.

At the top of the hill, Clare looks back at me. "No one deserves what he did to you."

The sobs come before I can stop them. Gregg. He did that to me. Now Daddy might be dead. I couldn't save him—or the little blond girls: Suzanne and Jazmin. Their names sting.

Clare touches my shoulder, her hand steady. "You're safe now," she says softly.

Can I believe her?

"But we've got to keep moving. There's more to this story, I can tell. But not now."

I nod, brushing at my eyes. No time to think. No time for questions. Nothing can be worse than Gregg.

For now, I'll go along with her.

She taps her chin thoughtfully. "Who do you belong to?"

"I think my parents are dead," I say before I can stop myself. The words fall out, heavy as lead.

She stoops slightly, her face unreadable. "Did the fat man kill them?"

"No, but he knows the people who did," I say. My voice breaks.

"Bad business," Clare mutters. She wrinkles her nose, looking down the hill. She points to the tent. "He left you for the wolves. Lucy, that's not right."

"Lucy?"

Clare shakes her head, smiling faintly. "Did I call you Lucy? Silly me."

She's not looking at me when she says it. She just keeps walking.

"Why did you help me?"

"I couldn't leave you there." Her fingers flutter in the air, light as moth wings. She turns, her red rubber boots crunching the ground.

I hesitate, my feet refusing to move. But I can't go back to the tent. Whatever comes next has to be better than that.

My legs tremble as I follow Clare.

"Come on, Angel." Her voice is steady like a compass. "We're not out of danger yet."

April 18, 1986
Dear Lucy,

If you're watching, you'll see a new you. She calls herself Angel and came out of nowhere, just like you disappeared into it. Odd little thing: wild hair, sad eyes, and a weight in her gaze like she's seen more than even tired old me.

She says her mother's dead, her father is missing. I was foraging for mushrooms on World's End when I heard shouting—sharp and ugly. I crept to the top of a hill and saw him: a porker of a man binding a girl's feet, tossing her into a tent like she was nothing. And—for all I know—he did worse. Papa would've shot him. I would too if I could still see straight. But the film over my right eye blurs everything. Everything but her. I couldn't leave her there, and I couldn't go for help. Still as stone, I waited until he drove off. Then I climbed down and pulled her out, before worse could happen.

For now, the child needs space to breathe. I can give her that. I want to hear her story before I call the authorities—not that I have a phone or any way to contact them. Until Max comes back, it's on me to keep her safe.

She's asleep on the sofa now, curled up one minute, tossing off the blankets the next, writhing like she's fighting shadows in her dreams. I'm trying to show her I mean well, but she's not having it. She won't eat, won't accept anything—except the couch and the heat from the stove.

The girl's bone-thin. Nothing like you. Oh, I hear you. "I still hadn't lost my baby fat," you'd say. But this urchin? She's all wiry tension, on high alert. She wouldn't land upside-down at the bottom of a pit like you did.

She mumbles names in her sleep: Daddy, Ivy, Gregg, Stone, Vixen. Then, clear as day, she starts reciting the alphabet.

I'll search through my books for remedies to help her set-tle—lavender, chamomile, eucalyptus. Something has to work.

Your loving sister,

C

FOUR

Angel

Gregg's jowls drip blood onto my face. His weight crushes me. His breath is hot and sour.

I twist and thrash. Mud sucks me in, pinning my feet.

"Help," I groan.

A soft voice cuts through the darkness. "No one's going to hurt you, darlin'." Gentle fingers swirl soothing O's on my back. "It's all right. You're just dreaming."

The words tug me back, pulling me from the nightmare. My body jerks awake. My face is damp—sweat or tears, I don't know. My hands clutch the blanket like it can anchor me.

Yesterday barrels back at me, full speed. My memories scatter—bits of me left behind in Hull, in the van, in that green tent. Now I'm here, in a tiny house on an island far from my attic room and my walls of letters.

The wind howls. A door creaks.

Someone's outside. Waiting. Watching. Ready to pounce.

"Gregg is coming! I hear him!" I shout, my voice raw.

"Angel," Clare's voice cuts through my panic. "It's just the wind. That predator won't find you here."

The voice snaps into focus. Clare—the old woman who hasn't

left my side. She calls me Angel. Agnes without the crushing S, adding the keep-going L.

Clare sits in a sturdy wooden chair, a shotgun across her lap. It's as long as she is tall.

She sets the gun on the floor. "I'm going to fix you some vittles."

Vittles? The nasty letter V slides down my throat and jabs me from the inside.

From a pot on the stove, she ladles out soup. "I added echinacea," she says. "It cures destructive forces and restores dignity."

The smell punches the back of my throat, earthy and bitter. No way am I drinking that. "Where's my backpack? And my duffel?"

Clare kneels, pulling my backpack from under the couch. "The duffel's in the skiff. Getting you up here was hard enough."

I lunge for the door. It sticks. I grab for the window, ready to kick it out and bolt into the woods, but Clare blocks me. "That bamboo is thick and dense. You wouldn't last five minutes. Stay put. I'll get your things."

She's right. The bamboo's so dense it feels like the walls of Gregg's van all over again—no light, no escape, just green bars keeping me trapped.

I remember Daddy's last words: "Stay put until I get back. But if something bad happens..."

"Nothing bad will happen, right?" I had asked him, clinging to hope.

"Of course not," he said, though he'd never believe what's happened to me. I'm far from Hull, from everything I know.

Two sleek dogs nose their way into the cabin. "Boy-Doggie. Girl-Doggie. Keep her company," Clare says.

Their cold noses nudge my arms. They're nothing like Apollo, the junkyard dog. These two are built for speed. If I run, they'll take me down. If Gregg's out there, they won't be enough to save me.

So I stay.

I recite the alphabet forward and backward, the letters keeping me steady, until Clare returns. She sets the duffel in front of me. I unzip it and pull out all the giant wooden blocks. Daddy's carvings. They're solid and familiar. I feel Daddy in my fingertips. I surround myself with the blocks, safe inside them.

Clare slumps into her chair, shotgun across her knees. The dogs settle beside her. She tilts her head back, mouth slightly open, exhausted or at peace—I can't tell.

I could leave, but Clare and her dogs—or Gregg—would still find me. I barely move as I listen to the creak of bamboo, the chirping of crickets, and the rhythmic breathing of two dogs and an old woman.

All night, I toss and turn. Gregg is everywhere: pressing me down, squeezing my heart, hurting my body. When I wake, the blankets are damp with sweat.

"You're burning up," Clare says, concern in her voice. She hands me warm soda from my backpack as she changes the bedding.

Questions batter me like the wind outside. Where is Daddy? Did Vixen finish him off? What will happen to me?

Gregg called this place World's End. Right now, it feels like my world is ending.

How can I escape? And if I do, will Gregg find me again?

Or worse—will Clare, with her dogs and her shotgun, decide I'm not worth saving after all?

April 21, 1986
Dear Lucy,

Angel must've had wing-dang parents—the kind who give you life, then spend their days draining it out of you. She's always ready to jump at shadows.

Her fever's high, and she's talking crazy. She clutches her wooden blocks, muttering the alphabet over and over, like she's possessed. Letters mean everything to her. Does she think they can save her? I wonder what mattered most to you before you passed? Paper dolls?

She won't eat. She's afraid I'll poison her, like that time with the mushrooms. Remember? I scattered them on the path and swore they were wild, though I'd bought them at the store. You thought you'd die. You spent two sleepless nights waiting for it to happen, until I finally told you the truth.

Papa said I was being mean and that I'd be punished. Maybe Angel is you, come back to teach me a lesson.

Your loving sister,
C

Clare chops wood, feeds the chickens, and bustles in and out of the house, the rifle slung sideways on her body like an extra arm. "If that Gregg comes around, I'll kill him," she says. I believe her.

She touches my face to check my fever; her fingers are like weights on my skin. She puts an icy cold rag on my forehead and stays with me for what feels like hours. Her knitting needles click softly, her pen scratches across paper, and sometimes she hums—faint, almost like a lullaby. I hear that sound, the L of it—like a ripple from long ago. I focus on that sound, hoping it will drown out the noise in my head and bring me to a place of peace. Something I haven't felt in oh so long.

Clare offers me tea, warm and golden, smelling of sunshine and summer mornings. "Crushed dandelions. Good for bringing down a fever." I taste it finally and realize Clare is trying to help me heal.

Nightmares creep in like shadows.

S's slither, winding tighter, choking me.

N's drop like endless pits, pulling me down. I'm drowning in them, struggling to rise again.

I reach out, but my fingers close on nothing. Children's faces rise from the mud, sinking before I can reach them. I throw a rope, but mud drags me under again.

When I wake, fog blankets the skylight and gray tiptoes around the windows. I hear the tap-tap-tap of branches on the roof pointing fingers at me, blaming me for trusting Gregg, for telling him about the hidden panels in the kitchen, for causing Ivy's death and Daddy's torture by Vixen, for not saving the little blond girls when I had the chance.

I don't think—I scramble off the couch-bed, my feet slamming onto the cold floor. The door is already open, and I'm outside before I can even make sense of it. I step into the morning, my first time outside in days, my heart hammering at every shadow.

The scream builds inside me, pushing up my throat. Sharp. Raw. A storm ready to break. When it finally comes out, it's so loud I feel the gray sky grow black and the windows shake.

For a moment, I freeze, breathless. Silence presses in. Then it hits me.

If Gregg is out there, he knows exactly where I am.

Clare

April 23, 1986
Dear Lucy,

    At dawn, Angel bursts from the cabin, screaming like the devil was chasing her. Good thing we're on an isolated island—or she'd have woken the entire town of Hull. As it was, every bird flew into the sky and the dogs howled.

    I wrapped her in a blanket and brought her inside, singing the alphabet the whole time. Letters affect her strangely, like a balm, soothing something deep inside. It's the oddest thing—each letter is alive to her, each one with its own spirit. That's the key! If I can understand how each letter has its own nature, then I can win her trust. I try to understand them through her eyes, even if I'm nearly blind. The B might be balloons tied to a stick, bouncing around, ready to be released. The E could be energy shooting out from a wall socket.

    Lucy, help me here. I need to show Angel that I care, that I will protect her. I cared so much about you, my darling sister, but I failed to protect you. I won't fail her too.

Your loving sister,
C

April 25, 1986
Dear Lucy,

A small victory—Angel ate today. Just a nibble on a blue-berry scone, but it's something. Papa always said, "We must have scones. Stress cannot exist in the presence of a scone." He had a way of making life seem so simple, didn't he?

Lucy, I feel like I have a second chance here to make things right. This poor urchin has dropped into my life, lost and alone. She's an orphan at fourteen. You left us when you were fourteen. Maybe I can help her grow. Maybe she'll bring me peace—the kind I've been searching for since you died.

Your loving sister,
C

*   *   *

April 27, 1986
Dear Lucy,

Max rowed over this morning with groceries and newspapers. It had been two Sundays since his last visit. He was thinner than ever, nothing like the virile hunk you knew. His skin's yellow and his cough hacks. That damn pneumonia again. Angel was asleep. Good thing. She's not ready for new faces, and Max is one of them. We sat outside in the sun by the stone pyramid I built for his granddaughter Lucille. I like to think she was playing beside us while we talked.

Then we discussed Angel. I told him that she came from Hull and is recuperating while I figure out what to do next. I didn't tell him she's the resurrection of you, Lucy. He'd say I was loony, but I know why she's here. I feel you in every breath she takes.

Max asked me so many questions, my head spun. 'Where

are her parents? Is she a runaway? Is she going to hurt herself or you? What happened in Hull to scare her?' Then he said the thing I've been dreading: we need to inform the police. I shook my head. Angel swears the police are involved, and not in a good way. Until we know more, I can't risk involving them.

We searched The Boston Globe for answers. There it was: a shoot-out on a Hull beach between a man named Gregg Bunkny and an unidentified woman with dark hair. The photo showed him on a stretcher. His bloated stomach bulged under a white sheet. Not dead. But barely hanging on.

I'm pretty sure that's the fat man who sealed Angel in the tent. The article said the woman had been shot in the gut and her face was unrecognizable. But she managed to fire a shot before she died, hitting Bunkny in the spine. Drugs were involved, of course.

The follow-up said Bunkny was on life support, but later, they said he was off the danger list. No one knows the full story yet. A Sergeant Evan Stone is leading the investigation. If anyone knows the identity of the dead woman, they're supposed to call him directly.

Max wants his son Tom to dig for more information, but I have no faith in that man. He finds trouble just looking at the sky. Max insists Tom knows people. Yeah, the ones who line up at the liquor store at 8 a.m. and again at midnight before closing. Still, Tom might have known Angel's parents. Doozies, the two of them. Anyone can birth a kid. But raise one? That takes sacrifice. Without it, doom!

D-O-O-M. How would Angel interpret those letters?

Your loving sister,

C

Lucy

On the front porch, Clare sits in a rocking chair, smiling like a storybook grandma. Morning light catches the white of her hair, making her papery skin glow. She seems so here, not distant like Ivy or Daddy, whose minds always drifted.

The books on her shelves make my brain explode. *Gone with the Wind. Tales of Egyptian Pharaohs. Ancient Mythology. The Complete Collection of Sherlock Holmes.* So many books. So much to figure out. More letters. More meanings. More secrets in the shapes of names and words. Has she read them all? Can we talk about them?

I open one and stare at the drawings of gods and goddesses, pharaohs and queens. I trace the name inside the front covers: Clare Brewer.

She even has a dictionary and a thesaurus—my old friends.

I pull my blocks from my duffel and line up her letters. C–L–A–R–E.

The C tells me she really listens, not like Ivy, where words just bounced off her.

L is the move-forward-and-don't-look-back letter. Clare has a lot of years to look back on, but she keeps on moving forward. I respect her for that.

A is all-powerful, like she owns this island.

I like the R because it has an independent mind and strong foot action. If Gregg came here, she'd put him in his place.

I'm still thinking about the E when Clare walks in. I scramble the blocks so she doesn't see what I'm doing.

She pours something steamy into a mug with a yellow smiley face.

"Roasted chicory root with cinnamon and goat milk, one of my specialties." She hands me the mug. "I'll teach you all about chicory and goats and wild carrots and Johnny jump-ups."

Johnny jump-up is a funny name. The J roots into the ground, then springs toward the sun.

"The woods offer everything we need," Clare says. "Tonight, we'll have dandelion stew. I'll teach you which buds are the best."

I nod, eager to learn. Most of what I know, I taught myself—just me, a book, and the alphabet. Sometimes Daddy would read to me for a few days straight. Then he'd turn into Wizz, and I wouldn't see him for a week.

"How do you know all this?" I ask.

"I've lived on this land for thirty years. Ever since my parents died. I call it Brewer Island to honor them. When I was young, I explored it with my father and Lucy."

The question that's been buzzing in my brain slips out. "Who's Lucy?"

Clare flinches, her chin lifts like she's trying to hold something in, but her eyes go sad, like a wave is crashing over her out of nowhere.

"My little sister Lucy will always be fourteen," she says, like each word is a struggle. "That's how old she was when she left me. I've never stopped missing her."

Fourteen. My age.

Her letters flash bold in my mind. L–U–C–Y.

L, sure-footed and steady.

U, the secret-keeper.

C, the listener.

And the Y—it plunges deep, forcing a choice between one path or another.

"I was supposed to keep her safe," Clare whispers.

"I don't trust safe. The S is a mean letter. It looks like a snake." Like Squid. Like Sergeant Stone. It's in sneak and screech, stash and banshee. S hissed whenever Ivy said my name. Ag-nesss. Ag-messss. Ag-Assss.

I hate the S.

"Snakes aren't all bad," Clare says. "They eat rodents, protect the soil. Their venom can heal."

Maybe. But I'd need a whole lot of convincing before I see the S as anything but evil. Still. . . Smile. Soothe. Sweet. Something to think on.

I sip the tea. It's spicy and warms my insides.

"How did she die?"

Clare takes a breath, but it stumbles on the way out. "We were walking home from school. I was teasing her, calling her Loosey Goosey. She hated that." Clare's chest rises and falls, like she's trying to hold herself together. Her hands wring in her lap. "She ran ahead, mad as a hornet. I let her go. The next thing I heard was a scream."

She pauses, swallowing hard.

"When I found her, she was face down in a manhole."

She covers her face with her hands, rocking slightly as if the world itself has crushed her.

"The damned gas company left it open. I—I couldn't reach her." Her voice cracks. "'Lucy! Lucy!' I called, but she didn't answer. I ran for help, but it was too late."

Clare cries now, full-on, her whole body shaking. I don't know what to do.

But then I do.

I wrap my arms around her. She's tiny, but her body holds a thousand pounds of pain. I feel it pour into me, heavy and slow, like I'm holding up both of us.

My father's hugs were stiff—like two I's leaning in—unless it was late and we were in the ocean, or Daddy carried me to bed. Ivy only touched me to hurt me. And Gregg's hug started out like the C, comforting and protective, until it became the G—the rod in the middle pressing into my backside. I can't think about that.

But Clare's hug is different. A true C hug that surrounds me but leaves room to breathe. A hug that makes me feel like I'm giving as much as I'm taking. Maybe I can stay here a little longer. Eat a few more scones. Drink more chicory coffee and dandelion tea. Chop wood, feed the chickens, play with the dogs. Read and read and read until the world makes sense again.

When I hug her, it feels like my broken pieces glue back together.

"What I've come to understand," Clare says, "is we can hope, we can dream, we can prepare, but we never know what's around the corner."

I never knew from one day to the next if I'd get to use a real bathroom instead of a litter box. Or if I'd have enough peanut butter sandwiches to last the week. I never knew what was around any corner—unless it was my letters wrapping around a ceiling beam.I cry then too.

"Let your tears come," she says, wrapping an arm around me. "They'll water your soul."

I stiffen. "I'll never be safe from Gregg. He'll hunt me down. And he'll hurt you too."

"Drink your tea and relax, Angel. He won't be coming around ever again. I promise." Clare walks to the bookshelf and pulls out a newspaper. "Read this."

My eyes land on a photo of Gregg strapped to a stretcher, a brace around his neck. Is he dying? Or already dead?

My fingers go numb, and the mug slips from my hands. The smile shatters into a million pieces.

"Don't move. I'll clean that up in a jiffy. Just read."

> HULL – A shootout Thursday evening on Beach Avenue between an unidentified female and Hull resident Gregg Bunkny, 26, left the woman dead and Bunkny hospitalized in critical condition with a spinal injury. Police suspect drug activity as the motive, according to Sergeant Evan Stone.
>
> Bunkny remains in critical condition and unable to provide further information.

The woman is unidentified? Could it be Vixen? That would be a miracle! But then—no. The article goes on to say that the woman had black hair, pale skin, and long limbs.

That's not Vixen. It's Ivy!

But she was already dead, wasn't she?

My brain spins. Gregg didn't kill her—Vixen did. None of this makes sense. Stone said Ivy was dead. Did he move her body to the beach? But why? To hide who was really responsible?

And where is my father in all of this? There's no mention of a skinny man with a snaggletooth and a head full of dreams and marijuana. No hint of where he might be, no indication that anyone is even looking for him. And there's not a single report about the missing girls, like they never existed.

Every unanswered question feels like a wound, making me feel helpless.

My neck gets hot, like I'm burning up from the inside. The words lie, just like Stone. But he's a policeman. He should be a good guy. I try to see him as anything else, but his letters show his true nature.

S slithers through him.

T spins trouble.

O rolls him on a wicked path.

N bends people to his will.

E spreads evil.

I hate Sergeant Stone.

The thought of him makes my hands curl into fists. Gregg's a monster, but Stone has the badge. The whole town trusts him. How is that fair? Stone's rotten through and through. The world needs to know what he really is. I'm just a kid, but I'll see to it— or die trying.

Clare sits beside me and wipes my tears with a rumpled tissue from one of her many pockets. "Darlin'," she says softly. "It's time you tell me the whole story."

I gather my courage, relying on letters to give me strength.

The N in my name won't sink me. I'll rise again.

I'll be more than a victim of the G—I'll be the one who fights.

I need the L to stay steady and move forward.

I whisper the alphabet under my breath, pressing my fingertips into my palm with each letter. The word rises like a promise. This woman is trustworthy. She will help me.

I begin.

"Vixen killed Ivy, then she and Stone dragged my father off to be tortured for whatever Ivy had been hiding." I can't breathe just thinking about it. "My father had secret places—inside and outside the house. I saw them, I knew they were there. Some hid drugs, some hid money. And there was the silver suitcase filled with drugs that I was supposed to protect. Gregg yanked it away from me and then downed pills and snorted powder and got nasty and mean."

The memory of him, his hands cold and greedy, makes me furious. He was in control. He liked knowing he could do whatever he wanted.

"And then..." I can't stop shaking, my hands twitch so bad I can barely hold onto the words. "...in the van, he pinned me down and rammed his body into my backside. I screamed at him to stop, but he wouldn't. He said I belonged to him and he was all I had left."

Clare puts her arms around me. "Did he undress you when he did this?"

"No, but he got my jeans all wet." I cry then, knowing that Gregg had it in his power to rape me and didn't. It makes my skin crawl. It makes me want to scrub every part of me clean.

"After he set up the tent, he tied me up and covered my mouth and threw me inside. He said he was going back to Hull. To confront Vixen. To find my father."

"But he got more than he bargained for," said Clare, shaking her head.

"And if it weren't for you, I'd have died in that tent." When I try to tell her about the missing girls, my throat closes up. The words get stuck when I try.

Clare listens, like the C in her name demands. I feel the steadiness of her presence, the way she grounds herself here in this moment, and it steadies me, too.

She exhales sharply, like the whole situation leaves a bitter taste. "Bad business," she spits out, her face twisted in disgust. She presses her lips together like she's trying to keep from saying more. Finally, she adds, "At least you don't have to worry about Bunkny. If the bullet hit his spine, that man will never walk again."

She's right, this old lady who really cares about me. I feel it in every word she says, every cup of tea she makes, every small kindness she shows. She's steady and real, and she actually listens to me. No one ever has. I think I remind her of her sister Lucy who died at fourteen. I'm alive at fourteen, ready to go back to Hull and find out if Daddy's still alive—and tell the world that Sergeant Stone is a butt-faced liar and a kidnapper of children.

Clare watches me closely, then says, "The S and the N are bad letters, aren't they?"

"The worst."

Clare reaches for my hand, wrapping her warm fingers around mine. And for the first time in forever, I don't feel alone.

April 28, 1986
Dear Lucy,

What this child has been through gnaws at my gut. Murder, abuse, neglect, drugs. I'm in my eighties and I've never experienced fear like hers. Who raises a child surrounded by such filth and degradation? Don't they know that children are our only hope? They need to be understood, nourished and loved.

If Angel's right—and if Sergeant Stone is involved—if he has even a hint that she can tie him to Ivy's death, her life is in danger. I need her to stay here until Bunkny is locked up for good, and I need to do some investigating about that duplicitous Stone.

I'm taking the skiff into Hull and doing some scuttling of my own. Who's going to notice a feeble old woman who can't see straight? That's the gift of age—people stop seeing me altogether. Besides, I don't trust Max's son to get the job done. Tom lacks his father's strength and conviction. Lucy, if you and Max had a child together, he would be strong and reliable. Not that Max's wife was weak, but she never held a candle to you.

Papa always said, "Patience and fortitude conquer all things." I'll try to remember that. I'll protect this child, Lucy. With everything I've got.

Your loving sister,
C

S E V E N

Max

The dogs dart into the bamboo maze, their tails flicking like startled deer.

"Must be a squirrel on the run," Clare says, retrieving her rifle. She pulls on her red rubber boots and descends the slope.

What if Vixen's coming for me? Or Squid? He has a posse of thugs who track down girls. But I'm not little anymore, I'm not blonde, and I've got purple birthmarks on my neck.

I lift my eyes just enough to peer out the window. The chickens peck, and the goats graze on the shed roof. Minutes pass. I recite the alphabet backward to keep my mind from spiraling.

Then I see him: tall, thin, back hunched, head tilted as if listening to the bamboo whisper. He moves carefully, bundles cradled like babies in his arms. My shoulders stiffen. My gaze locks on him.

"Angel," Clare calls. "Angel?"

I crouch beneath the window.

Clare enters and takes my hand. "It's all right. He's a friend."

His eyes—large, glassy blue, magnified by black-framed glasses—catch my attention first. He tilts his head down as I look up. His long nose, sloped forehead, and yellowed skin remind me of crumbling paper bags. Nothing about him screams crazy.

"Nice to meet you, Angel," he says, setting the bundles on the table. His hands are enormous compared to mine. "I'm Max."

I roll the letters around in my head and they make me smile. The strong M, the smart A, the independent X. Clare is close to him. Maybe I will be too.

His voice is deep, resonating from the island's core. Max pulls a package wrapped with a bow from one of the bags and hands it to me. "For you."

Why would a stranger give me a gift? It has to be a trick. But Clare nods, so I open it. Inside is a quilt with squares of sailboats, kittens, and balloons. Warmth creeps across my face.

"My wife made this for our granddaughter," Max explains. "The quilt is pieced together from her old baby clothes. Clare mentioned you might need something comforting."

"Doesn't your granddaughter still want it?"

Max coughs, a harsh rattle. "She's no longer with us."

Clare stands on a chair to slap his back. "Your cough's worse. Have you seen a doctor?"

"She worries about me," Max says, giving Clare a soft look. "Clare and I have been talking. Let's sit down and decide what to do next."

Next? We? Clare, Max, and me? Why does he care?My belly cramps. Can I trust him? Will he tell me the truth?

Clare dashes into the kitchen, returning with steaming mugs and a tray of freshly baked squash scones. No one speaks as we sip the berry-and-honey blend and bite into the flaky crust.

"As good as always," Max says.

Clare smiles, her lips curling gently—not the full, gum-baring grin she reserves for me. "Been making scones since I was knee-high. Crust's always in the icebox. Just add the flavor of the day."

Max sits heavily in his chair, his fingers steepled into an A-bridge, a sadness swirling around him like smoke. "My son Tom's a regular in Hull."

Clare grimaces.

T–O–M. The letters tumble in my mind—spinning, rolling, rising, falling. There's something about Tom that upsets Clare.

Max's voice slices through the silence. "Angel, I don't know how to tell you this, but I'm a straight shooter. When Clare found you, you were in a bad place. She told me about Bunkny and what happened to you in Hull. Now, Tom's hearing scuttlebutt that the house where you lived was a weigh station for human trafficking. And your parents? They weren't just selling drugs. They were in the business of kidnapping children and selling them."

My face burns. My head spins. Suzanne. Jazmin. "Squid took those girls, not my father." But the truth claws at me. I was there. I did nothing to stop it. And neither did he.

The marks on my neck throb.

How can I explain parents who locked me in the attic to keep me safe from Squid? That snake-headed monster who controlled Hull from a distance. Safe. That's what they called it. But I wasn't safe. Not from the hunger, the dark, the loneliness. Not from Ivy.

Daddy taught me my letters, carved blocks for me, brought me books, ran on the beach, swam with me. When he was sober, he was my hero. When he wasn't, he disappeared, slumped in some corner or gone for days.

When he wasn't home, Ivy took over. She was always angry. Always cruel. I called her Ivy—never mother, never mom, never mommy. She shoved me into the hidey-hole when we traveled in the van, sometimes leaving me there for days with barely enough food and water.

When I cried, she told me to shut up. When I screamed, she did worse. A cigarette pressed to my soles. A fist to my stomach. "That's what you get for making noise," she'd say. And when Squid came sniffing around to check on his property and collect his money, she fed me little white pills so I'd sleep through the worst of it and I wouldn't be a problem.

Daddy was supposed to keep me safe. And sometimes he did. But sometimes wasn't enough.

But she was my mother. And mothers—at least the ones in books—were supposed to be kind. Loving. They were supposed to brush your hair, tuck you in at night, kiss your scraped knees. Not shove you in a hole for days or lock you in an attic. Not burn you when you cried or look at you like you were nothing.

What was so wrong with me that she treated me worse than a dog?

There's so much I don't understand. So much that Daddy never told me. Could Max and his son Tom uncover the truth?

Max's voice is gentle, like he's afraid I might break.

"Angel, can you tell us what you remember? It might help us figure out what to do."

I try to swallow, but my throat is dry. My thoughts tangle, fighting to stay buried. But I push forward. I have to.

"We traveled in this old, broken-down van Daddy called the shitbox. Sometimes he'd invite little girls to play with me. I'd show them my blocks, and we'd make up stories. He said they needed a fresh start and that Squid would give them better lives."

Max's eyes narrow. "So this man Squid took the girls?"

"I don't know." My voice is small. "One day they were there. The next, gone."

I don't say how their giggles would echo through the van one night, replaced by silence the next. How Ivy told me to forget them. How I tried, but couldn't.

"When the van broke down in Hull, Squid offered us his house on the beach. Daddy said the ocean was the best way to move goods."

Max leans in. "You knew your parents were drug dealers?"

I nod. "People came and went constantly—buying, selling, shouting, laughing. I heard it all from the attic."

I don't tell them about the nights when the noise would stop, and I'd lie there in the dark, repeating the alphabet over and over, afraid Ivy would remember I existed. Afraid of what she might do if she did.

"Daddy kept me hidden, saying it was for my safety." I force my voice to steady. "But one day, when Daddy and Ivy fought, I snuck out and hid in the bushes. That's when I first saw Sergeant Stone."

I taste bile as the memory slams into me. "He threatened Ivy. He said she had something that belonged to him."

"What was it?" Clare asks.

I don't want to say it. I don't want to picture it. But I do.

"Ivy carried a blond girl out from under the house and gave her to Stone." My stomach heaves. "Later, I learned her name was Suzanne."

Clare's face darkens, her scowl like a storm rolling in.

"Sergeant Stone came around weekly," I whisper. "I wasn't allowed out when he was there. But Daddy..." I hesitate. "He said Ivy was doing what he told her not to—trafficking children. The night she died, Daddy told me we were leaving because of her."

Max and Clare exchange a look. Heavy. Serious.

Max's voice is firm. "We'll get to the bottom of this. For now, it's best you stay put. Tom can do some digging. If you know details about these kidnappings, Angel, you're in danger."

I don't say it out loud, but I already know. I've always been in danger.

The word howls in my mind. Danger.

The D drives forward.

The A perches high, reaching above the darkness.

The N drags me down, never letting me climb back up.

The G curls like a fist holding a knife.

The E—open, yearning for escape.

The R wants to run. But to where?

EIGHT

Girl-Doggie and Boy-Doggie

A few days later, the sharp crack of an axe splits the wood. The pace is relentless, the sound cruel and swift.

Then silence.

When I step outside, a man crouches beside a chicken, feeding it from his hand. Max hasn't been by lately—he's sick. This must be Tom.

"Good morning," I call.

He doesn't look up. "Nothing good about it," he growls, shooing the chickens away.

"The sun's shining," I offer.

"A hot ball in the sky. What else would it do?"

Tom stands, stretching his stocky frame. His eyes are dark, his forehead etched with deep creases. His stringy black hair is tied into a ponytail. Everything about him is shadows and dynamite, so unlike Max's easy warmth.

He lights a cigarette, sucking on it like it's a fight he's determined to win. The cigarette dangles from his lips as he picks up the axe again.

Tom catches me staring and barks, "What?"

I jump, and for a moment he grins—his straight, white teeth flashing. But the scowl returns as quickly as it vanished.

Gathering my courage, I ask, "Any news about Gregg Bunkny?"

"He's still in the hospital. No trial date yet."

Tom resumes chopping, breathing hard.

Clare comes outside, sniffing the air like a hound. "Mighty early to hit the sauce, isn't it, Tom?"

He just shrugs.

Clare pulls me inside, her hand warm on my arm, guiding me away from Tom's heavy presence.

"What's wrong?" I ask.

"Tom's not himself today."

From the window, I watch wood chips fly as chickens scatter. When the wood is stacked, he slinks to his boat, revs the motor, and disappears.

"Fill him up with high-test, and he's stupid," Clare mutters.

Even Ivy had a few good moments. Does Tom have more kind days than cruel ones?

Now that I know Gregg is still in the hospital and might never walk again, I feel safer. The island is isolated, and bamboo keeps the house hidden. Besides, Girl-Doggie and Boy-Doggie always announce anything that disturbs the shore.

Clare sits on the porch, pulling twine from old rope to create dreamcatchers. "Everything has a purpose, and it's our job to find it," she says.

Nothing is wasted here; Clare has the bulging pockets to prove it.

After a while, she disappears into the house. I hear footsteps in her little room. When she reappears, her rifle is slung across her back, and she pulls on her red rubber boots.

"I'm going to get us dinner. How's rabbit stew?" She doesn't wait for an answer. "I'll be back by dusk."

The greyhounds follow her down the slope, their bodies lithe and eager. Clare's voice cuts through the air—low and command-ing—and the dogs slink back.

I click my tongue. "Come on, Doggies. Play with me."

I've only ever played with one other dog back when Ivy and I slept in the van while a roofer fixed an attic leak. Daddy bribed her with quaaludes and weed so she'd quit complaining.

"Agnes, say hello to Cerberus," she said when we got to the junkyard where the shitbox van had been dumped.

"Can you spell Cerberus?"

Probably to shut me up, she spelled it.

After Ivy passed out, I wrote his name and studied the letters.

The plump C and B didn't match the bony dog.

His gentle eyes didn't suit the sharp S.

He needed moving letters, like the L.

Maybe an A for his pointy ears.

I focused on the L, the O, and the A, trying different combi-nations, playing with the letters until I saw him for who he was: Apollo.

I wonder if Apollo still guards the junkyard.

I crouch and write his name in the sand. Girl-Doggie comes close, licking my face in neat hellos. Boy-Doggie shadows me as I sip my honeyed chicory, and I break off chunks of scone, holding them out. He cautiously takes a piece.

Suddenly, both dogs freeze, necks arched, ears tilted. They bound away into the bamboo. Their whip-like tails flicker, and moments later, they return, satisfied nothing's amiss.

I sit in the sand and sketch the alphabet, glancing at the dogs. Girl-Doggie and Boy-Doggie are hardly names. I can do better.

"Tell me about yourself," I say to Girl-Doggie.

When I reach to stroke her, she steps back. Clare said they were rescued, shivering and thrashing in the current. Even now, they're skittish.

"I understand. You've had a tough time, and it still hurts." I offer her pieces of the scone. "But you're here now. You're safe. You're loved."

I study their forms, their movements. Tall and smart—they need A's.

They're connected and gentle, so each gets an H.

Sturdy and grounded, they don't need the twirling T or the secretive U.

Their long legs remind me of the R. I circle A, H, and R in the sand.

Boy-Doggie never relaxes. He's always on alert. He needs an O.

His head, shaped like Apollo's, looks like a P.

The letters grow before my eyes: P-H-A-R-O. I double up on the A and H, and his name emerges, like the photos I saw in Clare's books: Pharaoh.

Now it's Girl-Doggie's turn. She's softer than Pharaoh. Her grace, calmness, and strength surround her like a D. I write A-H-R-D and shuffle them until the perfect name appears: Darah.

I say their names aloud. "Pharaoh. Darah." They roll off my tongue like a song.

When they nuzzle into me, I stroke their fur, soft as beachgrass.

Clare returns with a striped bass in a net. Her cheeks are pink from the brisk air, her energy electric.

"I never could kill a bunny," she says, louder than usual. The dogs crowd her, sniffing and licking her hands.

"I've named them," I say.

"Of course you have," Clare replies. "You put your letters to good use, I'm sure."

"She's Darah, and he's Pharaoh."

"Pharaoh, the ruler—yes, a good choice. And Darah...the name isn't just a name, is it? It's compassion. Loyalty. Quiet strength. A perfect fit. You've got a gift, little sister."

NINE

Hull

May 1, 1986
Dear Lucy,

   I'll start easy so I won't scare myself in the telling, but I gotta get this out or it'll kill me. First off, I lied to Angel about hunting. I went to Hull. I don't trust Tom. He'll spew to the wrong nightcrawler, ask the wrong questions, and get himself killed. When he's sober, he's thoughtful and kind. But drunk, he's mean-mouthed and stupid. I'm making it my business to find out about these low-lifes myself.

   I moored the skiff at the A Street pier and walked to the F Street house where Angel lived with those selfish, rotten scum buckets.

   Even from a distance, I saw gaping black holes in the roof of this monstrosity. Obviously, there had been a fire. The house stood charred and angry, still smoking. Its frame buckled; its body festered. I got the feeling that ghosts spiraled around inside, caught in its smoldering remains.

   As I walked closer, I saw yellow police tape and no-trespassing warnings. Nevertheless, I slipped through the mangled hedge into the yard. Deep tire treads cut into the sand from fire engines and tractors. Shovelfuls of dirt slammed against the wooden stairs; it piled on the deck and toppled into broken windows. The house cried from the assault of hoses and sledgehammers. I stared up at the attic where Angel had lived. It gaped and yawed and gave me no answers.

I walked the circumference of the pitted yard, searching for that kernel of truth. At the back of the property was a rock wall, built with misshapen stones, bricks, boulders, and sticks glued haphazardly together like a story told backward and inside out. Did Angel's father start this messy border and never finish it? The wall looked as if it might tumble from neglect, but nothing else struck me as suspicious.

I shone my flashlight along the foundation of the house and saw a bulkhead with its door unhinged, the gaping hole leading to a basement. I climbed down several stairs to a dirt floor littered with ceiling debris. A hot water boiler had melted from the fire. Warped pipes clung desperately to the crumbling ceiling. No proof of evil, except its absence. Another room. Deeper.

Like a chamber of bleakness, a coffin of cement. In here, the ocean didn't exist. The birds had no voices. Even spiders and beetles and ants stayed away. I felt no energy. No life.

I shuddered back to the yard, feeling the softness of earth beneath my feet. The ocean spoke softly, whispering to get out of there before I drowned in sadness and fear and everything that made me human. My eyes squinted, having seen the inside organ of the house, its empty heart.

In the daylight, the crystal sands sparkled, the gravel twinkled, the sand crunched, and the tar and ash mixed. Among the pebbles were burnt oranges and black golds, like gems scattered in the dirt. When I examined one, I realized with horror that it was the tip of a mangled toe, its nail brittle and shriveled. I threw it away so fast that my fingers splayed and panic seized me. The *more I looked, the more digits I found, each in a different state of decay, discarded like seeds, growing like clones in the sand.*

How had the police missed them? Or was Stone the one who scattered them here as a warning to stay out of his business?

I bolted out of there like the ground was peeling up in flames. I gagged as I jumped in the skiff, thinking how I walked among the knuckles and bones. How they trailed me out of the yard. Hands and feet clawing their way toward me, yelling their stories. I didn't stop to listen. I rowed like an Olympian back to the safety of my island, feeling eyes on me the entire way, beckoning me to come back, to investigate.

Angel can't be anywhere near maniacs like Vixen, Squid, and Stone. I've lived long enough to know that what goes around comes around. But Angel doesn't deserve to be at the center of it.

Your loving sister,
C

* * *

June 1, 1986
Dear Lucy,

Every time I look at Angel, my tongue turns to steel. A lump of terror I can't swallow. No need to tell her what I saw. The burned house. The strewn fingers and toes. The room of dead secrets. The mystery wall in the backyard. How did Angel ever survive people like that? No wonder she was scared. She's better off here, protected. No one knows she's here. From what I understand, no one even knows she exists, except for Gregg Bunkny, and he's going nowhere.

I never expected to be watching over a teenager in my ninth decade. I hope I know what I'm doing because sometimes my mind plays tricks on me. I see things that aren't there. Like eyes

in the bamboo. I worry that I didn't cover my tracks. I left foot-
prints around the basement near the concealed room. But no one
saw me. And there were no boats near me when I rowed back
to the island. Or were there? With my eyes, I can never be sure.

I can't remember yesterday or last week or last year—but
there's not a single detail I can't recall about the sick remains
of that house.

Your loving sister,
C

TEN

Brewer Island

Max and Tom set up a mattress in the loft. No more couch. I can see into the downstairs, all buttery yellows and spring greens. Nothing cramped, closed, bruised, or broken like in my attic room. To come down, I have a ladder, not a fold-up, but a solid wood staircase that Tom nailed to the lip of the loft.

My room is shaped like the A of my attic, but there are skylights in the roof and paintings on the walls with the name Edward Brewer scrawled at the bottom. Ocean and rock formations, buoys and trees. The outside is inside. I have bookshelves, a bureau, and clothes that belonged to the Brewer family—wool sweaters, flannel shirts, and wind jackets. Max brought me pants and shoes that his wife once wore. Clare teaches me to thread a needle and mend a tear.

Each morning, I milk the goats and gather eggs. I empty cisterns of water into buckets and boil it for drinking. I mix berries or dandelions or beans into the batter that Clare prepares for scones and put them in the oven. I brew chicory coffee and wait for Clare to come out of her room. Then we preserve greens and can fruits before storing them in the root cellar, or we string necklaces, lace dreamcatchers, or polish bamboo for chimes. Clare boxes up whatever crafts we make and gives them to Max. He brings them to a gift shop in the center of Hingham, the next town over. Clare says they turn a pretty profit.

After being secluded for years in that attic when we moved to Hull, I love being outdoors. I'm discovering I'm in awe of trees and grasses and the changing currents. I bring my letter blocks outside and watch how the sun shines on them, like they're honoring Daddy. Sometimes I pretend Clare's sister Lucy is with me, and we talk about all that I left behind in Hull. She reminds me that I don't have to live like my parents did, immersed in drugs and selfishness. And I'm not alone. I think about how my letters have always been my best friends, how my attic had letters painted on every beam in every shape and thickness. With letters as my companions, I could escape to the sky, to the moon, to other solar systems.

That's the one thing I thank Gregg for. Daddy hired him to be my teacher, and I studied with him almost every morning, as long as Ivy wasn't around. Gregg peeled down the empty layers in my brain and filled them with the phases of the moon and the reason for the change in tides. He gave me an overview of Hull, its twenty-two neighborhoods, some so private few knew they existed, like Gunrock and Rockaway, Windemere and Hog Island. He described how food was absorbed in the body and metabolized. He taught me about chemical elements and molecular structure, foreign currencies, and weights and measures. I learned the difference between opioids and barbiturates, hallucinogens and steroids—all that a drug dealer's daughter might need.

To please Gregg, I studied the thesaurus from A to Z, memorizing fifty-one synonyms for cool, forty-three for anger, and nineteen for bored. I wanted to flabbergast him.

I used to be an O, with plain white space. Then Gregg colored me in. Now, with Clare, I have the chance to be a rainbow. With her, I read and read. We talk and I learn. I grow.

On Sunday, Max boats over with mail, groceries, and special somethings for me like strawberry soap and saltwater taffy. But most important, he brings *The Boston Globe* and *The Hull Gazette*. I search for mention of anyone resembling my father, but I find nothing. I search for articles on missing children; they too don't exist. Just endless stories about how wonderful Sergeant Stone is and how much good he does for the town. I want to barf whenever I see his name. Clare says he'll get his just rewards, but I'm doubtful.

And then one day I find it:

> Hull—The body of an unidentified male estimated to be in his mid-thirties was discovered wedged between boulders at Pemberton Point. It is estimated that he'd been lodged there for several months. His fingers and toes had been removed and his facial features were destroyed by a gunshot at close range. All that remained was a fang-like tooth in the man's jaw. Police suspect the killing was gang-related. An investigation is underway.

"Clare! It's Daddy! They found his body. He's dead. The newspaper says so!"

My chest tightens so fast I can't breathe. The words blur on the page. No. No. It can't be. But the tooth—his tooth—sharp and crooked, tells me it has to be him.

She sits beside me in seconds. "Angel? What are you talking about? Let me see—"

"There was a tooth. Like his. And they said he was shot in the face."

Clare's hand goes to her chest. "Oh no," she whispers, and then her knees buckle. "Help me..."

She collapses, eyes wide, sweat pouring down her face.

I drop the paper and grab her before she hits the floor, but I'm shaking so hard I can barely hold her.

"Clare! Clare! Can you hear me?"

I don't know what to do. There's no phone to call Max. There's no way to contact a doctor. No one is here to help. I am on my own.

Dogs and goats and chickens surround me. Barks and clucks and bleats. And I hear screaming. My screaming. I need to calm down.

C–A–L–M.

C–A–L–M.

C–A–L–M.

I repeat the letters over and over until my breath settles.

"Clare, come back to me!" I wrap her in my arms and help her into bed. She's like a bird, all bones and loose skin. I remove her red boots and socks and massage her feet, her legs, her hands. I kiss her forehead.

Clare's head wobbles and her eyes open. "Am I dead?"

I bring her water and wash her face with a warm cloth. I sit across from her, watching her sunken chest go up and down. My heart aches and I worry that she won't recover. How can I go on without her? She's been my life saver in oh so many many ways.

Hours pass, and finally the color returns to her face.

"Angel, help me up. I need to make dinner."

"You're going nowhere," I say, my voice aching with relief. "I'm here. I'll take care of you. You can trust me."

I keep vigil by her bed all night, watching her chest rise and fall, terrified it might stop. In the morning, she wakes like nothing happened. Just opens her eyes and smiles at me like I hadn't spent the night crying. I bring her broth with echinacea leaves, a pinch of mint, a swirl of honey. It's the only thing I know to do. My breathing eases, but my whole body feels jumpy and wound up. She could go again. Just like that.

Worry beads my face, wet and hot.

"Angel," Clare says, her voice thin and scratchy, "there's something I need to tell you before I die. It's about your father."

"He's dead, Clare. What else is there to say?" I choke on the words. "Vixen chopped off his fingers. His toes. Why would she do that?" I see his fingers in my head—his steady hands whittling my blocks, shaping the letter *A* from cedar, bringing the alphabet alive.

Clare's arms fold around me. Her skin is crinkly-soft, like old paper, like something that might tear if I hold on too long. Her lips press together, and the lines around her mouth cut deep.

"Fingerprints are used to identify people. Whoever did this didn't want him traced."

I blink, confused. "But his toes?"

She holds me like she won't let go no matter what.

"It's a warning. That's what monsters do when they want to scare everyone else into silence."

I know that Vixen branded Daddy with her knives, like she did on Gregg's wrist. No one is safe in Hull with Vixen and Stone running the town.

"Somehow I have to stop them from doing this to someone else," I say aloud to Clare.

"You're still a child, Angel, and they're organized killers."

And kidnappers who steal children and sell them. I'm too ashamed of myself to tell Clare how I couldn't stop Ivy from stealing children, how I didn't stand up for Suzanne and Jazmin. Where are they? Am I too late to help them? To help others? Are Stone and Vixen still out there selling children to Squid? My insides boil like mercury rising.

Clare holds her heart. I run to take her in my arms. Instead, she stands up to her full four-foot-five-inch height and breathes fire. "Monsters. Those people. How did you survive among them?"

I didn't.

July 1, 1986
Dear Lucy,

 The newspapers told Angel what I couldn't, including the gory details about the missing fingers and toes. What I found at the house had to belong to Wizz, that unhinged father of Angel's. What more can that child endure? She was finally settling in, and now that Gregg Bunkny's trial date is set for the end of June, she's worried that he will get off and come looking for her—and not by himself, but with Vixen. I assure her the bamboo is a labyrinth and no one can find their way through it. She says Vixen only comes out at night and can see through anything. She's superhuman and diabolical.

 Max insists on going to the trial even though he can't control his cough, and I could knock him over with a feather. He's eighty-six! How did we get so old? A few weeks back, I swear I had a heart attack. Angel hasn't left my side except to do chores around the house. She won't let me lift a finger. She even mashes my food. She has this uncanny ability to know what nourishes me.

Your loving sister,
C

ELEVEN

The Verdict

Gregg's trial started last Monday. I'm nervous and jumpy waiting for Max to show up with the verdict. I crack the eggs when I pick them up and wear a path to the shore, walking it while repeating the alphabet a thousand times.

Finally, we hear him. Darah and Pharaoh run down the slope; I'm close behind. Clare waits by the porch. She's frail, her eyesight weak, but she hears the ripple of waves and the gulls' wings, so she knows he's arrived.

Max anchors his boat and disembarks, perspiring in the summer heat, his face like drippy paste. When he sees me, he whoops, "Gregg Bunkny will never bother you again."

I crow like a rooster. Pharaoh and Darah wag their tails. When we tell Clare, she flaps her arms and chickens around the yard. Max laughs until his chest heaves and his cough hacks.

"You need a dose of my special brew," Clare says. "Then you can tell us the whole story."

In the house, she crushes mullein seeds and thyme, boils water, and pours honey. "Drink," she says, placing a steaming bowl of broth in front of him. The steam alone could cure him.

Max coughs—a throat-clearing sound, not bone-shattering like usual. "The verdict came in this morning. Bunkny was convicted of the manslaughter of the woman he shot on the beach. The bullets in Bunkny's gun matched those in the victim's body. It was a drug deal gone bad. The evidence was all around the crime scene."

I shake my head. "The description of Jane Doe in the newspaper matched my mother. But she was already dead. I heard Daddy's cries when Vixen killed her."

I know I should be crying for Ivy, but I'm not. She was a horrible mother—mean and vicious. She hurt me over and over again. Daddy tried to protect me, but he was no match for her. I hated her, and all I feel now is relief that she's gone. How awful is that?

Max coughs again, prompting Clare to stand on a chair and thump his back.

"There's more," he says. "The bullet in your father's body was traced to the gun Bunkny used on Ivy."

I'm confused. Didn't Gregg say he'd find my father and bring him to me? He had no intention of killing him. Maybe Gregg confronted him and things went downhill? That makes no sense—Gregg and Daddy were friends, and he trusted Gregg to be alone with me. Then again, Gregg stole the silver suitcase with all the drugs. Maybe he threatened Daddy about it? Maybe they fought over me.

My gut tells me Vixen is behind this. The night Ivy was murdered, I heard Vixen say she knew Wizz stashed drugs and money in false doors and floorboards. I let his hiding places slip during one of our lessons, at least that's what Gregg said. Did he tell Vixen? Was he responsible for Ivy and Daddy's deaths? Even if he didn't shoot them, was he guilty?

"Did Bunkny take the stand?" Clare asks.

"He never said a word. He sat there while the lawyer let the proof pile up. I saw the lawyer whisper in his ear a few times, and Bunkny would nod or grimace."

"How did he react to the verdict?" Clare asks.

"Like a building fell on him. I swear, he thought he'd get off."

"Someone raised his expectations," Clare says. "Then dropped the ball. I wonder if the lawyer was bought."

"Bunkny was railroaded," Clare says.

"What does that mean?" I ask.

"When someone is convicted without a fair trial or on trumped-up charges," Max says.

"Or fabricated evidence," Clare adds.

Evidence? Daddy said he had evidence against Stone, Squid, and Vixen. Something big enough to convict them. Where is it?

"Did the police testify?" I ask.

Max nods. "Sergeant Stone was in charge of the investigation."

Sergeant Stone. ButtFace. Lies on top of lies. "Gregg hated guns. He said guns offer easy solutions to difficult problems."

"That's the same Gregg who tied you up and left you for the wolves," Clare says. "What makes you think he was telling the truth?"

"Vixen killed my parents and pinned it on Gregg."

Clare scrunches her lips into a pruney-O. "Justice doesn't mean the bad guy goes to jail. It just means someone pays for the crime."

That didn't feel like justice. It felt like someone tilted the board and let all the pieces fall on Gregg.

"Bunkny deserves to be held accountable for hurting you, Angel," Max says.

"But Vixen is roaming free. And Sergeant Stone is in this up to his eyeballs. They are the evil ones."

Letters form in front of me: E–V–I–L.

Nastiness spreads out, infecting everything.

Then stands proud and lets loose more destruction.

My stomach lurches. I walk to the shore thinking about consequences...so anyone can be convicted of a crime if they're not properly represented? That seems wrong. Stone needs to pay. Vixen needs to pay. And Gregg? He's guilty of hurting me, but he didn't murder Daddy and Ivy even though he's been convicted of the crime.

I imagine Stone's face, his butt-crack cheek. I can hear his testimony from the stand, talking trash about John and Jane Doe. He knew damn well who Daddy and Ivy were.

I relive the night of the murders. I hear the beams shake when Ivy falls. I hear Vixen cackle and Daddy scream. Then he falls. Smashing wood. Shattered glass. Thuds throughout the house. Banging walls. Prying floorboards. Then Stone comes in and says, "Holy shit! Why didn't you wait for me? What a goddamn mess."

Vixen tells him to take Ivy to the car and wrap Daddy up. I hear grunts dragging their bodies onto the deck, down the stairs, and into the night. Could Stone and Vixen carry both bodies? Was Gregg there? Helping? He found me so fast—maybe he was in the house the whole time.

The only thing that lets me breathe is knowing Gregg will never come for me again. He'll be in prison for life for something he didn't do. But what can be done about Vixen and Stone? Is it up to me to bring them to justice and have the right people convicted of the crime?

I have so many questions for Max, but when I come back to the cabin, Max is asleep in his chair. Clare's head is down too. After their nap, Max shares more details about the trial, but his head wobbles. How much did he actually hear?

"Was there more about John and Jane Doe? Did anyone try to find their real names?" I ask.

Max shrugs.

"Were there any women in the courtroom? Someone with white hair and black lipstick?"

"The only woman I remember had short orange hair, a full figure, and sat in the back row. She cried her eyes out when John and Jane Doe's pictures were shown."

"That has to be Orange Head." I picture her and Ivy at the kitchen table, forehead to forehead, whispering and laughing. Ivy actually looked happy when Orange Head was around. "She loved Ivy. They were friends."

"I'm sorry about your parents," Max says. "But it seems like the town regarded them as drifters looking to score drugs and were in the wrong place at the wrong time."

So John and Jane Doe ran into bad luck. They didn't belong in Hull anyway. Clear and simple. Good riddance. My head spins.

And where are the girls? Suzanne and Jazmin. Are there more? Was that why Ivy was murdered? Did she keep trafficking children even after Vixen warned her to stick to drugs? If children are still being taken...how am I supposed to stop it?

September 1, 1986
Dear Lucy,

> *What Angel needs to understand is that no matter what has happened, it has brought her to this moment. This is the time she can choose to make everything new. Right now.*

> *Angel talks about letters as living creatures revealing human traits and secrets. Today is the V—the place of reckoning for her. She can live in the past or the future. That has been my problem. I got stuck at eighteen when you fell in that pit. I never moved beyond your death. Life passed me by.*

> *What haunts me is something Papa always said: Evil triumphs when good people do nothing. Am I guilty of doing nothing? I never told Angel the truth about what they did to her father's body. Why tell her something that would hurt her and encourage her to seek answers? She's no ostrich. She'd march into Hull and confront that despicable man and diabolical woman.*

> *No sense in looking for trouble. My job is to keep her safe and give her as much of me as I can before I leave this planet. I'll be seeing you soon. I feel it in my bones.*

> *Your loving sister,*
> *C*

TWELVE

The Letter Bible

Clare knows I've never been to school, but I share stories about all the books I've devoured and how I immersed myself in each volume of the *Encyclopedia Britannica*. I might have been stuck in an attic, but in my imagination, I've traveled the world, sat in classrooms, swum in the Indian Ocean, and even piloted a spaceship. Books opened the door to adventure. The letters came alive—unraveling mysteries, offering glimpses of the future, and bringing clarity to my sheltered life. Even so, Clare decides I need more education and devotes our days to my studies. She's nothing like Gregg. Her jowls don't shake when I give a wrong answer. Her eyes don't accuse, and her breath never reeks of acid or weed. She might be small, but to me, she's the universe. Unlike Gregg, Ivy, or even Daddy, she expects nothing in return.

Clare is magic. She sees molecules in the air and describes them to me. She hears more than the buzz of bees; she feels their drumbeat, their mission. She explains tectonic shifts, pebbles on the beach, the grain of sand, the gray of squirrels, slate, and winter skies. She understands prisms, rainbows, refracted light—things I hadn't thought to notice.

Each day, Clare follows a routine she calls Awareness. She

walks around the cabin with her hands clasped behind her back. I follow, afraid she might topple, but she moves slowly, perfectly balanced. Darah and Pharaoh trail behind us, then the chickens. The goats watch from shed rooftops.

"On my first walk," she says, "I measure what I have to do against what I've already done."

I've done so little, but I know what I must do: return to Hull and uncover the truth about the missing girls, even if it reveals dark secrets about my father and Ivy.

"On my second walk, I open my mind to the impossible," Clare continues.

The S's tell me that's a slippery road, that the more I investigate, the more I won't want to discover. But Clare knows what she's doing.

"By the third revolution, my body and spirit merge. I become mindful of what's inside and outside me."

"Like I'm inside the tower of the letter A, waiting to climb out and reach the top of the mountain?"

"Angel," she says gently, "letters are more than shapes. If you want to find meaning in them, you must study the interplay of air and light. You're so focused on the lines and curves, you miss the gestalt."

"Gestalt?"

Clare disappears into the house and returns with my favorite book—the dictionary.

Gestalt: a visual pattern that includes not just objects but the spaces between them. A childlike blue twinkles through the gray of her eyes, like the winter ocean on a sunny day.

"So a letter is more than it seems," I say.

"Look at the whole and how it interacts with its surroundings. Be the spaces between letters. Feel their weight. Their taste. Their sound. Notice what they stir up: love or irritation, friction or comfort, pain or intimacy." She hands me a bucket. "Come with me."

We walk through the bamboo to the shore. "Gather whatever catches your eye," she says.

For hours, we form an alphabet out of pebbles, feathers, crab legs, knotted twigs, and dried kelp. Each line and curve is fragile yet strong. We sit inside the circle of letters, knowing one gust of wind or a single misstep could destroy it.

Clare pulls a wrinkled piece of paper from the pocket over her heart. "It's something Emerson wrote. I think it matters right now."

> *Standing on the bare ground,*
> *my head bathed by the blithe air,*
> *and uplifted into infinite space,*
> *all mean egotism vanishes.*
> *I become a transparent eyeball—*
> *I am nothing; I see all;*
> *currents of the Universal Being circulate through me.*

She recites the words again, slowly, letting them sink in.

I picture the all-seeing O, an air bubble rising before me.

"Feel the O," Clare says, as though reading my mind. "Notice how silence and sound flow through it."

I sit small inside the circle of letters, trying to be the island, the earth, a single dot open to infinity.

But all I feel is sadness. Fear. Darkness. Need.

The sand pulls at me. I squirm and start to sink.

"Don't fight it," Clare says. "Let the currents flow through you."

I relax, loosening the questions inside me. Who has walked this shore? What lives beneath the surface? How deep does it go? Will the current preserve our circle of letters, or will time erase it?

"What are you learning?" Clare asks.

My body feels like it's floating above the ground, and I'm watching myself melt into the air. "That we have no beginning and no end. We are what surrounds us, what came before us, and what continues after us."

"Now you're listening."

Back at the cabin, Clare gives me a blank journal. "Start with the letter O," she says. "What's inside it? What's outside? How does it breathe? Who does it touch?"

I imagine a living O.

I talk, she writes.

She talks, I write.

And so, our work on *The Letter Bible* begins.

THIRTEEN

Renewal

April 16, 1987
Dear Lucy,

Today is Angel's fifteenth birthday—an age you never saw. And here I am, eighty-four, more than five times that!

Angel has grown into a beautiful, thoughtful young woman. No longer the skinny waif of last year, though her black curls remain a tangled mess. Mother would have snipped them off ages ago.

We've been working on letters—not ordinary ones, but exercises in form and substance. Papa would have admired her artistic eye. Don't worry, there's no need for jealousy; Angel is humble, eager to learn, and deeply appreciative.

Having her here renews my faith in the future—not mine, but hers. She was overjoyed when I baked her a layered fruit cake. We lit fifteen candles and another one for luck.

Max, Tom, and I each gave her a gift: knee-high waders from me (Mother's), a carved hand mirror from Tom (it belonged to baby Lucille), and tortoiseshell combs from Max (his wife's).

Angel danced in her boots, pinned back her curls with the combs, and admired herself in the mirror.

For a fleeting hour, we felt whole and alive. Then reality returned...my back ached, Max coughed blood, and Tom snuck off for a drink. But Angel went to bed happy.

Your loving sister,
C

* * *

May 16, 1987
Dear Lucy,

Max has had more bad days than good. Tom brings groceries and newspapers. Sometimes he sneaks supplies onto the porch at night—those are the drinking times, and he knows if I catch him, there'll be hell to pay.

Sometimes he sits on the porch with me and Angel, and he's all smiles and chatter in the middle of the day. He asks Angel about Wizz and Ivy. She tells stories about the strange characters who paraded into and out of the house, and how there were bowls of white powder and a refrigerator filled with vodka and beer. I see his eyes dazzle at the mention.

I wish I could trust him to stay sober. He has so many demons eating away at him. He blames himself for his daughter's death, believing his neglect worsened her leukemia. Such narcissism, the way he makes her suffering all about him. Max, in contrast, is steadfast and honest. But Tom changes like the wind, and I never know which version of him will show up.

Your loving sister,
C

FOURTEEN

Giant Blocks

I've been on Brewer Island for a year and a half, avoiding World's End. Clare says I have to face my fears even if it's like swallowing pine needles. Once I break the ice, I'll be able to grow again.

On New Year's morning, after my chores, Clare puts on her red rubber boots and I put on my birthday waders. We bundle up with parkas, hats, and gloves. She tells Darah and Pharaoh to stay and together we walk down the slope to the skiff. She leans on me the whole way. I am her support.

The current runs fast, matching my heartbeat. We climb into the small boat and I take up the oars. I try not to recall the last time—the day my parents were broken from the outside, the day Gregg broke my spirit from the inside, the day I left Agnes behind in the tent and became Angel.

Clare hums while I row, the alphabet repeating in my head with the rhythm of the oars. Rowing across terrifies me and frees me at the same time.

When we reach the far shore, I moor the skiff and secure the oars. The climb to the top feels endless. It's where Clare saw Gregg attack me, but nothing physical remains of the tent. The scars live inside me. She points out the roller coaster and the Ferris Wheel across the Weir River in Hull, both outlined like dinosaurs on the horizon.

"Every day may not be good," she says, "but there's something good in every day."

I nod. I believe her. What I'm experiencing isn't World's End—it feels like a new beginning.

I make a New Year's resolution: I'll help at least one kid, the way Clare helped me.

I am stronger now, more confident in myself. I am no longer a prisoner. No longer a victim.

* * *

On our way to the skiff, Clare finds a thick animal bone and tucks it into a pocket for the dogs. At the cabin, she tosses it into the air. Both dogs jump, but Pharaoh catches it and whizzes past with the bone in his mouth. Not wanting to be left out, Darah grabs a daddy-block from the porch table and bolts through the bamboo and down the slope.

I sprint after her, but she darts away just as I get close.

"Darah," I call. "Come back here, right now."

Clare hears me and gives a sharp whistle. Darah inches toward me, her tail low, her ears pinned back. A chunk is missing from the side of the B block.

"Drop it," I say quietly, patting her crown.

Darah lays the block at my feet, then scampers after Pharaoh, who tears around the yard with the knuckle bone.

Something green pokes out of the cracked block. I pick it up and pry it open carefully, keeping the wood mostly intact. Inside is a wad of money.

"Clare, look!" I hold it up.

"Where'd that come from?"

"Darah cracked the block open. This was inside." I pump my fist. "Daddy must have hidden it. He was a genius at camouflage." I sit on a stump and unwrap the roll. Twenty-six hundred-dollar bills.

"This is crazy," I say, running to show Clare.

"Hot diggity!" she says. "That's a lot of moolah!"

I haul the blocks to the shed and line them up in alphabetical order. That seems the fairest way. Then I get to work, prying each open with an awl. Each block holds a roll of cash. One has thirty hundred-dollar bills, another twenty.

"This is drug money," I say, flatly.

"Wouldn't surprise me, the way those two did business."

"But why stash it in the blocks?"

"He had you in mind?"

"I doubt it. He thought it would be safe. I remember his words. 'Pack your big blocks in the duffel and take them with you.' My father and I were leaving Hull together the night of the attack. Maybe this was money for us to live on."

Crazy Daddy. Hiding all this cash. If Darah hadn't chewed into it, I'd never know. Should I be happy or upset? For now, I'll pick happy.

I'm almost at the end of the alphabet when I reach the V block. I unroll the wad. A small metal object drops to the floor.

I take a slow breath and pick up a key. It's cold and solid—heavier than it should be—like it carries a piece of Daddy with it.

My mind spins. What could it unlock? A door? A safe? A secret compartment he never trusted anyone to find? One step at a time. I can't let excitement make me careless.

I finish the remaining blocks and count the total: $95,500, a fortune.

Clare watches me tuck the key into my pocket.

"Does it look familiar?" Clare asks.

"Maybe it has something to do with the second suitcase. The one my father said contained evidence against Stone, Vixen and Squid. The one I never found. But why hide it in the V block?"

"It's a mystery, Angel," Clare says softly. "One you may never solve."

FIFTEEN

Vixen

April 19, 1988
Dear Lucy,

It's been a hellish week. On Monday, Max came up the hill, hunched and coughing like his lungs might give out. Angel rushed to him, but he pointed to the shore. Through binoculars, I saw Tom slumped in the boat, swaddled in a blanket. Was he dead? Then he moved.

"He's hurt. Help him, please!" Max begged.

Angel and Max brought him into the house. I had no idea what we were dealing with until I removed the makeshift bandages. Tom's hairline was a pus-bubbling cut shaped like a V.

Tom's eyes rolled back. He was burning up. Angel stoked the fire. I put on broth with healing herbs, and we went to work on him.

Max said he and Tom had morning plans, but he was a no-show. Max went to Tom's house in Hull and found him lying face down on his bed. "I thought he was passed out," Max said, "but I turned him over and saw his bloody forehead. I wanted to rush him to the hospital, but Tom kept crying 'No, no. She'll

*kill me.' I went to call the police, but Tom screamed, 'No, no.
They'll kill me too.'"*

*Max thought Tom was delirious, but he cried and screamed.
Max didn't know what else to do, so he brought him here.*

*It's been three days and Tom's still between earth and death.
Without Angel, I don't know what we would have done. She's
been sleeping at his side on the recliner, just like I did when she
came here two years ago.*

*She keeps saying that Vixen did this. I thought we were
finished with Vixen-vicious and Stone-scum. I'm too old and
sick and tired to resurrect those monsters. Angel's come too far
to waste energy worrying on how Hull still suffers under their
domination.*

Your loving sister,

C

*   *   *

I watch Tom. He's restless, beet-red, and furious. His face glistens with sweat as he spits out words Ivy and Daddy used: *fuckers, shitheads, ball-crushers.*

"You'll be all right," I say, trying to steady him.

"Bullshit. I'll never be right again."

His scalp bears a jagged V where his hairline used to be. Vixen had to have done this. That's her signature—carving hair and flesh into a V, laughing maniacally with every pull. I know because I've seen it.

It happened when I was on the second-floor of my house, checking to see if it was safe to go downstairs when I heard scratching at the front door. Daddy had rigged the door to make extra noise, but he was snoring on the couch and didn't stir.

I pressed my eye to the vent. Moonlight spilled through the front window, enough to see a woman slip inside. She moved like a shadow, gliding toward Daddy. Two straps on her thighs bulged with something shiny. Her spiked white hair gleamed, and black circles ringed her eyes.

It hit me all at once: Vixen.

She closed in on Daddy, a knife glinting in one hand and a thin silver clamp poking out of the other. My throat tightened. I wanted to scream but knew better. Stay silent. That's The Rule.

She let out a sharp, gull-like screech.

Daddy jerked awake, eyes wild.

"Don't say a word," she hissed, slamming her fist into his chest and pinning him down. The knife hovered a hair's breadth from his throat. "I'll do the talking."

With her free hand, she brandished the silver tool, plucking hairs from his eyelashes and eyebrows, mangling them with cruel precision until blood trickled into his eyes.

"I've got a bad feeling about what's breathing in these walls," she sneered. "No one plays my game without consequences."

Daddy struggled, but the knife stabbed his temple and he howled in pain. "We're out. Out of the trade," he croaked. "It's all yours."

"You might be clean," she spat, "but your scumbag dirt-ball bitch isn't. Get Ivy under control, or I will."

Before she left, Vixen scooped white powder from a bowl on the table with her long fingernail, snorted it, and let out a banshee-like cackle. Then she vanished into the night, laughing as she went.

I rushed to Daddy's side, pressing a towel to his wounds. "Are you all right?"

He waved me off with a laugh. "I'm fine. I cut myself shaving."

"That's not true! You don't shave your eyebrows! We need to leave. We can't stay where she can find us."

But Daddy didn't listen to me. I was just a kid, a kid who shouldn't have been snooping. But I saw her and I'll never forget her insane laugh.

And now Tom—broken, beaten, and scarred—has met the same fate. This time, I won't let her get away with it.

SIXTEEN

Tom

My sixteenth birthday came and went, overshadowed by everything happening with Tom. Clare baked scones topped with tulip petals and cornflowers—plants I'd gathered during a rare moment outside.

Clare is struggling. She can barely stay upright, and fidgets when she sits, making Tom more restless.

"It's okay if you lie down," I tell her. "If anything changes, I'll let you know."

Most times when I check on her, she's asleep. Sometimes, she's reading or writing in her journal. I give her space.

Max can't bear Tom's suffering. "I've seen enough," he says, his voice breaking. "I watched my sweet granddaughter Lucille die. I watched my beautiful wife die. And now my son looks like he's on his deathbed. I need to get away."

I hear the splash of his paddles as he rows away. Alone, I sit by Tom and let his letters unravel in my mind.

T-O-M. T-O-M-M-Y. T-H-O-M-A-S.

The M's trouble me, the way they sink into themselves.

The Y feels like a funnel, pouring poison into his body.

The S in Thomas makes me think of sliding slopes, of inevitable falls.

Only Tom feels sturdy, like the solid T—a name that might help him stand tall and shoulder his burdens.

Tom clears his throat, snapping me out of it. "That creature, the psycho who killed your parents and got away with it. I thought I could make things right for you. Do something good for once."

It's the first time Tom's talked about her.

"Vixen branded you," I whisper.

Tears streak down his face. "She crept into my room while I was asleep," he says, his voice hoarse.

Every nerve in my body snaps to attention. Tom's eyes roll back, like he's facing death itself.

"Spikes in her nose. Vampire fangs. She was going to kill me."

She's not human. She's a monster.

"She wanted to know why I was asking about her at the bar," Tom says, his breath coming in short, uneven puffs. His moans grow louder, then taper off as he forces out the rest. "Strange things were happening. Prostitutes beaten. A little girl went missing from the carousel."

I drop to my knees, quaking at the thought of another missing child. "Was she found?"

Tom shrugs weakly. "I don't know," he sobs.

I want to ask more about the little girl, about the beaten women, but the words won't come. Who was she? How old? Was she blond? I can't ask. I can barely breathe. My teeth chatter uncontrollably.

C–A–L–M.

C–A–L–M.

C–A–L–M.

Tom's voice turns flat and distant. "I was at my usual watering hole in Hull when this guy sat next to me. Just another regular. He started complaining about getting ripped off—bad heroin. Said if he wanted adultery, he'd have stayed married. Then this bulldog of a guy walks in. Big, barrel-bellied, all strut and swagger. He sits next to my buddy, apologizes for the bad batch, and hands him a new bag. 'We want our customers happy,' the bulldog says."

Tom tries to sit up, veins throbbing at his temples. His voice rises. "That's when I got involved. I asked, 'Who's we? You and Vixen?' Bulldog gave me a long look, then bought me a drink and started calling me *amigo, compadre*."

I bite my nails; the sting keeps me focused. "The bulldog in the bar? What was his voice like?"

"Spanish accent. Deep, rough."

My chest pounds. Squid. He's in Hull right now, stealing girls.

Tom pushes on, his voice edged with tears. "I told him about your parents—the house on the beach, the drugs. I asked if he remembered Wizz and Ivy. He said, 'Yeah, Wizz and the Cher wannabe. Whatever happened to them? Thought they went south.' I said, 'I hear Vixen's a hot bitch with sweet smack. She could make me happy. Just like the good old days.'"

Tom swallows. "Bulldog asks where she can find me. 'I got a place on Strawberry Hill,' I tell him."

Why would Tom tell him where he lives? Why did he put himself in danger? He must've thought it was the right thing to do. But now he's branded, broken. All because of me.

C-A-L-M. Breathe, breathe, breathe.

Tom's words loop in my mind: the bar, the bad heroin, Bulldog, Squid, the mention of Vixen and my parents. Tom was tortured because he was trying to help me. These monsters still haunt Hull, taking whatever they want.

"So Vixen came looking for you?"

Tom nods, his voice cracking. "I woke up to her straddling me, a knife at my throat. She said, 'Wizz and Ivy got what they deserved. Now it's your turn.' Then she laughed—like an animal, like a howler monkey on speed. I blacked out while she yanked my hair out in clumps."

She killed Ivy and Daddy without blinking. Why spare Tom? Was it a message? A warning? Or is she not done yet?

Tom collapses, shaking. I cover him with blankets and bring him hot ginkgo tea with honey, but my mind races.

I pace the room. I could take Daddy's block money and head for the horizon like he told me to do. I'd never have to worry about Vixen and Stone and Squid ever again. But I know, down to my core, that Hull will never be safe from these scumbags and no one is doing anything about it. But Clare, Max, and Tom are my family now. I should be looking toward my future, not my past.

I can't stop thinking about the little girl who went missing from the carousel. Where is she? Is she still alive? And what about all the others? How many more will vanish?

I have to go back. I have to find her. I have to stop Vixen and Squid.

SEVENTEEN

Squatter's Rights

Clare shouts from her bedroom, "There's a man outside. I see him through the bamboo."

I rush into her room. She stands at the window, aiming a revolver across the inlet.

"I should take him out," she says.

"What are you doing?" I ask. I grab the gun from her and quickly close the curtains. What if it's Squid? Maybe he had Tom followed.

I peek through the binoculars and see a man with a tripod and telescope. He's wearing an official khaki uniform—except for the thigh-high waders and the long, straggly beard tucked between the buttons of his shirt.

Clare reaches for her rifle, struggling under its weight as she tries to hitch it onto her shoulder.

"Stay here with Tom," I say, setting the rifle in the corner. "I'll find out what's going on."

"Be careful," she warns. "He's not on our side."

Wrapping a scarf around my neck, I gather my courage. The L in my name propels me forward. It's like I'm absorbing Clare's strength. As she weakens, I gain strength.

"Hey!" I yell across the current. "This is private property!"

"No, Missy, it's not," the man replies. "That island belongs to World's End. It's conservation land. It's dodged the bulldozer for years, but time's up. The council met last week, and a decision has been made."

He scratches his head and looks away.

"But my grandmother lives on this island!"

"Doesn't matter. She doesn't belong there."

"Her family's been here for over fifty years."

He wades through the water and hands me his card: Massachusetts Registry of Deeds, Franklin Fontaine. So many N's! And the mindless F, with no consideration for others.

"Tell Granny it's a done deal."

I watch him cross the current, return to his truck and pack up his equipment. The letters DPW are emblazoned on its side: D-P-W.

The bloated D.

The head-banging P.

The forever-reaching W.

We have a problem.

I race back to the cabin. Clare is sitting on her bedroom floor, surrounded by an arsenal of weapons: a grenade, pocket knives, brass knuckles, two pistols, and her rifle.

"None of these will do me any good," she says. "Those councilmen mean it this time. Max held them off for years."

"With those?" I ask, incredulous.

Clare smirks. "Max? Our man of peace! No, by talking to the Board of Selectmen, convincing them I'm just an old lady who'll be dead soon."

"Why can't you stay here?"

"Angel, I'm a squatter."

S-Q-U-A-T-T-E-R.

Right off the top, the trouble-maker S is followed by the Q, a

wormy letter that infiltrates its way into things. Then the U conceals and hides the truth.

The hair on my arm spikes.

"What does that mean?" I ask.

"It means my father wanted a place to paint, close to home
but far enough to be alone. Back in the '30s, nobody cared about
a little island where only birds and fish lived. He built a lean-to,
and we've been improving it ever since."

"So, you didn't grow up here?"

"Nope. I sold the family home in the '50s after my parents
passed. When I decided to move here, Max was against it. He said
it would come back to bite me."

Clare pulls out a thick folder. "Here's the rub: *Massachusetts does
not recognize adverse possession claims against nonprofit land, conservation
companies, or property held in trust for public conservation purposes.* I have
no lasting claim."

"You must have some rights."

"I'm 84, Angel. I've lived here 36 years. That's something."

"But you belong here."

"Max tried to convince me to leave years ago, but then you
showed up. You changed everything."

"What do you mean?"

"Angel, before I rescued you, I was so tired. I didn't want to live
anymore. Then my sister Lucy came to me in a vision and said,
'Clare, you old fool. There's someone out there who desperately
needs you.' When I saw that Bunkny lowlife tie you up, I knew
I had to act."

"You saved me. Now it's my turn to help you. And Tom."

"Angel, you gave me purpose, but healing Tom isn't your burden. He has to take control of himself. You, though—you have a
future."

"I only have a future if I solve my past. Isn't that what you
always say?"

Questions rumble through me. Why was I locked in an attic, barely ever going outside to run with the wind? Why did my father and mother do that to me? To keep me safe from Squid? From the headbangers who took over the downstairs?

Or from themselves?

I look at Clare, who's kept me safe and made me strong. When did she get so small? So frail? So sure of me?

In the living room, Tom's wrapped in blankets, his forehead swathed in bandages oozing pus and blood. My chest swells with rage at what keeps happening in Hull while everyone looks away. It coils around me like the letter S, squeezing until I can barely breathe.

EIGHTEEN

Farrah and Nadia

"Tom said another girl has been stolen. I can hear her—scared, wounded, and suffering."

"Who is this girl?" Clare asks.

"I don't know her, but I'm sure Squid took her. She needs my help. I have to do something—now."

Clare places her wrinkled hands on my cheeks, like she's drawing out my pain. "Tell me about Squid again."

"Vixen wormed her way into Squid's circle, and my parents were pushed out."

Clare's eyes narrow. She's listening intently. "What proof do you have that children have been abducted?"

I think back to the night I snuck out of the house while Daddy and Ivy were distracted. Most nights, the attic latch clicked shut, locking me in. But one night, there was no click, and I overheard their muffled voices.

"She keeps asking about the children who disappeared," Daddy had said. "She hears the dopers talking. The whole town knows. Farrah Silvio's no hooker's kid—she's the mailman's daughter. There are posters everywhere. The crazy bitch overstepped this time."

I'd never heard the name Farrah Silvio, and I wondered if she belonged to Squid now. I listened to the letters: only the emp-ty-headed follow-the-leader F showed weakness. The other letters were strong and hopeful. They didn't feel dead, only trying to keep themselves above water, their legs kicking so they wouldn't drown.

At the time, I was afraid Squid would come for me next. But Squid liked blond girls. Tasty girls without neck stains. My hair was dark and I smelled like old wood.

The latch was undone and Daddy and Ivy were passed out. I grabbed my chance to see those posters. I knotted my scarf, put on my hooded sweatshirt, and took the flashlight by the back door.

I walked through the shadows until I reached Nantasket Ave. On the corner, there it was: a telephone pole with a tattered poster.

MISSING. FARRAH SILVIO.
Blonde. Blue-eyed. Age 5.
Disappeared from the L Street Playground. Wearing a white blouse, checkered skirt. She has a jagged scar on her left thumb.
Reward. Contact Sergeant Stone of the Hull Police with any information.

Farrah's image flashes before me now, just like on the poster I saw as a child. "They're blond little girls—kidnapped by Stone and handed over to Squid."

Tom's voice drifts weakly from the other room. "The rumor was your parents were the traffickers."

I press my fists into my temples. "Ivy might've been trafficking when she died! She called it her magic. Like it was fun to steal children and hand them to Squid."

Clare's face pales, her eyes losing color. "This Squid—he's the bulldog Tom met in the bar? Angel, your parents were no good. Avenging their deaths will only get you killed."

"It's not about them. I want children to be safe."

"You can do that somewhere else—away from Hull." Clare's voice rises, sharp enough to startle the dogs, who rush to her side.

"But it's happening *now*, in Hull." I glance toward the living room, where Tom lies barely conscious. My skin prickles, and my throat burns like I've swallowed lightning. "Another child has been taken. Prostitutes are being beaten. Tom said so."

"If that's true, Hull is Sodom and Gomorrah," Clare says, her voice heavy with sorrow. "Even Lot couldn't save it."

L-O-T. Those are marching letters. Strong. Triumphant. Lot must've been a good man.

"But I'm not living in biblical times. I can do something. Right now."

"What on earth can a sixteen-year-old do?" Tom mutters, his head sinking back into his pillow.

"I don't know." I feel my strength draining, sinking like the N in my name. "But I have to try."

Clare breathes deeply, then pulls on her red rubber boots. I watch her hobble to the shed and return with sheets of newspaper. "Let's start with the facts."

She grabs a magnifying glass, and we divide the pile, our fingers blackening as we sift through the articles.

On an inside page of *The Hull Gazette*, a headline stops me cold:

Child Disappears from Carousel

Nadia Jones, age 6, vanished yesterday while riding the carousel at Paragon Park. Her mother had strapped her in and stepped away for coffee. When she returned, Nadia was gone.

"She vanished into thin air," said Vanessa Jones, the child's mother.

Police sealed off the area but found no trace.

Nadia Jones has bright red hair, blue eyes, and

a mole on her left shoulder. Contact Sergeant Evan Stone of the Hull Police Department with any information.

"Nadia," I whisper. N–A–D–I–A. Two A's. She's clever. She has a chance. "Sergeant Stone knows exactly where Nadia is."

"With Squid?" Clare asks.

Tom groans from the other room. "What's done is done."

I reread the article. Nadia's a redhead. Has Squid changed his preferences, or is this Vixen's influence?

"If we let them continue," I say, my voice rising with determination, "no child will ever be safe."

N I N E T E E N

Strawberry Hill

April 20, 1988
Dear Lucy,

Tom's wounds are healing, and he hasn't had a drink since
that woman branded him. He paces the cottage like a caged
lion—though he's more like the cowardly lion, afraid to face his
fears until he's forced to.

Max went to the Board of Selectmen to plead our case,
claiming I'm enfeebled and ready to die. They said there's nothing more they can do. I must leave by Memorial Day.

Now to what I really need to tell you: how I can help Angel
have a real future, a way to carry on without me. I can't stop
her from going back to Hull, just like she can't stop me from
becoming a crippled old woman whose insides are eating her
alive. She's determined to uncover what happened to the missing
children, punish Vixen for murdering her parents, and see Stone
and Squid put behind bars. It's cockamamie, but she's set on it,
and I'm too weak to stop her.

Max has a solution to make her a person in her own right,
and Tom agrees. Angel exists nowhere on paper. She's never been

to school, never seen a doctor—she's a ghost as far as the system is concerned. But we can give her a legal name and an identity. With baby Lucy's social security number, she'd become Lucille Ledwith. No one would ever know except us.

Tom will open a bank account for her, as if she were his daughter, and I can transfer my savings. It's not much, but with the block money, she'll have some security.

It's time for me to bow out. I'm a burden to her, weighing her down.

Your loving sister,

C

* * *

I wake, knowing that Max and I are going to Hull today to clean out Tom's house on Strawberry Hill.

"No fucking way will I set foot in that town again," Tom says. His voice sounds like Ivy with her N–F–W ultimatums, her shut-me-up letters.

I can't blame him. Vixen could have torn his limbs and gouged his eyes, but something—footsteps, a door slamming, the world intruding—made her pause. She decided to just play with him instead. Now it's up to Max and me to erase him from Hull.

When we leave, Clare waves from the porch, her face a criss-cross of wrinkles, her tiny body dwarfed by the dogs.

We row the current to World's End, where Max's truck is parked. I've only been in two vehicles: Daddy's shitbox van and Gregg's van-cave. The high seat lets me take in the scenery: crocuses and lilacs, meadows of dandelions and clover. The ocean winks in bays and inlets, surrounded by sprawling houses and tiny shacks. Lawnmowers hum; gardeners dig; children play ball.

I watch them like they belong to another planet—their open yards, their bright shouts, their normal. These are places I've only read about in books, play I've never been part of, children I'll never meet. The world looks wide and happy, like something meant for other people.We pass a sign: Welcome to Hull.

H–U–L–L.

The H divides two worlds: sunshine and shadow.

The U conceals kidnappers, druggies, and smugglers.

I am the L's, ready to help this double-natured town put its feet on the ground, stand straight and move forward.

Max drives past the roller coaster and Ferris wheel, their skeletons towering high, twisting S's and rolling O's that swirl through my thoughts. My eyes scan for a scarred-faced sergeant, a bulldog man with silver necklaces and grills, and a white-haired, black-lip-sticked woman with a maniacal caw.

On Nantasket Avenue, we pass stores, playgrounds, empty lots, and broken houses. Max turns onto A Street, and the place feels deserted. At the top of a winding hill stands a green water tower marked S–H.

"Strawberry Hill," Max says. "Pardon my English, but S-H also means shit hole."

I never heard Max swear, but this place is worse than a snake pit. It drags you down, even from a hill with a name that sounds good enough to eat.

Max stops the truck in front of a dilapidated bungalow. No flowers, no greenery. Rusty leaves fill the gutters. Tar gunks up the roof.

We don't need a key—the door has no knob. Vixen had no trouble slithering in. Beer cans and whiskey bottles litter the floor, a miniature version of Daddy and Ivy's house.

"Take what Tom might want. Put it in boxes or trash bags," Max says as he disappears into a back room.

"What about the furniture?"

"It's not his—it belongs to the landlord."

I save framed photos: Tom with his daughter Lucille, his ex-wife Penny, his parents. Tom in a crew cut, dressed in a suit and tie.

It's like he lived in someone else's life, surrounded by truths that weren't his.

Max hauls out a box of books, clothes on hangers, and bloody bedding.

A hard knock interrupts us. "What's going on?" a booming voice demands.

A wiry young officer walks in, his red hair bright against his pale, freckled face. His badge reads R. Murphy.

Max enters the room, holding a television.

"Put that down now," the officer says sharply, placing a hand on his holstered revolver. "Stand over there!"

He shouts into his walkie-talkie. "B & E in progress. 10 Halvorsen Road."

A gravelly voice responds through static: "Check it out, Cowboy, before we send the cavalry."

Max stammers, setting the TV down. "This is my son's place. Thomas Ledwith. I'm Max Ledwith, his father. I have every right to be here."

"Identification, now."

Max hands over his license, and the officer scribbles in a small notebook.

"And who's the female aiding and abetting?" Officer Murphy's freckled face darkens as he eyes me.

My port wine stains throb, my hand flies to my exposed neck, and I'm back in Hull, where Ivy's rule lingers like a ghost.

"She's my granddaughter, Lucille Ledwith," Max says, his chin quivering but his voice steady. "She's here to help pack her father's belongings, not steal anything."

Lucille. Not little Lucy. Max called me Tom's daughter. He's covering for me, and I'm grateful.

The officer studies me, his gaze narrowing. "What's in the bag?"

"Photos." I pull out a picture of Tom and his real daughter.

"That you?" Officer Murphy asks.

The girl in the photo has curly brown hair and apple cheeks like mine, though she's just a toddler. Max nods.

I answer, "Yes, that's me."

Max shows him another picture, this one of himself with his wife and Tom. "And that's me."

Murphy's expression softens. "I recognize this guy. We call him Doubting Thomas—always questioning people. Hope he's all right."

"He's recovering from an injury," Max replies.

"At the address on your license?"

"Yes, Sir."

The officer jots more notes, then walks into the bedroom. Blood covers the mattress and the floor. "What happened here?"

"Tom hit his head and fell back onto the bed," Max says.

"When did this happen?"

"Five nights ago."

Murphy speaks into his walkie-talkie. "Family matter at 10 Halvorsen. Cancel backup." His tone carries a hint of disappointment.

A gravelly laugh filters back. "Write it up anyway, Cowgirl."

Murphy's face flushes red, blotches rising to the surface.

"Sorry to jump the gun, folks," he says, his tone apologetic. "Bad neighborhood. Never can be too careful."

"My son says there's a woman on the loose who assaults people at night," Max presses. "Have you heard anything about her? Are others in danger?"

Murphy shakes his head, smiling faintly. "You sound just like your son—question after question. Sorry, Mr. Ledwith, no answers here." He jots more notes, avoiding Max's eyes.

"Officer Murphy," I say, summoning Clare's confidence into my tone. "What does the R on your badge stand for?"

His posture straightens. "Robert, but most folks call me Robo—like Robocop."

R–O–B–O. The letters tumble through my mind. Is he firm and fair, or clumsy and clueless?

"How long have you been a policeman?"

"Since New Year's. Proud to serve Hull." He salutes.

My real question slips out. "Were you working here when Nadia Jones went missing from the carousel?"

Murphy's lips press into a thin line, like he's holding back a thought. "One week too late," he says solemnly. "Why do you ask? Is Tom Ledwith involved?"

Max steps forward. "We saw the article in the *Gazette*. Tom's a family man. He cries when he reads about children being hurt."

That means Nadia's been missing for four months, since December. "Are there any leads?" I ask.

"You folks sure ask a lot of questions. I'm the interrogator, remember?" He chuckles awkwardly.

We force polite laughs, but nothing about this feels funny.

After Officer Murphy leaves, I turn to Max. "Why did you call me Lucille?"

"It felt natural. Clare insists you have a legal name. My granddaughter had a social security number. Tom and I will open a bank account under the name Lucille Ledwith. It'll give you an identity and some security."

Lucille Ledwith. Tom as my dad. Max as my granddad. My mind reels at the thought. L–U–C–I–L–L–E.

The L's feels solid, marching forward.

The U lets me keep my secrets.

The C reminds me of Clare's quiet strength.

The I stands tall and independent.

But where is my A? Will this new name, not of my choosing, change me?

Outside of Tom's rental, a woman leans against Max's truck. "Sorry to see Tommy go," she drawls, her bushy hair frizzing in the breeze. Her thin clothes reveal curves that bubble over. "He was my buddy."

Max holds his head high, his shoulders stiff. "He's not dead."

"Could've been," the woman says.

"What do you know about it?" Max demands.

"The she-ghost comes late at night, stealing souls. I banged frying pans and marched around the house to scare her off. Must've worked."

Her words sound insane, but her tone feels true.

"Did you know a couple named Wizz and Ivy? They lived at the corner of F Street and Beach Avenue," I ask cautiously.

Her eyes widen into O's. "Don't say their names. The she-ghost will come for you too!" She spins on her heels and clicks away down the street.

"That was about Vixen, right?" Max asks as we climb into the truck.

"They're terrified of her." Hull will never feel safe if Vixen is everyone's nightmare.

As Max drives, letters float through my thoughts: the forward-moving L's in Lucille, the spiked letters in Vixen, the cunning ones in Evan Stone. And what about the O's in Robocop? Do they roll aimlessly, circling back without progress?

Max's truck winds down the hill, past rows of cracked pavement and weathered houses. The streets seem desolate, a ghost town where even the shadows cling to the edges, afraid to step into the light.

"Do you believe her?" I ask, my voice barely rising above the hum of the engine.

"Who?" Max's eyes stay on the road, his hands gripping the wheel.

"The woman. About the she-ghost."

Max exhales sharply, almost a laugh but not quite. "People around here love their stories. They make it easier than facing the truth. That Hull is rotting from the inside out," Max says grimly. "The drugs, the crime, the fear—it's all connected. People like Vixen feed on it, thrive on it. And the rest just. . . look the other way."

The weight of his words settles over me. I glance out the window as we pass the roller coaster, its wooden frame looming like ribs against the horizon.

"I can't look the other way," I whisper.

Max glances at me, his expression softening. "I know, Lucille. That's what scares me."

The name feels foreign on his tongue, but there's a strange comfort in hearing it. A new name. A new identity. Maybe even a new start.

TWENTY

Moving On

I'm confused when Max pulls up in front of a two-story house on a quiet street in Hingham on our way back to World's End.

"We'll unload Tom's stuff here before heading to Brewer Island," Max says.

"Where are we?"

"My place." He points across the street to a nearly identical house. "That's where Clare and Lucy grew up."

The house looks nothing like Clare's style. It's boxy and nondescript, stripped of color and character. Brewer Island's cottage is cozy and comforting, with clean lines and an inviting porch.

"Let's put the boxes and bags in my garage. There's no room inside the house."

The house looks spacious enough. I can't see why ten boxes, some clothes, a TV, and odds and ends wouldn't fit. We had ditched the bloody bedding in a dumpster.

"The house isn't ready for company."

I'm not company, I want to say. I'm the person who sits with your son for hours, trying to coax him back to the living. I'm the dark-haired, freshly-minted sixteen-year-old you've decided to claim as your granddaughter. Company? Hardly. I bite my tongue and recite the alphabet silently to calm myself. Max doesn't seem to notice my silence; he's lost in his own thoughts.

We unload Tom's possessions and head back to Clare's cabin. Max calls a meeting, his steel-hard gaze locking us in place. "I've made a decision," he announces. "We'll all move into my house. No Hull, no Brewer Island, no more looking for trouble."

I don't want to live in Max's house. I'm old enough to make my own decisions, though I'm not ready to live on my own. If I could decide, what would I choose? Head for Daddy's horizon and escape this mess? Return to Hull and root out its evils? Curl up with a good book and forget about the ugly world? Or wait, accepting my place as part of Max's family? At his house, I'll be Lucille Ledwith's ghost—caring for my granddad, cooking for my dad, and making sure Clare eats. Where's my A in all this? It feels like it's abandoned me.

"You'll need a tow truck to clear out all the junk," Tom says, smirking. "My father's kept everything since he was a kid."

"It'll give us something to do until the end of the month," Max replies.

Four more weeks to be Angel. I wonder how I'll hold myself together.

*　*　*

May 2, 1988
Dear Lucy,

> *The man from the DPW paddled through the current and marched up the hill, his scrawny body battered by the wind, his straggly beard flapping. "Ma'am," he said, "I have papers showing you can't stay on this property. You've got thirty days to vacate."*
>
> *I spat at his feet.*

Then Tom appeared at the door. The man froze at the sight of the angry V etched into Tom's scalp, like an accusation ready to fire arrows. The guy skedaddled, tripping over his own feet.

Tomorrow, Max and Tom are going to the bank to move money around and file the paperwork for Angel's official name change. After that, Tom will head to Max's house to get it ready for all of us to move in.

I don't know how I'll manage. Living there will feel like walking backward through time, staring at my childhood home. My insides churn. Angel would say my R is in conflict—my head pulling one way, my legs another. The E will decide.

Your loving sister,

C

*   *   *

May 10, 1988
Dear Lucy,

We're clearing out the cabin. Angel and Tom are chopping bamboo and tying the poles into rafts to ferry everything to Max's house.

At low tide, Tom tows the raft to World's End, and together he and Angel transfer the load to his truck. So much stuff! Bamboo furniture, framed mirrors, barrels of beach treasures: sea glass, shells, and gemstones. Papa's paintings. Hundreds of books. And the herbs: bayberry for luck, cinnamon for focus, clove for memory, and heliotrope for protection.

Angel's going to need buckets of heliotrope if she goes through with her wild plan to rid Hull of its demons. She's still a child, though she doesn't see herself that way. Every time she talks about Hull, I feel something inside me burn. How can I protect someone who believes she has to save the world?

Max and I sit on the porch, eating blueberry scones and reminiscing, watching as my world gets packed up. Neither of us has the strength to help. Max coughs, and I'm always cold. No cayenne pepper or mullein in our tea helps. Angel wraps me in baby Lucy's quilt. We nod off every twenty minutes.

We're relocating our world, little sister. I don't know if I can do this.

Your loving sister,

C

TWENTY-ONE

After the Storm

Max says a storm is brewing and insists we move to his house immediately. Tom has already cleaned a room for us. But Clare brushes off his concerns and tells me to batten down the hatches. I secure the skiff between bamboo stalks.

Before Max leaves, he shows me the bank papers. He and Tom will open an account in my new name, Lucille Ledwith. I skim the legalese, but understand little. I have no choice but to trust them.

"I have the cash Daddy left me," I say. "Can we add it to the account?"

Clare and Max exchange a glance.

"Sit down, Angel," Clare says gently. "When my sister Lucy died, the gas company was at fault. They left a manhole cover open, and my parents settled with them for a large amount of money. I've never been one for keeping track of finances, and I've lived off the grid for decades. Max has invested that money wisely under his name, and it's grown into a healthy sum. That money is now in a trust for Lucille Ledwith. You, my dearest child, will be its official recipient when we're gone."

"But that won't be for a long time, right?"

Max clears his throat. "Keep a few thousand dollars of your

father's cash for daily expenses and unforeseen needs. The rest should go into your account. Tom and I will handle the details tomorrow, before the storm hits. You'll never have to worry about money. We'll make sure of that."

Outside, the air feels charged, the sky swollen and heavy with warning. By morning, a gray-black world surrounds us, the wind rises from a low whistle to a full-throated howl that shakes the cabin. The trees thrash like combatants.

Clare and I lie on a makeshift bed in front of the wood-burning stove. She starts talking about a book she once read, *Their Eyes Were Watching God.*

"Janie and her husband Tea Cake were in the Florida Keys during a hurricane," she says. "The storm raged around them, and they stared at their door as if the Big Bad Wolf was ready to devour them." She pauses, her voice cracking. "But they thought God would save them."

Clare turns to me, her frail body shivering under the blankets. "I've decided I don't go along with the God concept. We live and die by our own free will."

"You're scaring me," I whisper. "What would I do without you?"

"When I die, I won't be gone," Clare says, her tone soft but firm. "I'll become part of the tides, the raindrops, the salty tears. If you want me again, look under your boot soles. You'll hardly know who I am or what I mean, but I'll be good help to you nevertheless, filtering and fibering your blood." She smiles faintly. "That's from the poet Walt Whitman, but it might as well be me."

I clutch her tiny hand, feeling the curve of her fingers, the roughness of her skin. C–L–A–R–E. She is my comfort, my love, my anchor. I can't imagine life without her.

Outside, the storm peaks. Trees splinter and crack. Goats scramble under the porch; chickens scatter in panicked circles. Darah and Pharaoh hide in a corner of the cabin. Bamboo snaps like peas.

When the storm passes, the sun emerges cautiously, peeking

out as though afraid to face the wreckage. I rekindle the fire and help Clare to the bathroom before wrapping her in blankets and guiding her to the porch.

The goats nuzzle into us for comfort. Feathers litter the ground, but the chickens are gone, swept away like autumn leaves. The labyrinth of bamboo looks like it's been hacked by evil scissors, with its bald patches and uneven heights.

"No use cleaning up," Clare murmurs. Her skin is yellow in the morning light, her eyes sunken and distant. "The bulldozers will be here soon enough. It's not my concern anymore. Lucille, I'm tired. Help me back to bed."

I spoon feed her soup and garlic tea, but she struggles to keep it down. She lies in bed, listening to the island cry.

"Go," she says, shooing me away.

I sit on the porch, her coughs rattling the cabin walls. The air around me is fresh, but I can't catch my breath.

Tom arrives later, climbing the slope by himself. His baseball cap sits low on his head, and dark circles shadow his eyes. A cigarette dangles from his lips.

"Dad's at the hospital," he says quietly. "He went out during the storm. Said he wanted to feel the wind. He caught pneumonia. I took him to South Shore Hospital when he couldn't breathe. The doctors. . . they said it's just a matter of time."

My stomach turns. Max, the pillar of our family—gone? How can that be?

"Don't tell Clare," Tom adds, his voice breaking. "I can't stay, but I wanted you to know."

After Tom leaves, I go to Clare's room. Her eyes are rimmed with red, her nose running. "I heard," she whispers. "My lungs may be failing, but my ears still work. Help me outside, Lucille."

I guide her to the porch and drape the quilt over her thin legs.

"Gather smooth rocks," she says suddenly.

"Rocks?"

"Humor me. Build a pyramid near that old balsam tree at the base of the slope."

I spend hours collecting and stacking rocks into a pyramid. Clare watches through binoculars, nodding her approval.

"Now find white rocks the size of eggs," she says weakly. "Circle them around the tree."

I search the island for smooth, luminous stones, placing them in an O around the balsam. When I return, she smiles faintly.

"Why did I do all this?" I ask.

The paper skin around her eyes crinkles and her lips upturn at each end. She tilts her tiny head and nods, her gnarled fingers intertwine and press against her bony chest. "Rocks remember and trees bear witness."

*   *   *

The next day, Tom returns. He smells of band-aids and vinegar, his eyes shadowed.

"Dad's resting comfortably," he says.

Clare's face brightens briefly as Tom hands her an envelope. She retreats to her room to read it in private. I want to follow, but she needs her space. Instead I head down the hill with Tom.

"What can I do to help?" I ask.

Tom's face darkens, and he pulls his baseball cap low. "It's out of our hands."

His words lodge in my chest. I want to say something to help, but Tom hates that kind of stuff. He pretends he doesn't care, but I know he does.

Tom strides ahead without waiting for me. When he spots the rocks around the tree, he drops into the grass and buries his head in his arms.

"When my daughter died," he says without looking up, "I built a Spirit Garden for her. I gathered pebbles and white stones, and arranged them around a sapling. Clare said it would bring me peace."

"And did it?"

"No. I was pissed as hell. Still am. AA says surrendering to a higher power brings peace. That's bullshit."

A–A. Higher powers, piercing the sky. My A's. The ones I abandoned to become Lucille. I must now look to the L for support. A's are no longer part of my identity. It hurts more than I expected.

"Angel, I'm a fucking mess. A shitload of white pebbles will never make things right for me."

"Or for Clare," I whisper.

TWENTY-TWO

The Current

"Make me a chicory coffee, please, dear. And cut me a slice of goat cheese pie," Clare says, her tiny head sinking into the pillow. "I want to taste our island."

I bring her the meal and help her eat, her frail hands trembling around the fork.

"Clare, can you tell me what Max wrote?"

Her lips pull downward, every wrinkle sinking into her neck.

"Max wrote that he would love me forever."

The finality of her words knocks the wind out of me. Tears spill into my coffee cup, spreading like ripples on the sea.

"Remember Jack Sawyer?" Clare murmurs, slipping in and out of consciousness.

"Tell me about him," I say softly, knowing she means Stephen King's Jack Sawyer from *The Talisman*.

"When Jack held the talisman in his hand, he lived in the world, but he was also the world." Her voice wavers, and coffee dribbles down her chin. I wipe it away as she continues. "He was dust and the space between the dust. He was Lucy and Clare. He was the bottom of the pit where my sister fell, and the air she once breathed."

I sink into the spaces of my own life: the shitbox van before Hull, the attic, the tent, the loft on Brewer Island, Tom's blood-stained bedroom, Max's memory-hoarding house. I am the pecking chicken and the protective dog. I row the skiff. I am the skiff. I am the oars cutting through the water. I am the bed where Clare lies and the pillow where she rests her head. I am Agnes, Angel, and Lucille.

Like Emerson's poem about the transparent eyeball, Clare's words flow through me, weaving themselves into the fabric of my being.

I fall asleep in the chair by her side as twilight settles. My dreams are strange—a jumble of rocks with eyes and scones that speak. When I wake, Clare's bed is empty. The covers are neatly pulled up, her pillow fluffed. Resting on it is a small silk pouch. Inside is a heart-shaped rose quartz crystal and a note. I open it, thinking it might be the letter from Max, but it's Clare's hand-writing—shaky but legible.

May 25, 1988
Dear Angel, my new Lucille, my private Lucy,

You have been my crystal, my light, and my talisman.

'All the means of action
– the shapeless masses, the materials –
lie everywhere about us.
What is needed is the celestial fire
to change the flint into the transparent crystal,
bright and clear.' —Longfellow

That fire is YOU.

Forever in life, Clare.

Clutching the crystal and the note, I rush outside, expecting to find Clare on the porch. But her red rubber boots are gone.

"Clare! Clare!" I shout, tripping down the slope. The dogs race beside me, their noses to the ground, sensing my panic.

I stop short beneath the evergreen. The circle of rocks I'd placed yesterday has been rearranged. Where there was once an O, there is now a C.

"Clare! Where are you?"

I make my way to the beach. The current is swift, the water dark and churning. On the shore, I find Clare's nightgown. I pick it up, pressing the soft cotton to my face, inhaling the scent of her.

"Clare! Clare! Answer me!"

I race around the perimeter of the island, the dogs sniffing and barking as they try to lead me forward. And then, I see it: one red rubber boot lying on the backside of the island where the water churns and the whitecaps wink under the sun, like they know something I don't.

"Clare!"

I pick up the boot, searching the shoreline for the other. But there is nothing.

I collapse onto the rocky shore, hugging the boot to my chest as the dogs nuzzle and prod me to keep going. But I know.

Clare is gone.

PART TWO

 O N E

In a Fog

Since Clare disappeared, I stagger like a drunk around the island, searching for signs of her. None appear. The dogs perk their ears, and I hear paddles cut through the water. I hide behind what's left of the bamboo until I make out Tom's silhouette.

"It's over. Max is gone."

Like Clare, Max is dead. I choke out the words: "I'm sorry," though the apology feels insufficient—for myself, for Tom, for Brewer Island, for the loss of two extraordinary people who taught me that my breath is sacred and mine to control.

"I'm worried about you, Angel," Tom says.

He doesn't call me Lucy or Lucille.

"The bulldozers are lining up on World's End. It's time to move into Max's house."

"I'm not ready."

He goes back to the skiff and retrieves a silver urn.

"I brought Clare a gift. Inside are Max's ashes."

"I want a part of him to lie with Clare," Tom says.

We stand together at the shore. Tom removes the urn's lid and tilts it slightly.

"For Max," he says.

"For Clare," I say.

Ashes scatter over the water, carried away by the current, vanishing into tendrils of morning mist. Parts of me disappear with them.

"Clare wrote a note to my dad. I read it to him, but I don't think he heard a word. It'd make a good eulogy."

We bow our heads, and he reads:

To Max, my beloved friend,

> *The day which we fear as our last is but the birthday of eternity.*
> *Let's blow out our candles and celebrate.*

> > *Always in life. Always in love,*
> > *Clare*

It is done. We step away from the water.

"Memorial Day's this weekend. I'll be here Saturday to get you," he calls, leaving me a pile of newspapers for kindling. He splits a few logs before heading back toward the shore.

I climb the hill with the dogs sulking beside me. Darah and Pharaoh stay close as he pushes off into the fog. It swallows what's left of the bamboo, the tree where Clare's rocks form a C, and the faint outline of World's End and Hull.

Lucille Ledwith

I sit in Clare's empty room, staring at the faded yellow closet door with green horizontal stripes. When I asked Clare about the design, she said Lucy had painted it that way, and she'd kept it as a reminder of her sister.

I never snooped through Clare's things. They weren't like my parents' floorboards, where drugs and money were stashed. Clare was open with me, like the C in her name. Yet the closet door seems to call: *Open me. Open me.*

The brass handle is cool against my palm as I turn it.

My jaw drops. Three boxes are stacked waist high, their cardboard edges worn soft with age. The musty scent of old paper fills the room as I pull one down, my shoulders tensing. Did Clare leave these for me to find?

Inside the first box, photographs spill out: a man painting by the shore, hunting, fishing in waders; a woman in a crisp housedress, her shadow long as she hangs laundry and scatters feed for chickens; two young girls—Clare and Lucy—all smiles and chubby cheeks—building sandcastles, swimming, holding trophies.

And Max. Always Max. At every age: young and dashing in his wedding photos, eventually silver-haired but still tall and dignified.

Dozens of photos show Max and Tom over the years. But it's the ones of Max with his granddaughter Lucille that catch in my throat—watching her transform from a vibrant child to one whose hair falls out in clumps, her face swelling like a balloon as the images progress.

The second box holds official documents: birth certificates, death certificates, yellowed and crisp. A family tree spreads across pages like roots of an ancient oak. I lean back against the wall, the texture grounding me as questions swirl. Who am I from? Did Daddy and Ivy have certificates? What proof exists of their lives?

A memory surfaces, sharp as broken glass: Ivy sprawled in the van on X Street, while Squid and my father did business at the beach house.

"Ever since I was little," Ivy had said, slurring her words, "I knew that I'd never have a fairytale life. My father," she took a long pull from the bottle, "loved me more than he loved my mother. He showed me that every fucking day." Her laugh was hollow. "And my mother just sat in her room, her door locked, leaving me to him."

"Where are they now?" I asked, my voice small in the darkness.

Ivy's face had hardened. "Gone. I gave them a proper burial. More than they deserved." Ivy's voice cut like a razor. "No more questions, AgMess. You're driving me crazy."

I'd once asked Daddy about his parents. He flashed that snaggletooth grin and said he'd sprung from the earth fully formed, belonging to no one but himself. Oh Daddy, there's so much I never learned about you, and now I never will.

The next box makes my heart stutter—old notebooks and journals, dating back to the 1920s. One labeled 1987-88 catches my eye—my first year on Clare's island. The pages crackle as I open them, and words leap out like accusations: *Sad. Skinny.* Clare's neat handwriting describes me, the S's slinking down the page like snakes.

You've come back to life, Clare writes, comparing me to Lucy, resurrecting her sister through me. *Angel doesn't know how to love.* The words sting like nettles. I want to argue with the pages—I do know love, I just don't trust it when it hides behind the treacherous V. *The girl learns fast.* That line, I cling to. *Papa would have loved her.*

Did Daddy love me? Images flutter through my mind like autumn leaves. His careful hands whittling miniature animals. The rhythmic scratch of knife against wood. His gentle voice reading bedtime stories. His fingers tickling my ribs until I squealed.

Then the memories darken. Daddy turning into Wizz. A vodka bottle glinting like poison, Needle marks tracking his arms like evil constellations. His body sprawled unconscious while I learn to feed myself. Maybe Daddy was never real at all. Maybe he only lived in my dreams.

The journal falls open to another page, and four words punch me in the gut: *I lied to Angel.* My palms sweat as I read Clare's account of the house on F Street after the fire, about a room behind the boiler that survived like a secret tomb. Her words bring that day rushing back with terrifying clarity—ButtFace's gun pressed into Ivy's stomach, the metal catching the light. Ivy disappearing into the basement, reemerging with Suzanne wrapped in a blanket, her small form too still.

Was there another child hidden in that concrete coffin? Was it the same child Stone discovered the night my parents were murdered? Or was it just another hiding place for their poisonous trade—drugs and money and silver suitcases full of despair?

Then I read about what Clare found outside, and bile rises in my throat. Among the burnt oranges and black golds of scattered pebbles, life was budding. But when she looked more closely, she realized with horror—it was a toe.

The vomit comes without warning, spattering across Clare's floor. Daddy's toes! Daddy's fingers! Each heave drags up another horrible truth from the depths of my memory until I'm empty, shaking, my throat raw. Now I understand why Clare lied—she was shielding me from nightmares. But I'm sixteen now, and I'm alone except for a few goats and Tom, who spins through space like the T.

I need truth more than protection. I need to know who my parents were and what happened to those vanished children.

Sleep takes me there on the floor, surrounded by scattered boxes and drying vomit, too exhausted to care about the mess. When I wake, my eyes are drawn to Clare's final journal entry, dated May 25, 1988.

Dear Lucy,

After you died, I wanted to follow. But I soldiered on. When Angel arrived, I found purpose again. But now I'm spent. My body betrays me daily. My mind wanders down paths I can't follow. Some days I'm not even sure these words make sense. I look at Angel and no longer see you. She's become her own woman, lovely and strong. She sits beside me from dawn until starlight, tending to my needs. But I won't have her waste her youth this way. Max has given her a new name, a fresh beginning, and enough money to build a good life.

Oh Clare! I don't need a new name or a clean slate. I just need you. Why did you leave me? My fingers trace her handwriting, trying to hold onto something of her. Tears blur the words as I continue to read.

Angel is officially Lucille Ledwith now. How do you like that? You might've carried that name if you married Max, like we used to giggle about we were little. Now Angel will live both as you and baby Lucille. She'll be free to move forward in safety. I will not be a burden to her.

I have a plan. When she's asleep, I'll hold myself together long enough to take the plunge. Unlike you, little sister, it's truly

*my time. I'll fill my boots with witness rocks and walk into the
water. What a beautiful way to become new.*

Your loving sister,

C

The journal falls from my trembling hands. Sobs rack my body
as I weep for all of them—Clare's sacrifice, Max's quiet strength,
Tom's broken promises, Lucy's stolen future, little Lucille's suffering. For Daddy, trapped in his own prison. For Brewer Island itself,
its bamboo bowing in surrender. For lost children everywhere. For
stolen children. For homeless children. For me.

A whimper breaks through my grief. Scratching at the front
door pulls me back to the present. When I open it, Darah staggers
out and retches green bile onto the sand. Her sides heave as she
pants. When I bring her water, she turns away, laying her head
between her paws like she's given up. Pharaoh circles her anx-
iously, tongue flicking out to comfort her, but she remains still as
driftwood. I sink down beside her, my fingers finding the soft spots
behind her ears, willing health back into her tired body.

The crunch of footsteps in sand announces Tom's arrival. He
sees Darah's collapsed form and covers her vomit with sand, his
movements jerky like a broken puppet. "Hey, pup," he drawls, his
words thick as tar. "Last minute jitters? Having second thoughts
about leaving the island?" The smell of alcohol radiates from him
like a toxic haze.

"I won't go until she's better," I tell him, my voice firm despite
my churning stomach.

"Then I'd better tell you the news now."

N–E–W–S. The letters surround me like a black cloud.

The N betrays trust.

The E makes an event last for decades.

The W fans people's fears.

And the S offers nothing in return.

My skin prickles with dread.

Tom drops heavily beside me; the brim of his baseball cap hides his scarred forehead. Whiskers dot his chin and upper lip like mold on bread. His leather jacket is frayed at the sleeves. His work boots, soaked from misjudging the shoreline, leave wet prints in the sand. Clare called him a slinker, a person who likes shadows and corners, who's afraid to stand in the sunshine. He guzzles openly from a flask.

"Angel," he begins, words slurring together like wet paint, "the bank book and Clare's money? They don't belong to you. Not yet anyway."

"They belonged to Max, right? He was the co-signer. And you and I are his beneficiary."

He downs more booze. His hands shake slightly as he wipes his mouth. "True. And it would stand to reason that all his possessions would automatically go to us when he died."

I'm following him, though his words slur, and visions of Ivy flash in my mind—rocking like a child, disappearing into mental caves where I couldn't follow.

"But something happened that I didn't expect." He turns away, and I hear the familiar snort of powder being inhaled, like Daddy used to do before he whittled a totem or dug up the backyard or made a closet inside a closet.

"What?" The word escapes me like a trapped breath.

"Clare and Max had this plan." Tom's words come fast, like he's memorized a speech and has to say it before he forgets. "They were going to transfer the gas company settlement money and Clare's earnings from dreamcatchers and chimes. Add a portion of the house since you'd legally be Max's granddaughter. Plus, the cash from your alphabet blocks." His fingers drum against his knee. "You'd be set for life. Except, of course, you'd have to stomach me as your father." Tom forces a strangled laugh, like a choke cut short. "We were good to go."

"How does Max's death change that?" The morning air feels suddenly colder.

Tom's fingers find his chin hairs, pulling at them like worry beads. "Well, that's the thing."

T–H–I–N–G. Each letter strikes like a tiny hammer against my skull.

"Now that Max is gone, I thought we'd inherit everything. Simple." He swallows hard. "But my ex, Penny, is claiming half of Max's money."

P--E–N–N–Y. The letters march across my vision like soldiers bearing bad news.

"But aren't you divorced?"

"Never got around to making it official." His voice shrinks.

"What does that mean?" Even though I already feel the truth settling like stones in my stomach.

Tom leans forward, his breath sour with alcohol and desperation. "It means she wants half the house and half the bank account. See, Max put Lucille Ledwith as the beneficiary. That might mean you, sort of." His words stumble over each other. "But Lucille Ledwith is also Penny's daughter."

My throat tightens. "How does Penny know about the bank documents?"

"Damn it all!" The words explode from him. "She found me at Max's house. She said she'd heard my place on Strawberry Hill was trashed, and thought something bad happened to me." His hands shake as he speaks. "She figured I was in jail sleeping off a drunk, so she went to the cops. Some busybody told her I'm at Dad's place."

His voice rises, bitter as burnt coffee.

"She barges in and the first thing she sees are the bankbook and legal documents right there on the kitchen table with Lucille

Ledwith's name. Next thing I know, she starts calculating what I owe her, just like that. I haven't seen the woman in years, and she comes in like she owns the place." He lets out a nervous laugh. "Which, legally, I guess she does."

"What are we going to do?" My voice sounds small, even to me.

Tom snorts more powder, not even trying to hide it anymore. "I'll hire a probate attorney. Let him figure it out. It's been six years since Penny and I split. That's got to count for something. And my little Lucille's been gone for eight." His voice catches on the name. "That money's mine, no matter whose name appears on the papers. When I get it, I'll share it with you. But you've got to lie low for now. You can't stay at Max's house."

"So I'm not Lucille Ledwith anymore?" The letters stop moving, like the L's forgot how to walk.

Tom stands, his body jerking like a puppet with its strings all tangled. "Sorry kid, I can't claim you."

The words sink into me like cold rain. I don't want to be claimed like a lost ticket. I want to exist as a real person—someone with a name, an identity, friends, parents, people who care about me. I've never had money before; I can survive without it now. Can't I? But I gave Max a lot of Daddy's block money to put in the bank, and now that's not mine either? Can I trust Tom to help me, or should I write him off like Clare did? Is he just another addict who cares only for himself?

Tom staggers down the hill, each step uncertain. "I'm heading west, Angel. Taking a job in Alaska on a fishing vessel. I'll be back after the summer."

"What about me?" The question hangs in the air like smoke.

"You're a survivor. You'll be fine."

S–U–R–V–I–V–O–R. The letters swim before my eyes, each one a verdict.

The slimy S writhes like a snake.

The secretive U hides shadows in its curve.

The V's pierces like an arrow through flesh.
The solitary I stands alone, untrustworthy.
The O rolls away like a broken promise.
Only the R's, sturdy and strong, offer any hope of rescue.

THREE

Angelica

Memorial Day comes and goes. The DPW has not shown up. Darah gets weaker every day. Pharaoh stays by her side, nudging her, licking her fur.

I chip away at the barrels in the root cellar. I still have potatoes, squash, apples and berries. I portion out packets of dogfood that Clare and I dehydrated. When I take the dogs to the water's edge, they flank me down the hill, as they always have. But today, they don't follow me back.

"Darah! Pharaoh!" I call, my voice sharp against the stillness. "Girl! Boy!"

I search the shore, calling again and again. No whimpers, no barks—no sign of them at all. Hours stretch like days.

In the morning, howling cuts through the air. I run to the shore and find Pharaoh curled around Darah's cold body. My legs buckle, and I sink to my knees, sobbing under the weight of loss.

Later, I bury Darah beside Clare's memory garden. Coaxing Pharaoh away from Darah's body is like tearing apart something sacred, but I have no choice. I lay my beautiful girl to rest, arranging white stones into a D to honor her, whispering every memory I have of her.

Pharaoh pines for her. He cries, refuses food, and slips away with each passing day. When he dies, I dig a grave for him beside Darah's and shape a P in the stones.

I thought I had nothing left to lose. I was wrong.

Now I am truly alone. Goats are not house companions.

I lie on the mattress and think about letters. Does that make me crazy? Did Clare truly understand, or was she just being kind, helping me believe in myself?

M–E.

The strong-shouldered M with its internal danger.

The forever reaching E.

Today I'm cold. The stove is full of gray-white powder, fine as confectioners' sugar. I've forgotten to eat. I've forgotten to dream. I've forgotten why I need to keep myself safe. I can't think past the moment.

I find old newspapers in the kitchen corner, shredding them to start a fire. A face appears from the print—long hair, head thrown back, mouth open. A spark of memory ignites. Jazmin? Suzanne? Farrah? Impossible. They disappeared years ago.

I snatch the article before it burns.

Child Washes Up on Gunrock Beach; Identity a Mystery

A girl, approximately eleven, with long black hair, and multiple wounds, was found unconscious on Gunrock Beach yesterday morning. Sergeant Evan Stone performed CPR, reviving her, but she remains unresponsive. She was rushed to South Shore Hospital where her condition is listed as critical.

Dated Friday, May 13—three weeks ago, before Clare and Max and Darah and Pharaoh died, before Tom left, when I was still

Lucille Ledwith. I skim the rest of the article, and read a detail that sends ice through my veins.

The young girl had jagged bruises on her stomach, back and thighs. A witness said they looked like V's.

V's. V-scars! This girl is connected to Vixen—just like Daddy's eyebrows, Gregg's wrist, and Tom's scalp.

I scour other newspapers for more information. Nothing. Gone. Yesterday's news. Stone appears again, though—praised for arresting a burglar, shutting down an underage bar, leading a cocaine bust, rescuing a child from a storm.

Only I seem suspicious of Stone.

How can I tell a town that its hero is a murderer?

Engines rumbling jolt me back to the present: the advance of an army of island-destroyers intent on leveling what's left of Clare's bamboo.

I pack quickly: my blocks, *The Letter Bible*, a few of Clare's journals, photos of her and Max. I hide the remainder of Daddy's block money in my backpack. I had given Max over seventy-five thousand dollars to put in the bank. Clare assured me it would be safe. I trusted her; it was Tom who couldn't be trusted.

T–R–U–S–T. The taunting word, its letters twirl around in space.

I consider taking a weapon, but realize that a gun is no way to solve a problem. I throw Clare's arsenal into the sea.

The pink quartz crystal Clare left me beats like a heart against my chest. I dress in layers, stash food and clothes in my bags, and roll little Lucille's quilt to strap onto my pack. On the way down the slope, I stop at Clare's rock garden and Darah and Pharaoh's graves and salute the witness tree.

"You'll be all right without me?"

The tree sways in the morning breeze.

"You won't let them cut you down, will you?"

Its branches rustle and nod.

I remember what Daddy told me. Keep your eyes on the horizon and you'll find the right road. I study how the water meets the sky. As Agnes, I used only my eyes to measure the horizon. A slightly curved pencil line. A gray rainbow. A far-away place where the sun sank. As Angel, I saw dancing shapes. Bouncing letters. Lying-down B's and D's. Ships and birds and dots of land. I discovered that the earth keeps going. Like the L. Then as Lucille, I realized how quickly clouds gathered and the jagged I of lightning strikes.

In the sand, I write A–N–G–E–L with a long stick. Then I go through the alphabet, selecting additional letters that mean something special to me.

Two I's were in Daddy's real name—William—and one in Ivy. I add the I to remind me of my father and mother.

And how can I move forward without the C honoring Clare? If I add another A for Agnes, I can blend past with present.

I rearrange the letters into my new name—Angelica Brewer. With Clare's last name, I'm ready to face a new horizon.

I cross the current and step onto World's End. I walk a trail that leads to the road that Max took when he drove to Hull a few weeks ago. How could so much change in thirty days? But I know the answer: one night was all it took for Gregg to change everything.

F O U R

Andréa

It's almost midnight when I make my way to the boardwalk at the beginning of Hull where the roller coaster soars and the Ferris Wheel turns. Neon signs blare and jukebox music spills out of bars. I'm big-eyed at the wonder of it all but want to stick my fingers in my ears. The noise is just too much.

I keep a lookout for an orange-headed woman, and a face with a scar from eye to chin. I listen for a screeching cackler and a barrel-chested bully. As I pass the hotspots, I see drunks and druggies, staggering bodies and slamming bodies, and hear laughter so loud that the ocean is quiet in comparison.

As I try to blend in, a frizzy-haired man grabs my arm, yanking at my backpack. I hold tight to its straps.

"Get away from me," I spew all the anger I've saved up and screech like a crazy-crazy. "Hull is full of scum like you, sliming through town, taking whatever you want without a second thought!"

I swear I won't be a victim again. I won't let him win, but even as I think this he charges at me. I let him get close, then jump away as he slams into a parked car. The man bounces off it then comes at me again, his eyes on fire.

I make like I'm reaching into my pocket for a weapon. "Come any closer, and I'll kill you," I snarl.

For a moment, he hesitates. But before he can react, a woman storms out of a nearby bar. She's tall, teetering on four-inch heels, her auburn hair shiny under the neon lights. She carries a purse big enough to double as luggage.

"Swizzle Prick, leave that girl alone," she hollers, whacking him with the bag. "Can't ya tell she's a child?"

I'm struck by the name she calls him and am reminded of Daddy's name Wizz. Adding the S makes this man dangerous, but this woman seems to know he's all bluster.

Swizzle Prick flinches but doesn't back away. "C'mon, Andréa, I was just messin' around."

Andréa? Nice letters—except for the N. Maybe her life dips sometimes, but the R and the A's say she's a survivor.

Andréa plants herself between us, her red nails like claws poised to strike. "Piss off, shit-for-brains." She glares him down, and with one final grumble, he slinks away, rubbing his head.

When she turns to me, her tone changes. "What the hell are you doing here alone at this hour?" She looks me over, her makeup exaggerated, her green eyeshadow shimmering under pencil-thin brows.

"I couldn't sleep," I mumble.

Her painted lips twitch downward, and she digs through her white leather bag decorated with a sparkly A stitched on its side. "Here," she says, shaking a handful of pills into my palm before popping four into her mouth, swallowing them like candy.

She dips into her purse again, pulling out a gold cigarette case. She fiddles with the lock and I hear a snap. Her fingernail splits in two, jagged as a broken heart. "Goddamn it. Why do they make these things so hard to open? Fuck it all," she mutters, sounding like Ivy.

I take the case and pop it open.

"Thank ya, darlin'. You're a sweet one, aren't you?" She lights a joint. I smell the familiar earthy smoke. She blows it in the opposite direction of my face but it floats heavy through the air.

I wonder how much I should tell her about myself. Clare's advice comes to mind: "Talk to her about herself. People love that."

"I'm not surprised you helped me. You have an A in your name, a sign of strength."

"I'm Ahn-dray-a." She tosses back her hair, revealing deep crow's feet around her eyes.

"You have several A's. You're not only strong, you're smart. How do you spell your name?"

"A–N–D–R–E–A. But I pronounce it the French way."

"The A's tell me you're adventurous, but clever about it. Like you wouldn't compromise yourself, but you still like a good time."

"Hot damn. I sure do like a good time. How do you know that?"

I recite the entry for the A from *The Letter Bible*: "A's have an acute awareness of their surroundings which allows them to ascend to heights that others are afraid to try."

"Jeez, kid. You're a wiz with words!" She inhales deeply from the joint. "Tell me more."

I almost cry when she says wiz, but I can't risk spooking her. I'm aching to ask her about Daddy and Ivy—she seems like someone who would have known them. I point to a bench across the street. "Can we talk over there?" I ask and she nods.

I pick up my duffel and backpack and cross the street together. When we're seated, I smile at her, wanting to keep her attention so that maybe she'll answer a few questions for me about Hull. "Like I said, the A is a special letter that lets you soar above everyone else. But the N can be aggressive. It tells me that you will mow down anyone who narrows your options."

Her eyes arch and the tips of her black liner stretch like wings. "I'm capable of mowing down anyone who opposes me. That's for damn sure."

"The D says you'll overcome the negative." I draw the D in the air, catching the red light from the bar's sign. "See how proud it is?"

"I'm seeing myself in a whole new way. Tell me more."

"The R is a mind-body letter. If you're in balance, the parts of the letter work in harmony."

"I'm a double-R," she chuckles, shimmying her chest.

I laugh like I know what she's talking about. "The E takes you to new territory, traveling up and down the coast, perhaps."

"I do a lot of moving." She snickers again. "You nailed my personality, kid. What's your name anyway?"

"Angelica." It's the first time I've said my new name aloud.

She grins. "So you have a lot of the same letters as I do! No wonder you know so much about me."

Andréa downs another two pills and reaches into her bag for lipstick and a mirror, swearing again about her broken fingernail. She takes her time painting her lips scarlet. Then she digs into her mega-bag and tosses out candy wrappers, tissues, and empty cigarette boxes. "What a mess."

She looks like she's going to dive in head first. When she comes up with her keys, she jiggles them. Then she stands and wiggles her backside. "Lemme drop you off somewhere," she slurs, but it sounds more like "lemon drop my underwear."

"Maybe you shouldn't drive."

Within minutes, she's gone from clipped words sprayed fast to slow talking. Those pills are not valium. They're quaaludes, like Daddy and Ivy used to pop.

"I don't need a pint-sized squirt telling me what to do," she snaps, laughing like a tired goat.

I remember how quickly Ivy would turn on me. One minute I was Agnes, the next Ag-mess.

A police car pulls up to the curb.

The passenger window lowers, revealing three stripes on a white shirt. My breath catches.

Could it be Sergeant Stone? I want to shrink, to disappear, but if it is him, he doesn't know who I am, and he's the one who should be afraid.

"Well, well, well. What do we have here?" The cop grunts.

I bend low to see his face, but it's backlit.

"Sergeant, Officer, Sir," Andréa says with a drawl. "Are we doing something wrong?"

"Andréa, you're off early tonight. You got my cut?"

She reaches into her bra and hands him a wad of cash.

"And what about your sidekick? I haven't seen her around. Is she your protégé on the streets and if she is, she owes me a slice of the action too."

"She's my niece visiting from out of town," Andréa says smoothly.

I inch in close behind Andréa to get a good look, but he's still in silhouette.

"Yes, Sir, she's my auntie," I chime in, forcing a sing-song tone.

The sergeant narrows his eyes. "She's your auntie like I'm the fucking Pope."

"Popes aren't allowed to fuck," Andréa giggles.

"You smell a little funky, ladies."

Andréa shields me. "Now you don't like my perfume?" She leans into the car, puffing out her chest, and hiking up her skirt to reveal her thighs. "Check it out."

The sergeant shifts forward, his face fully lit. It *is* ButtFace Stone, his doughy cheek as scary as in my nightmares. My hand flies to the stain on my neck, throbbing underneath my hoodie. I can barely breathe.

"I'll let you off tonight. But tell your niece she's looking for trouble."

"Yes, Sir." Andréa pulls me away. "Keep walking. Don't look back."

I don't. I only want to look forward and stop that disgusting man from hurting anyone else. If Andréa weren't dragging me along, I'd be frozen with that face still staring at me. In the flesh. Not in my nightmares. But real. I could touch his scar. Slice it open. Make it bleed.

He said Andréa was hooking me. So she's a prostitute? Could she know anything about Suzanne or Jazmin? Their mothers were hookers too.

Andréa stops short at a dented red convertible. "Go home to mommy, and don't come around here again."

"But I have more to tell you about your name!" I shout. I have so many questions aching to be asked.

"I'll find you." She gets into the driver's seat, slams the door, and revs away.

FIVE

Hornet

After Andréa leaves, my world shrinks around me. But I vow to see this through, by myself if I have to.

Stay calm.

C–A–L–M.

The letters shout orders. Listen. Think. Move forward. Be strong.

I can do this.

Down the street, saxophones, trumpets, and fist-pumping music blaze through the doors of bars, but I tune into the call of the ocean.

From my attic days, I know the sound of the tides. I fell asleep to them every night for ten years. They were always there.

I curl up against the seawall under my quilt, hidden from sight, and finally feel safe. I think about Clare on Brewer Island, alone but not lonely. She showed me how to rely on myself and not let dark thoughts take over.

I trace letters in the sky. A and L appear everywhere, and they give me courage.

Sleep comes with the rush of the waves and the distant sounds on the boardwalk.

I wake before dawn and dig through my backpack for the food I stowed: dried vegetables, an apple, cheese, and dandelion scones—the flavors of Brewer Island. I eat, then sort and repack my few belongings, saving the apple for later. I adjust the straps on my backpack and swing my duffel over my shoulder. Everything I own weighs heavy on my body.

I walk down the beach, a magnet pulling me to F Street. Even from afar, the house looks burned and dead, like something waiting to eat me.

Sweat breaks out as I near the house. I strip to my underwear and plunge into the June water for relief. But when I climb out, I'm still shaking—and it's not from the cold. It's fear of what I might see if I get any closer.

Are Daddy's toes still scattered there? Is the basement room crawling with slimy sea creatures? And what about the silver key that bumps against the rose quartz in my pocket? What if it opens something? What if it's a clue I'm meant to find?

I can't go there. Not yet. I don't want to relive seeing Suzanne rolled up in a blanket, carried out from the basement and given to Stone. I don't want to hear Ivy hissing my name or Daddy slurring his words. I hear Vixen's cackle and Squid's heavy accent drifting up to my attic from the deck. I consider walking on to X Street, where the van might still sit and Apollo might still guard the junkyard.

My body refuses.

The A and the L abandon me. I can't go forward. Instead, I go back to last night's spot and curl up.

By the afternoon, I'm steadier. Still not strong enough to revisit the house on F Street or the junkyard on X. Instead, I cross Nantasket Avenue to the bay side where I can see World's End in the distance and it gives me courage.

I can do this. I repeat it until I believe it.

I sit at a picnic table outside a fast-food place and watch the world, trying to figure out the next move.

Then I see him.

A ragged man rifles through trash bins, stuffing bottles and cans into a green plastic bag. He slings it over his shoulder and continues down the road to other receptacles, looking for anything he can redeem for cash.

I remember him.

Hornet. Daddy's snitch.

* * *

The last time I saw him, I was seven. When he came through the front door, Daddy made me hide real quick in a kitchen cabinet. Through the latticework, I had a clear view of the yellow-and-black bees tattooed up his calves, tiny egg-shaped dots along his heels. A ponytail pulled his hair tight, and a tattooed eye peeked at the back of his neck.

"There's scuttle that V is back in town," he said, his loud voice shaking the walls.

The letter V stabbed me even then as they sat at the table.

"Who's V?" Daddy asked, rolling a joint.

"Psychopath bitch named Vixen. White hair, goddamn spikes in her ears. She eats testicles for breakfast."

V–I–X–E–N. Someone like Ivy but ten times worse. Badness in every direction.

"What's she into?" Daddy asked.

"Coke and heroin's all I know, maybe bolting some crazy bastard to the wall and abusing him." His voice buzzed with B's.

"Vixen likes action," the hornet-man said.

"What kind of action?"

"Light that doobie and I'll tell you."

Daddy struck a match, and the sweet smell filled the kitchen.

He passed Hornet the joint. "Tell me about this Vixen before I lose patience."

"You'll hear her before you see her." Hornet roared out a sound like he was grinding gears with pieces of glass.

Daddy's eyes popped and his snaggletooth cut into his lip.

"She cut into my tattoos," Hornet said, lifting his shirt. "Said she wanted the bees to cry blood. Carved a V into my stomach—connecting the dots."

"The bitch must be big."

"Skinny but strong. Like an Albino cockroach."

Daddy shuddered. "How'd you get mixed up with her?"

"Vixen was night prowling the beach and found me. She said we were soulmates from a former life, before I went to Vietnam. We stayed high on booze, pills, pot, heroin, whatever we could find."

"Vietnam? No wonder you're fucked up."

"I prided myself on being the ghost in sky, dropping bombs on villagers. When each mission was over, I tattooed a hornet on my body, so I wouldn't forget what I had done."

"But there are dozens of bugs on your body," Daddy said, rolling another joint.

The man squirmed in his seat, the bugs jumping around his legs, the eye winking. "Guess I got carried away. The more demons, the more tattoos."

My father lit the second joint. "I want to know more about Vixen, and less about you."

"At first we had fun. She'd stalk the dunes looking for someone to hurt. Knives in her jacket lining. Twin revolvers in a holster—real, not toys. She'd leap out screaming, waving the guns or flinging knives. Made grown men crap themselves."

"And you watched?"

Hornet chuckled. "Had the fuckers running scared. Funny as all hell."

Daddy passed him the joint. Hornet drew on it and let the smoke out like it was the best thing he'd had all day.

"Dude, what else do you know about Vixen?"

"She only comes out at night, like a vampire bat. When she wants something, she goes after it. I'd watch out if I were you."

"I've been here four years, and she hasn't bothered me. Besides, pot and pills sound like short money for her."

"Haven't you been listening? She's been away and now she's back. She hates competition. Someone told her you're a big dealer with a hot chick who's got Stone in her pocket and Squid in her ear."

*   *   *

Now, watching Hornet dig through trash on the beach, I know he's my only link to Daddy, Ivy, and that house. I follow from a distance until nightfall, when he slips beneath the wooden ribs of Paragon Amusement Park's roller coaster. I settle into a sheltered corner, unroll my quilt, bite into the apple and fall asleep.

I wake to a live rat gnawing on my apple core less than four feet away. Before I can react, a knife flies through the air, nailing the rat between its eyes. I scramble backward as Hornet comes into view.

"It was his territory too," he says, flinging the rat over a railing, "but he was getting too close to you. Even I don't eat varmints."

"I've been searching for you!" I blurt.

"And you are?"

I step out. At five-three, we stand eye to eye. His back stoops, his eyes are glassy, and his long hair pulls his body down so that he looks like a dirty Christmas elf.

"My father was Wizz. My mother was Ivy. They lived in the beach house on F Street. Do you remember them?"

I figure I should ask him up front.

His bees ripple with tension. "Those people been dead for years. I forgot about them the minute they hit the ground."

"So you know how they died?"

"Don't mean shit. I'm still kickin' and they're six feet under."

"But you were Daddy's snitch."

Hornet looks around. "That aint no word to be spreading."

"You told him about Vixen. And Vietnam."

Hornet's face turns bright red like I punctured a vein. "Don't go talking what you don't know." He changes the subject. "You hungry? I got doughnuts."

He leads me to his cardboard shelter under the coaster. On a three-legged table sits a Dunkin' Donuts bag. He pours dark brown liquid into a plastic cup and offers it to me. I refuse. He studies me like a ghost.

"Wizz and Ivy, you say? You're their kid? Jesus H. Christ. Always thought big eyes were following me. Didn't know if they were real."

"My father trusted you," I say.

"Damned stupid Wizz. Nice guy. Just didn't have a whole lot of business sense."

"So you believe me?"

"As much as I believe there's a moon in the morning sky and silver fish jumping out of the ocean."

He picks his teeth with the same knife that stabbed the rat. He sucks on the scraps like they're sacred.

"Did ya know that house you lived in had a fire a few years back? Still a fucking eyesore. Sometimes, I hole up there in the winter. You lived in the walls?"

"In the attic," I admit, then hesitate, ". . . and I saw you buzzing into the house when the crazy-crazies weren't around. Daddy rolled you joints and you told him stuff about the druggies in town."

His jaw buzzes with tension. "I knew there was something secret going on, like with Wizz and Ivy and the kidnappings."

I gasp. "Of Suzanne and Jazmin?" The names slip out like breathing.

Hornet narrows his eyes, his tongue working his teeth like he's about to swallow them. "You got a big mouth for a ghost. What are you doing here anyway? Wizz and Ivy been gone almost three years. Don't make no sense coming back."

"I read about a girl who washed up unconscious on Gunrock Beach a few weeks ago. I need to find out who she is and if she's alive. I can't rest knowing she's another victim of Hull's predators."

Hornet twitches. "Girly, what you don't know will get you killed. Best be on your way."

He knows something. I can feel it.

"Ivy thought you were okay too."

"Now I know you're bullshitting me. Your mother ate nails for breakfast and laughed at me whenever I got near."

She called him Whornet. Said he sold himself cheap and couldn't be trusted.

"Ok. I'll give you that," I say, shrugging. "My mother wasn't nice, but I am."

"What's it to me? I saved you from a rat. My job is done."

"All I want is to know about the girl who washed up on the beach. I can't let her be another victim."

Hornet chews his bottom lip, like it's hiding secrets. I stare at him and wonder if he's passed the last few years dumpster diving and eating hand to mouth.

"I know why you call yourself Hornet. You told my father that you tattooed yourself so you would never forget what you did in Vietnam. But you got carried away," I say. "The more demons, the more tattoos—those were your exact words."

Hornet eats more of his lip. "So I should help you because you know why I'm called Hornet?"

"No. Because Hornet isn't your real name. You hide behind your bees."

"I'm ok with that."

"Names matter. They reveal who we are."

"I was born to be a bug, easy to squash."

"But you weren't born Hornet."

He opens his mouth but only stale pot-smoke air comes out. Then he straightens his back and squares his shoulders. "I was born Ira Trapper in 1945 in Hull, Massachusetts."

For a second, I forget to breathe. Ira. A real person.

"I had no tattoos. No bugs circling my wrists and ankles. I wasn't a buzzing annoying hornet. That came later."

I study his letters: I–R–A.

The I stands alone.

The R tries to move forward.

The A is smart.

He could have been so much more.

"You know Hull better than anyone. I need to know the truth about the missing girls." I say.

Hornet's jaw jumps, a small muscle working near his ear. The bees on his skin seem to shift, like they sense danger. "You don't want that truth, girly. Some things are best left buried."

Hornet paces under the roller coaster beams. The buzzing starts up, low and angry. "You have some fucking nerve, coming into my home and demanding answers. Who do you think you are? The secret daughter of a dead man and his psycho wife. I owe you nothing."

I look around his so-called house: stained cardboard, piles of blankets, and a tilted table under the wooden dinosaur ribs of the coaster. What brought him so low? Drugs? Daddy? ButtFace? Something else?

"I can't go to the police," I say quietly. "Sergeant Stone is involved. He'd find a way to blame me."

"And what if you woke up with the rat eating your toes instead of the apple?"

"But that didn't happen. You intervened. The Ira in you. Some-one who is good and thoughtful."

"I can't help you, girly. I can barely help myself."

"At least tell me where I can stay. I'll handle the rest."

Hornet's eyes pop. "I know someone. I'll take you to her when the time's right."

DeeDee

I tuck myself under the roller coaster in a shadowed corner of Paragon Park where Hornet makes his summer nest. At night, he covers himself with newspapers, like his tattoos are renewed with ink as he sleeps.

At dawn, I watch him climb the lattice of the coaster, inspecting every inch of the wooden giant. He tightens bolts, replaces screws, and traces his fingers along the grain of the beams like they're alive.

"It's a beautiful, breathing creature, and I keep it young," he says, his Ira-face bright. "I've been doing this from Memorial Day to Labor Day ever since I got back from 'Nam. Ain't a curve or bump I haven't caressed."

I eat scones and cheese, another apple, and accept a coffee from Ira as the coaster roars to life. Wheels and wood. Click and clack. A beast chasing its tail over and over again.

I know how Clare's Island must sound as dump trucks and bulldozers rumble through it.

Hornet disappears for the day with a garbage bag slung over his back. I'd like to explore the town, but I stay hidden. No sense asking for trouble. When the park's hum quiets and the ocean's laughter returns, he reappears, signaling for me to follow.

If I think of him as Ira, he becomes a man.

I gather my belongings and trail behind him through the empty park. The O of the Ferris Wheel looms overhead, while the double-S of the coaster loops around me with its turns and camel humps. We pass the canvas-hooded Caterpillar, the floating swings, and finally the carousel with its carved horses and Roman chariots.

I imagine Nadia Jones going round and round on one of those horses, her laughter mingling with the carousel's music until the moment she was stolen away. How had she been kidnapped in broad daylight? Why didn't she scream? Did she know the person who took her? Was it someone to be trusted? Someone in a policeman's uniform? I want to ask Ira these questions, but he's made it clear he doesn't want to talk about missing girls.

"Tonight you'll sleep under the merry-go-round," he says matter-of-factly. Under? U–N–D–E–R. The letters close in, pressing down on me.

I'm stuffed away. Abandoned.

Never to rise.

Never to grow or explore.

Never to be part of the sky and earth.

Then, after a pause, his tone softens. "It's a cool place. I've spent many nights there."

And that makes it all right! I bite back my frustration. What choice do I have?

"Tomorrow you'll meet Dee, a friend of Wizz and Ivy's."

Dee? I search my memory for the name. The D is not a crazy-crazy letter or one that I distrust. D's can be filled with self-knowledge and determination, puffed out in a good way. But, it can be bloated and unable to share, always looking for more. I won't understand this person until we meet, until I know the whole name.

Ira leads me to a circular space beneath the carousel. The thick center pole is anchored deep into the ground, and grated windows let in air and light. It doesn't feel smothering or confining. Ira points out the door.

"You can leave whenever you want. You're not trapped here."

This isn't a hidey-hole. Except that I'm hiding. I lay my quilt on the floor, which is surprisingly clean, and settle onto the cement, curling my legs against my chest. The air smells faintly of carousel oil and sea breeze, and I trace the light patterns on the grated windows with my fingers. For the first time in days, I let myself breathe.

The sound that wakes me in the morning is something I never imagined: chimes, bells, horns, flutes, cymbals—happy music that trills through me.

I picture Clare and her sister Lucy as little girls, soaring on the carousel horses among princes, rainbows and pots of gold, never realizing that Lucy's life would end in a few short years, and Clare would think she was to blame. Did Tom and Max bring little Lucille here too? Carousel dreams. Short-lived.

I worry that everything happens beyond my reach, always through a window: the shitbox van's grimy glass, the attic's small portal, the tiny cottage with its narrow skylights, surrounded by rock and bamboo, cut off from the mainland.

I pull blocks from my duffel, arranging them in random order. For a second I wonder what I'm even doing here—trusting a stranger, sleeping under a carousel, chasing ghosts instead of heading for the horizon like Daddy said. Maybe I should just let Hull rot on its own.

But I can't. Not yet.

I select the H block. I study the upside and the downside. Sky. Sun. Earth. Darkness. The letters whisper: *Don't give up. You can do this.*

For a moment, the world holds its breath with me. Then the

day grows growly, like a storm brewing. The carousel music stops, leaving only the sound of cars along Nantasket Ave. A shuffle breaks the stillness, and I gather my belongings, pressing myself into a corner.

Ira slips into the room, barely pausing. "Time to move on."

He gestures for me to follow, and I obey without question, slinging my backpack over my shoulders and carrying my duffel.

We walk along the avenue. As cars drive by, we duck into doorways. Both of us know how to be invisible. At the corner of Kenberma and Nantasket Ave, we stop at a beauty parlor: DeeDee's Salon.

D–E–E–D–E–E. The woman who lives here pays no attention to boundaries. No attic rooms for her. There's too much to see and do.

Ira leads me through an alley to a step-down door. He knocks. A wide-bodied woman with poofy orange hair opens it. The sharp tang of her perfume and the faint scent of smoke hit me before she speaks.

"Come in," she says to me in a husky voice. "You, stay out." Ira lowers his head and slinks away.

I enter a dark narrow hallway, getting far enough away from her to bolt out the door if I need to. A blue light shines from an inner room and silhouettes the woman in front of me. Her thick neck disappears into a black robe, her body round like a pot-bellied priest. She comes nose to nose with me and squints. "You're her, aren't you?"

My throat feels like it might burst. Jittery bumps crawl up my arms, like ants, crawling and not stopping. I'm stuck between wanting to yell and just trying to get through it all.

It dawns on me who this is—the woman who looked like a man and rolled around with Ivy in the back bedroom. Orange Head!

"You're not a bratty little kid anymore, creeping around the house, watching Ivy and me. Ivy never told me much about you, but I knew. I saw it in her eyes—something she was hiding, protecting." DeeDee looks me over from head to toe. "I figured you'd resemble her or Wizz, but your face is round and simple. . . and you're curvy."

I jump back against the door. She's going to stick me with those fingernails and scoop me into her blubbery mouth.

"Don't worry, Agnes, I'm not going to hurt you."

The name punches a hole in my stomach. A cannon goes off and pins me to the wall. Did Ivy tell her about me? How is that possible? I was nothing to Ivy, ever. Or was I?

DeeDee's waiting for me to say something. "I'm not Agnes anymore. My name is Angelica."

She shrugs. "It's been almost three years since Wizz and Ivy died, may they rest in peace. Where've you been hiding?"

I could answer Ivy-like and tell her it's none of her fucking business. I could say I've been eating out of dumpsters and sleeping in doorways in Boston. The way I look, all ragged and dirty, she'd believe me. Or I could tell her the truth. I have to begin somewhere and it seems that this DeeDee person knew my parents and loved Ivy. That's got to stand for something. My eyes fill with tears. "I've lived near World's End with a wonderful woman named Clare Brewer. She passed away a few weeks ago."

"So you have nowhere to go?"

I nod.

"How old are you anyway?"

"Sixteen."

"You're just a baby. How can I let a child like you roam out there? You'll end up on the streets and god knows who'll prey on you." She looks up to the sky. "Ivy? Are you listening? I'll watch her for the summer. Like she's the daughter of a long-lost cousin coming for vacation before school begins in the fall. That's the best I can do."

I wonder if she knows I've never been to school. How I'm here in Hull to find out about the girl who washed up on the beach and the others who vanished. And to prove that Daddy wasn't a bad man. He just made bad decisions, like keeping me locked in the attic or in a hidey-hole, like paying off Stone and not listening to Vixen when she told him to keep Ivy out of her business.

The crying startles me. It's coming from the bullish woman in priest's clothes, her orange hair shaking with each sob. She blows her nose like a foghorn, then grabs my duffel and backpack and waddles toward the blue light. I scramble after her—I can't let her disappear with my things. She goes into a small room with high windows and shelves stacked with bottles of shampoo and conditioner, hair spray and mousse, nail polish and glitter. She puts my things in a corner beside a couch.

"First order of business—strip." Her lips curl into something between a grin and a sneer. My legs wobble.

"And take a shower." She laughs, thick and rich from the depths of her belly. "No need to worry about me. I like mature women, preferably bony and hard-assed like your mother."

I smell like crust and mold. My hair is knotted and my body is stained with anger and fear, worry and sweat. But Clare is here beside me in this stall shower that seals me in like a coffin while a woman named DeeDee stands guard.

DeeDee leaves a white t-shirt and socks beside a towel, their clean scent foreign to me. "Your clothes smell like rotten armpits. I'm throwing them in the washing machine."

A washing machine? Something new to learn how to use.

In the kitchen, she sets out two peanut butter and jelly sandwiches and a glass of milk.

"How did you know about me?"

She opens a bag of chips and sits beside me. "I saw you through the vent in the ceiling, so Ivy had to tell me. People said Ivy was mixed up in all sorts of things, but I never believed it. Not my Ivy. She was too smart for that—too careful. But Wizz? He was reckless, a dreamer with no sense of danger. If they were hiding girls... God help them."

I hear Clare warning me to be careful: "Small steps are better than bold leaps."

DeeDee knew about the kidnappings and Squid? And she thought Ivy was innocent? Was she?

"So my parents had nothing to do with stealing Suzanne or Jazmin."

DeeDee looks like she ate a ghost. "Saying those names around here is like playing with fire in a room full of gasoline. People have died for less, Angelica. If you want to stay alive, you keep those questions locked up inside."

"So if I say Vixen I'll die?"

She slaps my face. "That's from Ivy."

Tears sting my eyes. My cheek burns. I feel like AgMess again—tiny, voiceless, with nowhere to feel safe. I want to run out the door, but I have nowhere else to go.

"Listen, Angelica, I run an honest business. You have to forget Squid and Vixen and whatever else you think you know about Hull if you stay in my house."

"But there are people walking who deserve to be punished."

"And you'll be their executioner?" She laughs like thorns scratching iron.

I calm myself by saying the alphabet in my head. I imagine sitting beside Clare, willing her strength into me so I won't break, reminding myself that I am no longer Agnes, no longer a child without choices.

DeeDee wedges herself into a recliner in front of the TV. I finish one of the sandwiches and watch a man on the screen argue a murder case in front of a jury. His voice pounds out words: justice, honor, truth. The scene gives me courage.

"You were at Gregg's trial, right?" I remember how Max said a big woman with short orange hair sat in the back and cried her eyes out. "You knew that Jane Doe was Ivy and John Doe was Wizz. Why didn't you identify them?"

DeeDee rubs her stubby fingers against her arms. Each of her nails is painted a different sparkly color. "That wouldn't bring either of them back."

I hate what Gregg did to me, but he was sent to prison for the rest of his life for killing my mother and she was already dead. That's just wrong. "So you let Gregg be sentenced for killing them?"

"I didn't let him. The evidence convicted him. The gun, the bullets, the blood."

E-V-I-D-E-N-C-E. A word with mixed messages. The stabbing V and the inconsistent N, but the other letters have promise. Yes, somewhere out there is evidence to prove that Stone and Vixen killed my parents and are involved in child trafficking.

"So Gregg planned their murder?"

"Might as well be that fat fuck. Besides, Ivy hated him. He was a snoop and a snitch. Bunkny blabbed about Wizz and Ivy's hiding places. That's what got your parents killed."

My eyes tear and my flesh flushes bright red. "It's my fault that Gregg knew. I showed him."

DeeDee turns off the television and sits beside me. "You're not the only person who knew Wizz had hiding places. When he got drunk, he did a lot of boasting. Foolish man. He trusted the wrong people. Ivy told him to stay away from Bunkny, that she knew what was best. But Wizz wasn't listening." DeeDee shakes her head. "She had a plan in place, but it never happened." DeeDee crushes me with a full body hug. "I gotta keep you safe, Angelica. You're my only connection to Ivy now. I did love that woman."

S-A-F-E. The letters coil inside me, the S sharp and cold, the F empty and hollow. My insides churn like acid.

How will I find out what happened? The girls' names are like stones in my chest—heavy, unmovable. Suzanne. Jazmin. Farrah. Nadia. Each deserves better, but what can I do? I'm homeless.

Lost. And yet, I can't let this go. I can't let them disappear into the shadows forever.

Go slow. Go slow.

C-A-L-M.

Listen. Think. Move forward. Stay strong.

"I read about a girl who washed up on Gunrock beach a few weeks back? Do you know anything about her?"

"Saw it on TV. Didn't give it much thought."

"Is she still alive?"

"Couldn't tell you."

"How can I find out?"

"You can't. It's old news. Let it go."

I cry for real. Tears plop onto the bread and spread like ocean foam.

"I got a relative who's a cop," she says, her voice dropping. "He's good at digging into things—or burying them, depending on who's asking. I'll see what he knows. O.K.?"

O-K. A closed circle, an open mouth. There's hope.

"Your relative's not Sergeant Stone, right?"

"That goddamned lying cheating bastard." She fires out the words like a machine gun.

"I call him ButtFace."

DeeDee laughs, loud and long and hearty. "That's the perfect name for the asshole! Listen, Angelica, you're here now and I'll do my damnedest to appease Ivy's spirit, but you gotta meet me half way." She puts her chunky hand over mine, her eyes locking onto mine. "No talking about Vixen or Squid or children who disappear. Got it? None of that matters here in my shop."

I squirm under her gaze, but she holds my hand steady.

"I'll try to find out what happened to the girl who washed up on the beach. In the meantime, I'll find work for you to do and you'll be fine. Trust me."

T-R-U-S-T.

I've been tricked by that word before.

I hate the S. It searches and spins and sneaks up on me and is never satisfied.

I'm thinking T–R–U–S–S–E–D. Hog-tied. Boiled in hot water. Then eaten limb by limb.

S E V E N

The Drag Queens

I sleep restlessly, like I'm tossed around with my clothes in the washing machine. When I wake, the first thing I see is a note written in bold letters:

Angelica,

> *Eat breakfast, put a black robe over your clothes*
> *(in back storage room), and come upstairs.*
>
> *DeeDee*

I pour a cup of coffee and butter some bread. On my way to the storage room, I pause at an open door. DeeDee's bedroom. A round bed with a puffy white comforter and rainbow-bright pillows sprawl in the center—so different from the stained narrow bed that she and Ivy shared in the house on the corner of F Street. Three wooden birds perch on the bureau, each carved with Daddy's touch. One stretches its jagged feathers in mid-song, all angles and sharp beak. Another sits plump and proud like a peahen, while the third spreads its wings in a perfect W. Ivy, DeeDee, and Daddy, captured in wood.

I pick each up, feeling Daddy in my fingertips. My throat goes dry. He never carved one for me. If he had, would it have been scrawny and open-beaked and needy with purple lines on its neck? Or would it be like a goddess—pure and unblemished?

I don't poke around in DeeDee's closet or check for loose floorboards. I back out of the room and walk down a hallway filled with framed photographs—pictures of dunes, ocean, sunsets, sailboats, and Paragon Park; a poster of fish found in the waters off Hull: haddock and cod, bass and bluefish, scup and flounder; a detailed pen and ink drawing of the town. I'm surprised to see Hull shaped like an L. My lifeline letter L. It's never afraid to walk the walk. Isn't that why I'm back here? Because L's live in me?

At the back of the apartment, shelves hold a dozen white molded heads with shallow eyes, bumped out noses, and pouty lips, each topped with a wig: bushy black, spiky white, curly red, and flowing brown. Shadows shift with the hair, giving each face a new personality. I grab a black robe from the stack.

Back in the main room, the TV is still on. I turn the knob, and a blue puppet fills the screen, singing about cookies. *C is for Cookie, it's good enough for me.* He sits inside a giant orange C and rolls his ping-pong eyes. Then a gigantic yellow bird and a monster elephant sing the alphabet. It's magic.

In a far corner, I find my refuge: a shelf of magazines and books. The titles are unlike anything from my attic or Clare's— *Woman's Day, Playgirl, Glamour, The Handmaid's Tale, The House of Spirits.* So much to discover! I could spend hours reading here. Clare always said, "A word after a word after a word is power." Letters hold that power for me, but now isn't the time for that.

Voices upstairs grow louder—laughter mixing with the hum of a hair dryer. I tuck my duffel and backpack under the couch, slip into the oversized robe, and climb the stairs. Each step brings a swirl of scents: strawberry, vanilla, apple, coconut—a dizzying sweetness guiding me into DeeDee's Salon.

I walk through an arched doorway to a high-ceilinged room with two swivel chairs, long mirrors, and shelves with wig-heads like the ones downstairs.

Posters of women hang everywhere. Names are written in fancy letters: Dolly Parton, Bette Midler, Marilyn Monroe, Tina Turner—draped in sequins, feathers, hot-red lipsticks and pushed-up breasts. Up close, I see signatures in the corners: Peppermint Patty, TuTu Titan, Hedda Lettuce, Chi Chi Cha.

Lots of P's and T's and C's. Twirling and dancing letters.

Weaving ribbons through the curls of a sandy-haired customer, DeeDee nods good morning. She bursts with color: orange spiked hair, purple shadowed eyes, and yellow lips outlined with white. As she works, she talks non-stop. "That prune-faced bitch called me a flaming dyke." She snaps her gum and throws up her hands. "I put a curse on her: May her face freeze and her titties sag."

The sandy-haired client fans herself likes she's heating up. "You're so naughty, girl." Her voice surprises me, deep low, what Clare would call a baritone.

"Meet Lacy LaRue," DeeDee says and hands me a broom. "Angelica is my new assistant."

And then I see them—tiny whiskers on Lacy's chin!

The man smiles at me with dazzling white teeth. "I need a shave."

DeeDee laughs so hard she cries. "The expression on your face, Angelica. I'm gonna wet my pants."

"DeeDee," he says, "come to my show tonight. Bring the kid."

DeeDee sweeps the robe off Lacy. He wears a silky V-neck sleeveless shirt. Muscles bulge from his hairless arms. His jeans are slung low and flare out at the bottom. Sparkling red platform shoes finish the look. Lacy LaRue is toweringly tall. Then he kisses DeeDee on each cheek. "See you later, lovelies."

With a wide grin, DeeDee watches him leave. "He's a gorgeous woman. You should see the others!" She sweeps her rainbow fingernails toward the wall of pictures. She looks outside and groans. "Oh, damn it all."

A police car pulls up beside Lacy LaRue. The three V's on the officer's shirt send a chill through my spine. My fingers find the edge of my robe, clutching the fabric as the letters come automatically: C–A–L–M. Each one a breath, a shield, the way Clare taught me when the shadows grew too dark. Listen. Think. Move forward. Be strong.

Scowling, ButtFace yanks the wig off Lacy's head and grinds it into the ground. Lacy backs away, arms raised in surrender, just as Stone spits—a blob arcing through the air to land on Lacy's cheek. As Lacy flees, and Stone crashes the salon door open, I race to the back room. "What the fuck, Two-Ton?"

His gravel voice digs into me, burying me like old bones. Suzanne, Jazmin, Farrah, Nadia—the names pulse in my head.

"You know better than to let that freak walk around in daylight. No homos in my town. Ever."

DeeDee opens the cash register. "That should take care of today, Sarge. It won't happen again."

"Fucking better not, or I'll close you down."

ButtFace stomps around the salon. Glass breaks, he yells some more, then a door slams. I peek out to see nail polish dripping down the side of the counter and splashing onto the floor. Red gobs, like blood.

"Bastard," DeeDee says. She pulls the shades and puts up a "Closed" sign.

I pull myself together and tiptoe into the salon to help her clean the mess. "Why does Sergeant Stone hate Lacy?"

"Stone's a homophobic, misogynistic, chauvinistic pig. I've known him since I was a kid."

I store the I–C words away to look up later. "Why does he call you Two Ton?"

T–W–O T–O–N.

The T's on alert.

The W welcoming.

The O's eye-opening and aware.

It's the N that's worrisome.

"He thinks it hurts me. Stone's all about pain. Besides, I got something on him. From a long time ago. His daughter Victoria and I played together in grade school, if you could call it that. She was a mean kid, always bullying, making me do stuff for her. She tortured Hornet too. The two of us idolized her. We did everything she wanted until one day she just up and disappeared."

Like Suzanne and Jazmin and Farrah and Nadia.

DeeDee's eyes grow distant, like she's been hypnotized. "Hornet and I were walking past her house one day when we heard screaming. Next thing, Stone flies out the door, holding the side of his face, blood dripping through his fingers. Behind him Victoria's mother stood with a knife, yelling, 'You touch her again and I'll kill you.'"

DeeDee leans closer. "Hornet and I dove into the bushes. Then out comes Victoria, running to Stone and hugging his waist. 'I didn't tell her! Don't be mad at me,' she said. That was the last time anyone saw Victoria. My guess? She's at the bottom of the ocean—wherever he dropped her to cover up his sins. It's been twenty-five years, and I haven't heard a peep about her since."

"So that's how he got the scar from his cheek to his chin?"

"Yup, I saw it happen."

"And you never asked Stone what happened to Victoria? Did he give her to Squid?"

DeeDee's spiked hair bristles. "Angelica, it's enough that I bribe Stone just to run my shop. If you throw around names you know nothing about and if the wrong ears hear you, you'll have more than him to worry about."

A sharp knock at the door makes me jump.

"Open up! I gotta see you. Now," a nasally voice calls. "I got a goddamn broken fingernail."

DeeDee unlocks the door and yanks the woman into the shop. "Stop with the drama, Andréa. Stone's on the loose."

Andréa! The same Andréa who saved me from Swizzle-Prick?

"That piece of shit Stone?" Andréa huffs. "Almost got me the other night, but I outsmarted him." She hikes up her skirt and waggles her butt. "I met this cheeky kid asking all sorts of questions. She told him I was her auntie. Funny as all hell if she wasn't such a sad little guttersnipe. Be on the lookout for her. Dark hair, big eyes."

I step forward and wave.

Andréa blinks. "You? What the hell are you doing here?"

"She's Wizz and Ivy's kid," DeeDee cuts in.

Andréa whistles. "Well, sonofabitch. Those two kept more secrets they didn't live to tell. What's she want with you?"

"Angelica," DeeDee says, giving me a hard look. "Get us some coffee."

I pout, but DeeDee gives me a stink-eye Ivy stare. When I return, DeeDee is fixing Andréa's nail.

I set the coffee next to the women and see an opportunity. "Do you notice when you pull the pinky and thumb back how your fingers form the letter E?"

I hold my hand sideways so the letter E is prominent.

"Yeah, I see it."

"Remember how I said you're a traveler and the E in your name will take you up and down the coast?"

"Yeah, yeah. I remember."

"There's more to reveal about that letter."

Andréa wiggles her fingers. "Go on. I love hearing about me."

"Sometimes you go high up the ladder of success and sometimes you fall low. The trick is balance."

Andréa smirks, holding out her middle finger. "I know all about tricks."

DeeDee laughs. "I've got E's in my name too, but I don't turn tricks."

Grabbing paper, I write their names in bold letters: ANDRÉA and DEEDEE.

I study the letters with the two women looking over my shoulder.

"The E reacts differently depending on what surrounds it," I tell them. "In Andréa, the aggressive R kicks the E—sometimes it soars, sometimes it sinks."

Andréa frowns, her makeup settling in the creases. "Are you saying I'm in danger?"

I'm ok with her being worried. I want her to ask me what she can do to make the E soar, so I can tell her to expose the dangers in the town and work with me to get rid of them.

I need back up. I can't do this alone. DeeDee and Andréa are a good start.

"What about me?" asks DeeDee. "My E is at the end of my name. What does that mean?"

"You've got four E's in your name—a quadruple threat that your E's will be buried."

Andréa's voice sharpens. "How do we make the E soar?"

I hear Clare whisper in my ear: "Offer honey, not venom."

"You're both smart," I say, pausing for effect. "But you're surrounded by people who want to bring you down. Your letters say you need to take charge of your future—and the future of those around you."

Will they realize I'm talking about Stone? Will they help me destroy him?

DeeDee's eyes gleam. "You're psychic—a living Ouija board."

"I'm not psychic. I just know how to read people's letters."

"Hot damn," DeeDee says, her rainbow nails drumming the counter. "We're gonna make a frigging fortune. Time to make you over, Angelica. No one wants a snot-nosed kid telling them their future."

"I'm not a fortune teller!" I protest, clenching my fists.

"Doesn't matter what you call it. This gift of yours will not go to waste." DeeDee sees Andréa out the door and takes me to the sink-room to wash my hair. "Lie back, Angelica. It's your time to relax."

I can always bolt out of the chair, but I know my hair is a tangled mess, and no amount of combing tames it. And I see the posters of sleek velvety hair on the walls. I want that too. Besides, this is a hair salon. DeeDee does this for a living, and her clients keep coming back. So, I let her.

I rest my neck on the hard porcelain sink as I brace for hot water to drench my head. Memories of Ivy hit me—shampoo stinging my eyes, water soaking my shirt, sharp fingers stabbing my scalp. "I should chop it all off, Ag fucking Tress, but Wizz won't let me. He likes running his fingers through your curls. It makes him feel sexy." Then she'd attack my head like it wasn't attached. If I complained, she'd leave me dripping.

DeeDee's first touch jolts me. Then her fingers move in gentle circles, massaging one spot, then another. Not even Clare touched my head like this. It's my A—my crown, my private center of thought.

DeeDee's energy flows through her fingertips, and I feel myself softening despite the voice in my head screaming *Don't trust her. Don't relax. Don't let her.*

Her movements are hypnotic—caressing circular O's, waves of calm unraveling the knots in my head and my neck. Oh, my neck! She's seeing it up close. Are my port wine stains angry red or quiet today? Can she feel their texture under her fingers?

My thoughts spiral inward, like she's found a secret passage from my skull to my heart. This is the DeeDee that Ivy loved. The DeeDee Daddy tolerated. The crystal around her thick neck catches the light. Did Ivy fasten it there with those same bony fingers that only knew how to hurt me? I can feel my crystal in my pocket, Clare's gift, loosening the tension inside me.

A warm tingle spreads through me, like when I pet Apollo or Darah or Pharaoh and they respond with soft pants. I almost purr. When she wraps the towel around my head, I feel a layer of protection rise around me, like I've been naked for the last ten minutes and she's seen my most private parts and now she's covering me up and I'm less exposed.

"Come on over to my chair," she says, like nothing intimate has just passed between us. But I'm floating—weightless, lifted above everything.

I'd never had my hair done. Clare trimmed it sometimes and so did Daddy, but nothing like this. Nothing meant to change me. I hear the snip snip snip of the scissors. I feel DeeDee's breath surround me. She giggles—a light, airy sound from a woman as solid as a mountain.

"Don't cut it short," I say. "I don't like my neck to show."

"Don't you worry. I know how to cover up birth defects."

Birth defects? I never thought the purple patches were a defect. Daddy said they were a sacred sign telling him I belong only to him. He'd kiss them, and call them his tasty plums.

I shrink under her words, feeling smaller with each snip.

DeeDee dabs something cool on my face and my neck, then dusts my cheeks with pink powder. "You look like an angel!"

Angel!

A–N–G–E–L.

What happened to my I–C–A?

Have I moved back in time, removing my independence, carrying away Clare, erasing my extra strength?

When DeeDee swivels my chair, I brace myself. In the mirror, a stranger stares back. A girl with soft curls framing her face. Smooth skin. Round eyes. Full lips. And muted lines on her neck.

I blink, half-expecting my old self to ghost through the mirror.

She doesn't. I touch the curls—light, bouncy, nothing like the tangled mess I've always battled. It's me. But not me. DeeDee beams behind me, proud of her work.

"I can't get over it," she says. "There's not a speck of Wizz or Ivy in you. No one would guess you're their kid."

Nothing from Daddy or Ivy looks back at me, not their hollow eyes, their sunken cheeks, their zig-zag smirks and stick-straight hair. I'm more of a cursive alphabet: full and flowing, with places for air to circulate and sway.

"DeeDee, I feel like I only knew the mean Ivy and you knew someone different than I did."

I see DeeDee's reflection in the mirror. Her eyes roll upward and she blows out her cheeks. "Your mother was complex. To me, she was like a diamond with a dozen facets."

She pulls up a stool and sits beside me.

"Ivy was born Ina Vee Yunis. Her father called her Venus, her mother barely spoke to her. She hated them both. In school, she started calling herself Ivy, using her initials, always capitalized. She was a shouting kind of woman, but I quieted her down. My name for her was Blue."

My head spins hearing all these letters. I-V-Y was I-N-A.

The N is cradled between the I and the A—protected, steadied.

She would have been a different person if she'd stayed Ina. Still troubled, sure—rising, sinking, hurting people—but maybe the I and A would've kept her from slipping so far.

Her father called her Venus. Deep-seated secrets and back-sliding dreams.

And DeeDee called her B-L-U-E.

The B is friendly and kissable.

The L shows a desire to move on.

The U still hides things, but the E seeks out new adventures.

No wonder Ivy loved DeeDee. DeeDee brought out the best in her.

I remember Ivy saying her father loved her too much, and her mother didn't interfere, how she gave them a decent burial even though they didn't deserve it. I want to ask DeeDee more, but the door opens and a client walks in.

DeeDee hands me the broom to sweep away my yesterdays. "Dust the shelves, clean the mirrors, and brew some coffee."

Later, when the salon is empty, DeeDee unveils a sign:

MEET YOUR GUARDIAN ANGEL
Psychic Readings.
Solve all matters of life and love.
Come in today for a better tomorrow.

She sets up a table in the front window with a flowered divider behind it.

"What do you think, Angel?"

What do I think! Maybe this is a backdoor into the town's secrets.

So I become Angel again, surrounded by my blocks and *The Letter Bible*, slipping into something almost familiar.

EIGHT

Robocop

Customers come in waves—A's, J's, B's, W's and D's.

Amanda asks about love. "The A shows strength and intelligence. You're in control of your own emotions," I tell her.

David wants to know about his future. "The D shows a huge capacity for success."

I let their letters speak, sharing *The Letter Bible's* wisdom, and watch their faces shift when something lands.

After a week, DeeDee counts the money, her rainbow nails clicking against each bill. She keeps a hundred for room and board, puts two hundred in an envelope for savings, and hands me fifty. "You're a miracle worker, Angel," she coos.

Growing up, money floated around the house on F Street, but I wasn't allowed to touch it. I wasn't allowed to touch much of anything.

With my earnings, I buy Hull shorts and t-shirts, sunglasses, M&Ms, and alphabet soup. I feel like a cannibal eating the letters, but they taste delicious.

I write Tom at his address in Hingham. He might never receive it, but I try.

June 24, 1988
Dear Tom,

I've been in Hull for a few weeks living downstairs from a hair salon on Nantasket Avenue. DeeDee, the owner, knew my parents. She's nothing like them and nothing like Clare either. I miss all of you—Clare, Max, you, Pharaoh, Darah, the bamboo, the rock garden, the quiet.

Hull is loud—street noise, customers, the TV blaring whenever DeeDee isn't working. But she's kind and that matters.

I worry about you. Please write.

Lucille Angel Ledwith

I sign all three names, hoping he'll see there's still a chance for something between us. I don't tell him how nervous I get every time I read a customer's letters and sense danger in the V's, the N's and the S's. I don't tell him how I walked to F Street but lacked the courage to get too close to the house. I don't tell him I know nothing about Nadia beyond the newspaper article about the kidnapping from the carousel, or that no one knows anything about the girl who washed up on the beach. I don't mention my loneliness, even though DeeDee's trying to make me feel at home.

But my letters tell me I'm in the right place at the right time.

A, N, and G ruled my first thirteen years as Agnes.

Now I'm working off the E and the L in Angel. Exploring. Evolving. Moving forward.

Between readings, I ask customers questions. Have you heard of Farrah? Nadia? No one knows anything. They're more interested in baby names and cheating husbands.

Lacy LaRue comes in for a new wig. I read his letters.

L–A–C–Y: Smart, caring, but pulled in different directions.

"Do you have another name?" I ask.

"Carol, but only my mother calls me that."

"Carol's letters are more grounded. The L at the end gives you direction. The Y in Lacy is like a fork in the road."

Lacy grins. "Inside, I'll be Carol. Outside, I'll be Lacy. Best of both worlds."

"That'll work."

Other entertainers come in for readings: Pooky, TuTu and C-C. I tweak Pooky to Pookie for hope, TuTu to Too-Too for flow, and leave C-C alone.

At night, I fall into bed, and negative letters invade my dreams.

The S slithers.

The G pokes.

The Q invades my body and leaves me achy.

The N sinks me into sadness and I can't crawl to safety.

I search for my L. Why can't I find it? Sometimes an R kicks me out of a funk and I wake up feeling better. Best of all is when the E arrives to save me and I face the day refreshed.

DeeDee's birthday is Thursday, so we go to Mama Mamie's for breakfast. We're settling into the back booth when a freckled, red-headed cop comes in. I recognize him immediately. Robocop!

"Bobby! Baby!" DeeDee cries, waving him over.

"Auntie Dee!"He gives her a bear hug. She tips up his chin so he can see me.

I recite the alphabet to stay calm.

"Meet Angel," she says.

"Pleased to meet you," he says, blushing.

He doesn't seem to remember me as Lucille Ledwith from Tom's house on Strawberry Hill. I look older; my hair is shorter and curly. My clothes are psychic chic, according to DeeDee—peasant skirts and frilly off-the-shoulder blouses. She taught me to tie a scarf in a French knot to cover my neck stains if I haven't used the liquid makeup.

They chat. I force myself to breathe evenly, to stay still, to not fidget. Then DeeDee lowers her voice and asks if he's still dating Melanie.

His blush creeps down his neck. "No, no, that's over."

My foot twitches. This is the moment. I nudge DeeDee's hefty leg.

DeeDee takes a beat, then says, "Bobby, any news about the girl who washed up on Gunrock Beach a month or so ago?"

"She's been in a coma since Sarge found her in May." He leans in closer to his aunt. "I'm not supposed to tell you this—Sarge gave the order to keep the case quiet—but you're a hairdresser. The kid's roots are yellow. Weirdest thing—watching them grow out. Why would a kid dye her hair black if it's blonde?"

A chill spreads over my arms, the fine hair rising. Squid's involved. I'm sure of it.

"So no one knows who she is?" DeeDee asks.

"She doesn't match any runaway profiles. Why do you want to know?"

DeeDee coughs. "Angel saw the newspaper article and felt bad for the girl. It got her curiosity cooking."

Robocop's freckles pop. "Curiosity killed the cat."

I finish the line, "and satisfaction brought it back."

His gaze lingers on me a beat too long.

"If anything changes, I'll let you know," he says.

"Thanks for the favor," DeeDee says and rubs Robocop's flat head. It must be a left-over endearment because he grins like a puppy.

"Speaking of favors, before I forget, can I put a poster in your window? We're planning a retirement tribute for Sarge."

"That man's overstayed his welcome in Hull," mutters DeeDee.

"How can you say that, Auntie? Sarge puts himself on the line every day." Robocop's freckles darken with pride. "You name it. He apprehends felons, saves children from drowning, and takes young guys under his wing. Like me."

DeeDee's fingers tighten around her coffee cup. "There are two sides to every story, Bobby."

Robocop isn't deterred. "That scar from Korea—he's a real war hero."

H-E-R-O. The word expands in my mind.

H rises above the line but also digs below it—just like Stone. One face for the world, and a hidden one for the dark stuff. If he retires now, he'll slither off to another town and keep hurting kids. I have to expose him before he disappears.

"I'll be right back," says Robocop.

Moments later, he brings DeeDee a giant poster of ButtFace, his good cheek in profile, set against a perfect sunset.

Summer Fling
Sunday, July 17, 4:00 - 8:00
Fort Revere Amphitheater
Honoring Hull Hero
Sergeant Evan Stone
for his 35 years of service

"Thanks, Auntie. The event is going to be one heck of a send off." Robocop hugs DeeDee and leaves after a nod to me.

"Why doesn't he realize what a horrible man Stone is?" I ask.

"I'll tell you a story about Bobby," DeeDee says. "When he was in sixth grade he got blamed for cheating. He stormed out because he was innocent, but his mom made him go back and apologize. From then on, Bobby decided adults deserved respect—even when they were wrong."

I think about respect and who deserves it. Robocop never questions Sarge—just like he never questioned that teacher.

"Aren't we supposed to challenge others when they're wrong?"

"Like I'm supposed to challenge Stone when he stomps on Lacy LaRue? What will that prove? Where will that get me?"

"But if you don't, Stone will keep on taking from you."

"But I stay in business."

"But you become less of a person."

"You have to go along to get along."

"So Robocop goes along with Sarge and he's a better person?"

DeeDee grimaces. "Bobby's kind. He's on the side of helping people."

"But Stone acts like that too, and he's a snake." The S in his name hisses in my mind.

There's no double-dealing letter in Robocop, but all those O's roll him along, following whoever's in charge.

How do I make him see Stone for what he is? That he shouldn't trust him, that he shouldn't let him distort things? He needs to open his eyes now—because to refuse to see is to give permission.

NINE

Constance Hill

DeeDee puts the poster in the window like she promised, but she spits on it first. "Stone's a fucking piece of shit," she mutters, then shrugs. "But Bobby's a good kid."

"He'd be smarter if he were Robert," I reply.

I get back to work, doing a few readings: Jeannette with her midlife crisis; Roz, convinced she has dementia; and Ruth, who hides her deepest thoughts and can't get out of the U.

For the most part, I feel good about my fortune telling. I meet nice people and give them hope. I stay away from the negative unless it's glaringly obvious, and then I suggest a nickname to ease their situations.

Late in the afternoon, a woman walks in for a mani-pedi. "A Thursday regular," DeeDee says.

The woman's face is framed by a stretchy band that holds back her dark shoulder-length hair with bangs hanging low over her brows. She wears oversized sunglasses that make her nose look tiny. A turtle-neck, a belted maxi-skirt, and a loose long-sleeved cardigan complete her look. No make up. No jewelry. Not even earrings.

"Constance!" DeeDee greets her with a wide smile. "So good to see you. Angel, come meet Constance. She's true to her name.

She's only missed one appointment in ten years. Let's see, that was in May if I remember correctly."

"Family matter," Constance says, her voice flat.

She selects a sheer polish and they head to the back room where DeeDee works her magic.

C–O–N–S–T–A–N–C–E.

The listening C's clash with the negative N's and that slippery S.

I hope she never goes by the name Conny. I can't imagine her enjoying life much if she did.

DeeDee talks as she works. "The girl is psychic. You wouldn't believe the number of customers coming in because of her."

"Uh-huh," says Constance, distant and cold.

"Aren't you curious to know what your name means?" asks DeeDee.

"Nah, not interested."

I peek into the room. Constance's head is tilted back; she has a V chin and hard angles in her hollow cheeks. She reminds me of Ivy. DeeDee sits on a low stool massaging the woman's feet, her hands working slowly. Her toes cross over each other, the knuckles raw and swollen. I wince just looking at them.

"You're missing out," DeeDee says. "It's fun, really. Your name tells you so much."

Constance gives another disinterested "Uh-huh," and DeeDee shifts to talking about her own letters, how they make her an explorer, always hungry for adventure.

"Where'd you find this kid?" Constance asks.

"She's family," DeeDee says, her tone softening. "Her parents passed away not long ago—may they rest in peace. I took her in after that."

"Must've been young," Constance murmurs. "Hull people?"

"Locals."

Does this woman Constance know something about Daddy and Ivy? She doesn't look like the crazies who used to drift through our house. If I check her letters, maybe I'll get a better read on this town and its secrets. I pull out my blocks and mark her letters in *The Letter Bible*.

Constance comes out wearing flip flops, her feet red and blotchy from DeeDee's pumice and oils. "I hear you used to live around here. Whereabouts?" Her voice is raspy now, like she's swallowed chicken bones and can't cough them out.

"Big Victorian on the beach," I say, brushing my fingers over Daddy's blocks.

Her eyes take on a beady squint, her lips puckering like she's holding something back. She straightens her shoulders, like she's pushing against an invisible force. She picks up the C block and turns it in her fingers before setting it down again. "Nice carving. Looks handmade."

"My dad whittled it."

"How'd you learn to read people's letters?" she asks, running her fingers over the blocks.

"I've made a study of it." I flip open *The Letter Bible*. "Have a seat. I'll tell you what Constance means. It's an interesting name, full of contradictions."

She scowls and flicks the C block. It bounces across the floor. "A bunch of crap," she mutters, turns and walks out.

"She's a weird one," DeeDee says, watching her go. "Been coming here for years. Wears the same uniform whether it's ninety degrees or nine. Every Wednesday at four I massage her mashed-up toes, then rub a heated stone over her calluses. They're as big as quarters! I file her fingernails into points, polish and buff them. She tips me big and walks out like she owns the place."

Through the window, I watch Constance slip into a boxy car with wooden sides. Two white, fluffy cats leap onto her. She kisses and coos at them.

The C's in her name should stand for caring, compassionate, considerate, like Clare. But she's got a wall of ice around her—at least when it comes to people. DeeDee locks the door. "Thank God we're done for the day." She plops into a chair with a sigh, kicking off her shoes. "My piggies are killing me. Maybe you'll give my feet some attention?"

I nod and straighten up my space, stacking my blocks and closing *The Letter Bible*.

DeeDee waddles into the sink room, calling out orders. "Fill the bucket with warm water, add soap. Heat the towels. Get the lotions ready."

I wait for her to settle into the recliner, then say, "DeeDee . . .what else can you tell me about Ivy?"

DeeDee's legs twitch and the water ripples. "Did you see how Constance parts the air when she walks in a room? Nothing pleases her, like she's above everything. Ivy was like that. All I wanted to do was make her happy," DeeDee says, her voice soft, regretful.

"I remember the two of you forehead to forehead. My mother never warmed up to anyone except for you. Not even Daddy. Especially not me."

DeeDee turns on the back massager and closes her eyes. I think she's done telling me about Ivy, but then she whispers, "Ivy only talked about you once, the day I saw you through the vents. I wondered why you were up there, but she said Wizz wanted you to be separated from the druggies and boozers. He wanted your babies to be pure with no pollution coursing through their veins. She said he was waiting for you to come into your own."

I go twitchy. She's telling me what I already know—just dressed in different words.

"I wanted to meet you," DeeDee says, almost wistful. "But Ivy said she'd made arrangements for you to visit some relatives and hang out with cousins your own age."

"But that never happened," I say, swallowing hard. "She was lying. They hid me so Squid wouldn't take me."

"I met Squid once," DeeDee says, her voice hardening. "A big boorish dude. Boasting about the little girls in his life and how he loved them all."

I want to grab her and make her understand what she ignored. "He loved the profit they brought him," I say, my gut twisting. "Those girls were his victims. Didn't you realize that?"

"I heard the rumors, but Ivy said that was bullshit. She told me if I wanted to stay close to her, I'd better keep my nose out of it."

"So you did nothing?"

"Ivy said it was none of my business. If I spoke up, it'd get her killed. So I kept quiet."

I want to blame DeeDee, to make her suffer like the children who went missing, but all my books say that love is blind. In Ivy's case, DeeDee totally removed her eyes.

I crawl to my room. My chest feels empty and heavy at the same time. Why don't people listen when someone is hurting? Why do they cover for bad people? Make excuses? Even love them?

I may only be sixteen, but I know one thing—kids are the most valuable thing in the world. If no one protects us, how is anything supposed to grow right?

TEN

Vasya Jones

I need a separate room for my readings. The hair dryers roar, people never stop talking, and I hate sitting in the front window. There's a decent-sized closet at the top of the stairs with supplies and junk.

"Let me clean it out and paint it," I say.

DeeDee hesitates for a second, then nods, "Go for it, kiddo."

Over the Fourth of July holiday, I remove the shelves and reinstall them along the walls of the staircase. Maybe I really am my father's daughter! It feels good knowing he actually taught me something about carpentry. Now I have a space all my own. I sit in its center and let it spin around me, talk to me, and tell me what to do next.

Nothing will ever be like my attic, where letters covered every wall because I didn't want to feel alone. Here, I want it to look intentional.

I paint the walls and ceiling white. Clean. Open. It feels right—how I see space now, how Clare taught me about infinity and possibility. Before Clare, I'd have picked black—closed in, like a trap.

I grab every color of acrylic I can find and paint letters—huge ones, tiny ones, ones that tilt or droop or sneak into corners. They pop off the walls, twisting and dancing. When I step back, it's like the room finally knows me.

As the paint dries, DeeDee and I watch *E.T.* on the VCR downstairs. What a name for a character!

E-T, so perfect: energy, adventure, future, other-worldly, twirling into space.

And to watch it on a V–C–R!

The V pulls me in—it could be dangerous, but this V feels gentler.

The C makes me listen.

The R sets everything in motion.

I'm officially a modern woman. I can answer a phone, use a washing machine, dishwasher, and microwave. I know how to shop for bargains. Maybe I'll learn to drive a car and pump my own gas!

DeeDee stoops and rewinds the tape, fast-forwarding to our favorite parts. I watch her work the machine, making it do what she wants. When the movie ends, I go to my wall of letters. I trace the sharp lines, the angles. Each stroke hums with power.

In the morning, DeeDee hands me an envelope. "You must be Lucille Angel Ledwith," she says, reading my name. Her purple eyebrows shoot up in surprise.

I sit on the floor of my new room, my letters chattering and dancing around me, and open it.

My own Lucille,

I'm in Alaska on a fishing expedition! My lawyer sent your letter along with the rest of my mail. You'd love it here—more islands than I can count, and big, friendly dogs everywhere. I'm working on a trawler out of Juneau. Maybe you'd say I'm running away from myself, but it's the opposite—I'm finding myself. Somehow, I know you understand.

I'll be at sea for three months. Eventually, I'll make my way

*back to Massachusetts. By then, the courts will have decided our
fate. Your money should be available to you by the fall, I hope.
No matter what, you'll always have a home with me if you need
it—just not now.*

Your out-of-step Dad,

Tom

I examine the slanted M's and the narrow O's in Tom's letter. There are erasures and smudges, like he had more to say but
changed his mind. His words sound optimistic, but his handwriting tells a different story. I reread the last sentence: You'll always
have a home with me. I believe him, but do I even want that?
I wouldn't be his daughter—just an intruder in his private life. I
compose a letter, sharing my deepest feelings:

July 5, 1988
Dear Tom,

> *You're chasing things you can't catch. You won't find peace
> until the M in Tom takes over and you balance sadness with joy,
> longing with fulfillment. I won't count on you until then.*

I don't mail it, even though every word is true. Clare would say,
"Never cut a tree down in winter." So instead, I write:

Dear Tom,

> *Catch a lot of fish! Get rid of those demons and come back
> refreshed.*

Till then, Your Lucille

I drop the letter in the mailbox outside the salon. I see
an old bearded man pulling a suitcase by a braided rope. He's

square-bodied with yellow skin and droopy eyes. A child trails behind him like a shadow. They don't look like summer residents.

"Can I help you?" I ask.

The man halts suddenly, then leans against the corner post of DeeDee's shop, breathing heavily. He pulls out a wrinkled piece of paper, his thick finger pounding an address: "2 Bluff Road." His voice is rough and guttural. "You know where this is? You take us there?"

The child, moon-faced, with a fleck of gold in her light brown eyes, lowers her hoodie. Her bright red hair hangs limp, cut with jagged scissors. The man, too, might once have had red hair, but it's faded with time.

"My grandpa don't speak English good," the child says.

She can't be more than eight, many of her baby teeth are still intact. "I'm not familiar with all the streets in Hull," I tell her. "Come into the salon. My friends will know where Bluff Road is."

The man and child follow me into DeeDee's. I grab water from the small refrigerator in the sink room and pour two glasses. The man nods in thanks and drinks deeply. Andréa takes the paper, squinting at the address. "Sonofabitch, that's across from my house in Gunrock."

DeeDee's voice drops to a hushed whisper. "It's one of the Cat Houses!"

The word tugs at my memory: Cat Houses.

Ivy storms into the house, screaming about Sergeant Stone. Her voice carried through the floorboards, sharp and furious. She was that loud.

"That scar-faced monster threw me into the squad car, blindfolded me, and shoved his foot into my back. 'Stay down or I'll kill you,' he said. 'I have a little surprise for you.'

"When he stopped the car, the goddamned bastard yanked me out, unlocked a door, and pushed me up a set of stairs. 'Get a good look at this,' he said, in that creepy voice. Then he pulled off my blindfold. 'I left her here, just for you.'

"A blond hooker, stone-cold fucking dead, was sprawled out on the floor."

"Jesus," Daddy whistled.

"Fuckhead Stone said we're responsible for her death. That the dope she smoked was cut with poison. But that woman was strangled. I saw the marks around her neck."

"He's sending us a message," Daddy said. "Do what he says or we're next."

"I hadda puke," Ivy said. "Stone let me use the bathroom. I looked out the window and saw where I was—on a bluff in Gunrock. I turned on the water to mask the noise and searched the room for anything I could use against him. And lookie lookie what I found."

Daddy stammered and I swear I heard his witch tooth click. "I wonder what the fuck is on it and why it was hidden."

Late that night, when Daddy came up to my room, I pretended to be asleep. He went to his corner of the attic and pulled up the floorboard. After he left, I snuck over to the hiding place. It wasn't drugs. It wasn't money. It wasn't photos. It was a small, black rectangular box with two holes in it.

Whatever it was, it mattered. But the night Daddy and I were leaving for the horizon, I checked under the floorboards one last time. It was gone. Still, I remember Ivy's words: Hooker. Gunrock. Cat House.

Yanking me back to the present, a small hand tugs my shirt. "We are looking for my ma."

The man pulls a worn photo from his wallet. The woman is freckle-faced with gray eyes; her red hair is pulled back, her long neck bare except for dangling hoop earrings.

"Vasya Jones," he says, his voice a coil of heat and anger.

V-A-S-Y-A.

I'm already fearful for her. The letters tell me she's knee-deep in quicksand and sinking.

The child looks at me with hopeful eyes. "Do you know her?"

Nobody knows your ma, I think. Her letters tell me she's beyond saving, gone already.

"You can help find my daughter?" the man asks.

Andréa pulls DeeDee into the sink room. I hear their shrill voices.

Andréa walks out first. "I'll take you. I live nearby."

"I'm coming too," I say.

DeeDee balloons her body in front of me, but Andréa takes my hand.

"Don't be so possessive with the kid. She's got to get out from under you once in a while," Andréa snickers.

DeeDee scowls, "We'll all go." She hustles to lock the door and put up the closed sign.I sit in the back seat beside the old man and his granddaughter. "What's your name?" I ask the girl.

"Talia."

T-A-L-I-A. Promising letters.

"And your grandfather?"

The old man re-enters the day and looks around."You good women. Not like Vasya."

"My Deduska's name is Anatoly." Talia's pale face is dotted with pink freckles.

A-N-A-T-O-L-Y.

A mixture of highs and lows. And now that he's at the end of his life, he's at a fork in the road.

"And what's your name?" she asks me.

"She's Angel," DeeDee yells from the front seat. It cracks me up that DeeDee makes it a point not to call me Agnes or Angelica. She wants to have named me herself. Ha ha on her.

Andréa drives along Nantasket Avenue, past Paragon and the Sea Mist. She takes a left on Atlantic Avenue. We drive past the town hall and the police station. I see massive posters for the tribute for Sergeant Stone and want to gag. A raggedy man hauls a green plastic garbage bag: Hornet being Hornet. I want DeeDee to stop so I can thank him, but she turns at the Gunrock Beach sign, then again onto Bluff Road.

B-L -U-F-F.

Lips and legs.

Secrets.

Unfulfilled dreams.

This is not a good place to live.

Andréa parks in front of a square house with a wide porch and a double front door painted red. "This is my house. Vasya Jones lives on the other side."

Andréa's home looks out to the ocean and the horizon, but just across the street, a row of boxy houses, all the same except for the door color, overlook a small junkyard of trashed automobiles, their parts tossed around like mangled bodies. The five of us walk up a dusty entranceway of pebbles and weeds. Anatoly knocks. A tall beauty opens the door. Her red hair is lush and newly brushed. Her lips are scarlet and her eyes metallic gray.

"Vasya?" The old man asks, the guttural sounds eating each letter. The man takes out the crumpled paper and points to the address. "Vasya. My daughter. You are her? Dah?"

The woman blinks and shrinks back. "Papa? Is it you? I thought I was dead to you."

Tears stream down the old man's face. He wipes them away with the back of his hand, mottled with red blisters and ropey veins. "I am dying, Vasya. Your daughter needs her *matooshka*."

Vasya's face melts. She sobs into her father, who pats her back and strokes her flaming curls. Talia jumps between them.

"Nadia!" Vasya says, "You have returned her to me! Papa, how have you done this?"

Nadia? The Nadia who was stolen from the carousel? Is this

woman her mother? I flash back to the newspaper article and recall that Vanessa Jones was the name in *The Hull Gazette*.

"I am Talia," the little girl says.

Vasya removes the child's head scarf and drinks in a long look. Then she sweeps her into her arms and they twirl wildly, their red hair interweaving, their tears overflowing. Anatoly clasps onto both of them and they hold tight to each other.

I want to ask about Nadia, but I hold my tongue. Clare's voice is firm: "Wait and listen. Patience and fortitude conquer all."

I see a black truck crest the hill. Vasya sees it too. She pulls us inside and slams the door.

"HIDE!" she shouts. "Especially you Talia!"

We freeze where we stand.

"Now, damn it. Hide!"

We scatter. Talia and I stretch out between the wall and the couch. Dust and grime, ash and regret surround us. DeeDee and Andréa race to the rear of the house. Anatoly trudges around until I hear a door close.

A light knock. "Vanessa, Sweetie," a gravel voice calls.

I know that sound. ButtFace Stone. That disgusting man is everywhere.

"Showtime," he says, drippy like slime.

Vasya opens the door. "Hey."

He comes in.

I hear the whoosh of a jar opening, and money being counted out. "I got it here for you," she says.

"And I got it here for you."

I hear a belt buckle loosen and a zipper slide. Then grunting. I shrink with the sounds. Talia hardly breathes.

"You're such a good girl, Nessa," he coos.

"Just tell me she's safe," Vasya says.

"One-eye is on her all the time," he laughs. "All you gotta do is keep the money and the men coming. Maybe I'll bring you a picture next time." I hear him knock her against the wall. "But don't do anything stupid, Sweet Face, or she's a goner." His voice is brick-hard.

Vasya shuts the door and I hear the pound of her fists. After a minute, she calls us into the parlor. Her lipstick is smeared and her face puffy.

"You are not well," Anatoly says to her.

"Neither are you, Papa. But you, my Talia, are so beautiful."

Talia puts her arms around her mother's waist. "I have waited so long to see you and Nadia." She looks up at Vasya. "Do we still look exactly alike? Will she be home soon?"

Vasya hangs her head. "She doesn't live with me anymore."

"I don't understand why she does not live with you. I'm a bad father to have such a bad daughter. We should have stayed in Ukraine."

A long speech for a man with a face like ancient rocks.

Vasya talks quietly to him in Russian. I hear words like *nyet* and *prostitutka* and see him shake his head. She gives him a wad of money and turns to Andréa. "I've got clients booked all evening. Will you take my father and daughter to the motel at the bottom of the hill? I'll call ahead for a room."

"No!" I shout. My voice is usually quiet but they hear the urgency. "Vasya, are Nadia and Talia identical twins?"

"Dah," Anatoly answers. "This one was puny. She couldn't travel. Vasya went ahead with Nadia to make money. Dirty money." He spits in his hands.

"Sergeant Stone knows what Nadia looks like."

Vasya nods.

"Then how can she stay at a motel? If Stone sees Talia in Hull, he'll figure she escaped from wherever he's hiding Nadia. He'll kill her or kidnap her again."

Vasya pulls Talia close and strokes her hair.

"How did this happen?" Anatoly asks.

Vasya's lips quiver. "I owed a man money."

"Squid?" I ask.

DeeDee skunk-eyes me.

Vasya nods. "He threatened to kill us both, but if I whored for him and dealt drugs, he said he'd keep her alive. What choice did I have?"

"What about Vixen?" I ask.

DeeDee gasps.

"I don't know anyone named Vixen," Vasya says, but her hands shake and her eyes shift.

I don't believe her. She thinks she's protecting her daughter, but doesn't she know she's just a pawn in their scheme? They'll do what they want because no one will stop them.

"I'll tell you how this happened," Vasya starts, like she's about to tell a fairy tale. "Last month, Stone knocked on my door. He said I'd be paying him directly instead of Squid. I begged him to tell me about Nadia. 'What's in it for me?' he asked.

"'Give me twenty percent up front before I give Squid his cut, and I'll keep her safe.' I begged him to tell me where she was. 'Bring her to me. A picture, a recording of her voice, something!' He slapped me up and down. I let him. I couldn't stop him.

"When it was over, he said Nadia was so close I could touch her. I pleaded with him, and he said he'd see what he could do, but only if I played his game."

Vasya breaks into sobs, her body heaving. Andréa wraps her in her arms. "It's ok, Sister. We'll find a way to get them. Tonight, I cruise the boardwalk. They can stay at my place. Tomorrow, we'll come up with a plan." She looks at DeeDee.

"Aint none of my business," DeeDee shrugs.

I remember something I read in Clare's journal: "What is necessary for the triumph of evil is for good people to do nothing."

"DeeDee," I say, "if you loved Ivy, now's the time to prove it."

DeeDee lowers her orange head, her white roots showing.

"You're a lot like your mother. Nervy, pushy and a pain in the ass. I knew Ivy had some shady dealings with Squid and Stone, but she told me to mind my own business. I didn't want to lose her. Isn't that a slap in the face." DeeDee looks up, her eyes runny with mascara, a clump of eyelash stuck to her cheek.

"DeeDee, if you don't help rid this town of these predators, kids will never be safe. You said it yourself—if Ivy was involved, she was scum. What does that make you if you turn away? Children's lives are at stake. My life's at stake. I'll go after these dirtbags by myself if I have to. No one's going to take freedom away from another kid in Hull if I have a say.

"You let Stone walk all over you and your friends. Sure, he's retiring from the force, but not from being a monster. He and Vixen will be out there, stealing kids for Squid. Destroying lives."

Vasya cringes.

I want to punch the walls and kick the doors. I need to make her understand. "Don't you want to live in a town that protects its children?" I try not to shout. "DeeDee, I'm counting on you."

DeeDee crushes me in a hug that takes my breath away. "I'm with you, Angel. I'll be damned if I let those bastards get away with abusing another kid. Not this time. Not now."

Maybe one child can be saved.

ELEVEN

The Islands

Andréa drops DeeDee and me off at the salon. We go down the alley and into the apartment. DeeDee glares like someone set a plate of bugs in front of her. "Ivy, wherever you are, you'd better be thanking me!"

DeeDee might be loyal to Ivy's memory, but she also cares about me and Hull's future. I'm thankful, and I want to show it. Without being asked, I start putting away the clean dishes stacked on the drying rack.

Then I hear a rap at the side door. DeeDee peeks through the peephole.

"Hornet, you bastard. What the hell do you want?"

"I gotta talk to the kid."

DeeDee hesitates but opens the door. "She's in the kitchen."

I expect to see the usual scruffy Hornet, but the man who steps into the kitchen is different. His hair's slicked back, his face smooth, and he's wearing a button-down shirt and clean jeans. Even his bugs go quiet.

"You look nice today, Ira. What's going on?"

He meets my gaze, eyes steady, brows raised. "No one's called me Ira since I was a boy. I've been invisible all this time, and suddenly you show up and all my bugs start twitching. They're buzzing at me to pay attention. My mother would never approve of Hornet, but she'd still have faith in Ira. You've reminded me of that and I'm grateful."

"You've got strong letters," I say. "You could live better taking that name back."

"I've been scared in this town since I was ten," Ira says. "I blame myself, but I blame Stone even more. If it weren't for him, I might've stood taller. But he was always in my head. 'Hornet, no one cares about you but me,' he'd say. 'I've got your back. I'm keeping you safe from yourself.'"

Ira's face twitches, his shoulders bunching, the skin on his neck wrinkling. "I gotta tell you something, Angel. You too, Dee. I don't know what can be done about it, if anything. But you've been asking, and I've been quiet. Now you need to know."

He pauses, breathes out slowly, his face finally settling into calm.

"There's these caves in the bluff on Gunrock where I crash when I'm coming down from a high. One morning, I wake up to buzzing. And it ain't me doing it, like someone's poking my ass with static. I pop up fast, but there's nothing—no bees, no hornets, no wasps. Just *buzz buzz buzz* fast and slow. Like a signal going off."

Ira tilts his head, tuning into that moment. "I crawl to the ledge. Nothing. Then I hear a truck rumbling, stopping at the cliff. Stone gets out, binoculars in hand, watching along the beach. I'm figuring there's been an accident. But then, he pisses down the hill."

DeeDee pours him a cup of coffee. He nods quick and keeps going.

"That's when I see something crawl along the beach, like a giant crab, only with long black hair. Stone runs over, lifts it up, and tosses it into the ocean. Then I realize it's a girl. She's flailing her legs, her arms, turning her face to catch a breath. Stone grabs her and pushes her head under water. Something snaps in me, and I shout in this deep God-like voice. 'Leave that girl alone.'

"Sarge looks around, and I duck into the cave. Then I hear another voice, 'I'm coming, Sarge! Hold on.' It's Robocop. Stone yanks the girl out of the water, flips her over, and gives her mouth-to-mouth."

"So you're saying Stone was trying to kill the girl?" DeeDee asks.

Ira's pacing now, his footsteps heavy. "Looked that way. When Robocop caught up, he called for an ambulance and backup."

"What caused all the buzzing?" I ask.

"My gut. Telling me something was wrong."

DeeDee grumbles. "Maybe it was a signal?"

"Or an alarm?"

Ira's face lights up, like a lightbulb's switched on. "Stone knew she was on the beach. Someone alerted him."

My chest heats up. "Take me there. I need to see where she washed up."

DeeDee plants her fists on her hips. "No fucking way. What's that going to prove?"

N–F–W. Ivy's letters. Her favorite answer to everything. Time to crush them.

"All I know is that Stone will be honored by this town in less than two weeks. Then he's off to run things on his own, with no one to stop him. He's poison. He has to be stopped."

"You're just a kid," DeeDee mutters, shaking her head.

"Yeah, I am. But you're not, DeeDee. And you're right, Ira Trapper. It's time to stop watching and do something. Make up for dropping bombs in Vietnam. Be the man your mother would've been proud of. And you, DeeDee, should know by now Ivy was a lying, rotten—"

"Enough!" DeeDee snaps, cutting me off.

I shrug. The silence hangs in the air. The tension thickens, like no one wants to say the thing we're all thinking.

DeeDee and Ira exchange a look. I can't tell if they're silently agreeing or if they're about to toss me into a hidey-hole.

Ira sighs, breaking the silence. "TwoTon, I've known you a long time. When we was little, everyone picked on us. You was the fatty, and I was the pushover. We always backed down. Let's do what the kid wants."

DeeDee grunts. "Fine. We'll go before dawn, before anyone in this goddamn town sees us walk into hell."

H–E–L–L. H–U–L–L.

What is this town about? Its secrets? Or exposing them before it's too late?

I lie awake, staring at the ceiling, trying to figure out what tomorrow might answer.

*   *   *

I'm dressed and ready before the sun. I wake Ira first. His bugs twitch when he stirs, and he's eager to get going.

DeeDee hesitates. "I've got clients this morning. Tomorrow's better."

Clare's words slip in: "To lose patience is to lose the battle." So I give DeeDee a quick kiss on her cheek. "I really need your help."

She huffs but doesn't argue, slapping a Be Back Soon sign on the door. We pile into her car. Her hands grip the steering wheel like she wants to snap it in half. "What the hell do you think you'll find out there?"

"I don't know yet, but something's off about where that girl washed ashore. That buzzing sound? It wasn't Hornet."

We drive up Bluff Road, past Andréa's house and turn onto Summit Ave.

"Victoria's Grandma lived over there," DeeDee says, pointing to a house that looms like a dark cloud. "Used to look a whole lot friendlier when we were kids."

"There wasn't no wall back then," Ira says, sticking his head out the window like a dog. "Victoria would dive off the rocks and swim to the islands. You and me was too scared to follow. She called us chicken shit."

"And fag dung," DeeDee adds with a smirk.

A streak of sun breaks through the clouds, and their eyes crinkle remembering when they played together as kids. I never had that—just my letters and books...and Gregg.

DeeDee parks the car on a dirt path surrounded by ruts and brambles.

"I walk out there a lot," Ira says. "The place has music to it."

We get out and take in the view. From the cliff's edge, Hull stretches out like a long L, lunging into the ocean.

"That's where Stone tried to drown the girl," Ira says, pointing.

"We're going down there," I tell DeeDee.

"I'll stand guard," she says.

"Shout out if you hear someone coming."

DeeDee sits on a flat rock at the top. "I can hear Victoria calling us to jump in. The balls on her, even as a kid."

I remember DeeDee told me that Victoria's body lies deep in the ocean. It's the V that pulled her down. She never got to live out the rest of her letters.

Ira focuses on descending a narrow path, thorns biting at his ankles. My feet fit better on the path, and I stay close to his lead. When we get to the bottom, the tide has pulled back enough to show a stretch of pebbly beach.

"Right here. This is the place," Ira says.

I stand still and listen. A plane drones. A fishing boat hums. The tide has risen and fallen so many times it's erased any sign of a girl with blond roots and probably V-shaped scars. I don't know her name, but I hope it's something strong—something filled with A's and E's and L's, positive letters that help her move forward.

To my right, I notice the islands off the coast, four rocky and one with vegetation. They don't look like Clare's island. They're battered by the open ocean, not part of the Weir River. Strung together, they resemble a W—jagged and forbidding. "Have you been on those islands?"

Ira shakes his head. "They're haunted."

"What do you mean?"

"Noise travels at night. Screams, cackles—like banshees ready to suck out your soul. But no one's ever seen 'em."

Daddy told me once about a woman with pasty skin, spiky hair and black lips. "She's called a banshee," Daddy said, his voice low, like he was sharing a secret. "She creeps around, putting death spells on people. But . . ." He dropped onto my bed and tugged my earlobe, "you can hear her coming. She has a high-pitched wail." Daddy screeched like a crow. "Her laugh's a shrill cackle." Then, he opened his mouth, went CAW, CAW, CAW, so loud it made the bats in the eaves twitch their wings. "Beware of her. She'll destroy you. So stay in your room where you're safe."

But I'm not in my room anymore and I'll never be safe with these monsters on the loose.

I study the islands. Something bad seeps from them, like they're soaked in poison. "How can we get over there?"

"We, Kemosabe?" says Ira, raising an eyebrow.

"Yes, Ira. This is a team effort."

"I didn't sign up for this."

"Where can we get a boat?"

"Nowhere, that's where. DeeDee would never allow it."

"Then we won't tell her."

I spot a canoe moored in the summer grass, the oars resting inside. "Let's do this."

"No fucking way," Ira says, his bees buzzing in agitation.

I'm not about to let Ivy's words, or anyone's, stop us now.

"Can't you hear Victoria's voice making fun of you? It's time to stand up for yourself. Just get in the boat and help me paddle." I drag the canoe into the water.

I'm used to paddling across Clare's current, but the open ocean is a different beast— denser, meaner. I shorten my stroke, grip the oars tighter, and start to make ground. The wind's at our backs, helping to close the distance quickly. Soon, we're approaching a horse-shoe shaped island with clumps of bushes and scraggly trees.

Out of the corner of my eye, something moves along the back side of a rock. A rat? No, it's a cat! A cat couldn't swim that far. Could it?

I row the canoe to the leeward side, pull into a shallow cove and moor the boat.

"Are you with me?" I ask Ira.

"I'll stay right here, thank you very much. I'm not setting foot on that haunt."

I don't tease him. "Wait here."

I glance over my shoulder before heading off. The shoreline's quiet, the vegetation sparse—short bushes, thick vines, nothing that looks like it's been disturbed. There's a faint path. As the sun climbs higher, it spills light across the landscape, guiding me forward.

I reach the bottom of a rocky wall. It looks like someone's been here recently. Creating a hiding space was Daddy's signature. This looks like one of his.

I kick the dirt around, and metal catches the light. Digging deeper with my hands, I uncover a heavy door, the kind you find on a root cellar or an underground hatchway. I tug at the handle, but it won't budge.

What's down there? Drugs? Girls? Something worse?

I back off and retrace my steps. I skirt around the backside of the island, moving toward an overhang made of rich, dark earth. As I get closer, I see large and small footprints scattered across the ground. I want to look more, but then an alarm sounds, far-off. My stomach drops. Did I set that off?

I don't wait to find out. I scramble back to the canoe, my feet moving faster than my thoughts.

Ira shivers, sweat trickling down his face. "I thought the banshees ate you." His bees buzz harder, like they feel how freaked out he is.

"I found something suspicious," I say, still out of breath. "A concealed door buried under the soil. It was too heavy for me to open, but the earth around it shows it's been used recently. And there's more. There's a cave on the other side of the island, some sort of lookout. It's filled with footprints. Ira, if drugs are being smuggled, or girls are being traded—if this is the main drop-off point, how do we ever prove it?"

He scoffs, the weight of his words dragging him down. "We? I'm an invisible homeless nobody. Ain't a person in town gonna listen to me. And you're a bossy kid who thinks letters can talk. We're chicken-shit outta of luck."

His words pull at me, but I won't let them bury me.

N-F-W.

The letters that trapped me, now fuel me.

A downslide won't stop me.

Ignoring the truth won't stop me.

A fake welcome won't stop me.

I row toward the other islands. They're all the same—barren, like nothing wants to live there.

We head back toward the mainland where I see the remains of a foundation against the cliff. "Was there once a lighthouse there?" I ask, pointing at the crumbling structure. Something about those cliffs bothers me—the way they rise like they're guarding a secret.

Ira puffs up, full-on Hull historian. "During the Revolutionary War, they built lookout towers. Some are still standing, like at Fort Revere, where they're holding Stone's tribute."

A ray of sunlight slices through the morning haze, hitting the bluff. Below the ruins, a bumpy ledge juts from the rock. A glint of glass flashes in the dirt.

"Ira, what's underneath the tower? Is that one of your caves?"

"Nope. Mine are over there." He nods toward the ledges. They're jagged and dark.

He calls them caves. I call them rat holes.

"But look there under the tower, in the cliffside. What do you see?"

He shrugs. "Heard people made bomb shelters like bunkers back in the '50s, in case of nuclear war."

Bunkers? Hidden spaces. Underground.

The B feels like a barrier.

The S hisses with secrets.

I stare at the shape buried in the weeds. Everyone's so busy staring at the tower, they never notice what's under it.

I return the boat and walk along the shoreline, keeping close to the cliff. The rock vibrates, faint but steady, like something's alive inside. How do I get close enough to find out?

A sharp caw slices through my thoughts. I look up just as a flock of seagulls swoops across the sky.

Ira shudders. "Haunted. The whole place is a coffin."

"Go back to DeeDee so she won't worry. She has clients this morning. Meet me at the salon later."

"She won't like that. Neither do I."

"Just go."

Ira doesn't argue. He hightails it up the beach and disappears into the shadows. DeeDee would never come down, which means I'm alone and free to explore.

I press into the bluff again. Nothing shakes or caws. My foot slips, and I hit the sand hard.

I get up, hugging the rocks, testing my footing as I move upward.

Bit by bit, I climb to Summit Avenue, slipping behind a row of bushes. No DeeDee. No Ira. Just me.

A black truck rolls down the road, slow and careful. It stops in front of Victoria's grandmother's house. The driver hits a button, and a gate swings open. The truck disappears inside.

Is it a garage? A back entrance?

I inch forward. A fence of interlocking X's blocks my view, with thick bushes behind it and a high cement wall beyond that—like a fortress. Near the base of the shrubs, a chunk of earth is missing, clawed away by some animal. I crouch, peering through, and see a gap in the cement wall.

I reach for the fence.

The shock blasts through me, white-hot. It hits again and again. Then an alarm shrieks, ripping the air open.

I need cover. Now.

I roll into the brambles, pushing through the roots and bushes. When the shaking slows, I crawl backward, sliding down the cliff. Thorns snag my skin. My legs burn and bleed. My head spins.

The alarm stops.

And then—

CAW.

The sound slices through me, sharp as glass.

Not just any caw. *That* caw.

The one I can't forget.

Vixen.

She's here. Somewhere. I can feel her.

Something slashes through the bushes, fast and angry. No barking. No search dog. Just swearing—a high-pitched wail.

I crawl through the last thorny bushes, legs shaking. The stone wall snakes along a narrow path, and just beyond it, Andréa's gray house perches above the seawall.

I slip around the side, careful not to make a sound. I pound on her door, the knock echoing faintly off the cliffside.

"What the hell happened to you?" Andréa pulls me inside. "Did you fall into a rabbit hole?"

"I set off an alarm scoping out a house on Summit Ave."

"You stupid girl." She shoves me into a chair. "You wanna get eaten by vampires? Trouble finds you when you let your guard down."

"There's something off about that place. And Vixen's at the center of it. I need to let DeeDee know I'm all right."

"This is gonna end bad, kid," Andréa mutters, shaking her head. "Just know you heard it here first."

She picks up the phone and dials.

DeeDee's voice is strained with worry. "Come home. Now. It's not safe out there."

"I need to know what they're keeping out there."

"Now, Angelica," DeeDee says again. And again.

Home.

The letters vibrate.

H. A bed where I can rest.

O. A circle holding my life together.

M. Shoulder-strong, keeping me from falling.

E. Smiling, promising I can climb high and still be safe.

There's no L in home. But the E offers escape.

"Put Andréa on," DeeDee says.

"I'm on the extension."

"Bring her. Now."

When we get to the salon, DeeDee runs to the car and pulls me into a hug—not a fake Ivy hug, but a real one. Solid. Warm. Like she means it.

"Don't scare me like that again," she says. "I promised Ivy I'd look after you."

I stiffen. "When did you do that?" My voice feels thin.

"The night you showed up at my door." She pulls back, her hands firm on my shoulders. "You're family now."

TWELVE

Getting to Safety

"Lemme in!" Ira pleads at DeeDee's back door. "Stone's gunnin' for me."

"What the hell are you talking about?" DeeDee shouts.

Ira rushes past her into the apartment. "Turn on the local news."

DeeDee switches the channel. *Breaking News* scrolls in a blue banner across the bottom.

Our jaws drop. Ira's mug shot flashes on the screen.

A news anchor with perfect hair and ice-blue eyes leans toward the camera, his voice smooth and serious: A teenager was attacked tonight by a grizzled man covered in insect tattoos. Witnesses say she had just exited the roller coaster at Paragon Park when he approached her.

The police have identified the suspect as Ira Trapper, known throughout Hull as Hornet. He's a homeless drifter, considered mentally unstable and potentially dangerous. If you see this man, contact Sergeant Stone at the Hull Police Department.

The mugshot blasts across the screen again. Ira's oily hair is matted. The bees inked onto his skin glisten like demons. From the side, his crooked nose and pointed chin make him look like a storybook witch about to eat children.

Ira takes a shaky breath. "I didn't do it. Stone set me up."

DeeDee folds her arms. "Start talking."

"After Angel and I rowed to the islands, I ran to tell you to go back to the salon, that we'd meet you there. But when the alarm went off, I crawled deep inside my cave and stayed put. After a while, I crept to the edge. Stone was there, scanning the shore with binoculars and saw me." His voice trembles. "He knows I was the one who shouted when he tried to drown that girl. I'm a witness to what he did."

My stomach clenches. What was Stone searching for? The person who set off the alarm? Me? Now he's pinning something on Hornet to cover his tracks?

DeeDee shakes her head. "That fucker." Her voice hardens. "Ivy hated him for a reason. Blackmailing her. Wizz, too." She presses her lips together, the yellows and greens of her gloss melting into blue. Then she disappears down the hall.

She comes back with a pair of jeans, a white T-shirt, scissors and a makeup case—the same one she uses when she paints Lacy LaRue's face.

"Hornet, my friend, it's time for a make-over."

Ira blinks. "Are you serious?"

"Shower and shave. Let's see what I can do."

When he's clean, DeeDee gets to work. She chops his hair short, layers foundation over his skin, and blurs the edges of his tattoos.

When she's done, the guy in the mirror isn't Hornet. He's someone else.

Ira stares. His mouth opens. His fingers hover over his jaw, his cheekbones. Then his face folds, tears streaming down his cheeks.

"Shit, Hornet," DeeDee mutters. "You're gonna wash the pancake off if you keep bawling."

Ira laughs—a broken, breathless sound. "I never knew..." His throat works like he's swallowing glass. "I never knew what I looked like without my bees."

His eyes meet DeeDee's.

"I might have had a woman."

*　*　*

Carrying pillows and a blanket, DeeDee and I take Ira downstairs to a subbasement where a small boiler room is sealed off from the elements. A safe place to hide.

"Not much different from my usual digs," he says as he settles in.

"I'll bring you breakfast," I tell him. It's the least I can do.

I'm making eggs with bacon and cheese, toast and jam, and chicory coffee with cream— not from goat's milk like on Brewer Island, but close—when there's a knock at the kitchen door. Andréa bustles in, followed by a stoop-shouldered Anatoly. Talia trails behind, her red hair tucked under a baseball cap.

"I got guests all weekend, and so does Vasya. No place else for the old man and the granddaughter to stay but here." Andréa snatches a piece of bacon and chews it like gum.

DeeDee throws her hands up, then glares at the ceiling. "Ivy, you bitch. I'm hating you right now." She waddles back and forth, trying to figure out what to do. Andréa keeps pace, clicking across the linoleum in four-inch heels.

I take Ira his food. The boiler room is steamy, and the inky bees on his skin drip like they're melting. "Tell DeeDee not to use the hot water," he mumbles through a mouthful of egg. I remember how he said he likes peanut butter sandwiches and plan dinner.

Upstairs, Anatoly sinks into a chair, his chin touching his chest. "My girls need help," he mutters. "I count on you good women to take care of Talia and find my Nadia."

DeeDee mutters as she paces. "What to do? What to do?"

Then it hits me. I didn't give Max all the daddy-block money. I still have a stash, tucked safe in my backpack.

I tell DeeDee and Andréa my idea. "The three of them can use the block money. I've seen *For Rent* signs all over town."

Andréa pauses, mid-chew. "Block money?"

"My father hid money inside blocks," I say, leaving out the part where Clare put most of it in a bank account under the name Lucille Ledwith—and how it's in probate waiting for a judge to decide if Tom's wife has any rights to Max's inheritance.

DeeDee gasps. "Be right back."

She hurries off and returns with a thick wooden block. I examine it. No letters and no etchings. No clues. Just a chunk of wood. "I forgot all about this. Ivy gave it to me just before she died. She said to keep it safe."

I grab tweezers and work them into the block. The wood gives, just slightly, then snap, the side pops open. Inside is a roll of money. A key drops to the floor. It's small, like it opens a briefcase but doesn't match the other key I found. Did Daddy leave this with DeeDee, planning to grab it if he ever made it back to Hull? Why two keys? Why hide one in the V block and one with no clue at all? This second key is more of a secret, more of Daddy's hidden side. What was he trying to tell us?

I hand the cash to DeeDee. She unfolds it, eyes widening. "Four grand."

She exhales sharply. "Why didn't Ivy tell me about this? I could've died with money stuffed inside a damn block on a back shelf. What the hell was she thinking? And what the hell does this key open?"

I stare at it, my pulse picking up.

Daddy had two silver suitcases. He grabbed one the night we were supposed to run. Did he leave the other behind? And if he did—what's inside? Does this key open it?

I compare it to the key on the chain around my neck. "This key is smaller than the one I found in the V block."

I sink into a chair and force my mind to work.

DeeDee waves a hand in front of my face. "So what's with the letter V?"

The answer is right there. Why didn't I think of this before?

I snap back to sitting on Daddy's lap, tracing the letters on the Volkswagen's steering wheel—V-W—while he stroked the marks on my neck.

Very wonderful. Very wealthy. Very well born.

The van. The abandoned one at the X Street junkyard. Is it still there? And if it is, what's inside?

But that's a mystery for later. Right now, we have a family to save.

"We'll use the money to get Anatoly and Talia a place," Andréa says.

DeeDee folds her arms. "Hey, that's my money. I get to decide."

Everyone stares at her.

She lets out a breath, then shoves the cash at Andréa. "Ivy, see this? I'm doing something good."

With DeeDee's help, Andréa tones down her usual look. In flip-flops and a shoulder-length brown wig with wispy bangs, she looks like a chill beach mom. She heads to Bambi Realtors on Nantasket Ave with a wad of cash and comes back an hour later shaking a set of keys.

"Walk-up, fully furnished," Andréa smirks. "Charmed the pants off the salesman."

DeeDee wags a finger. "You didn't!"

"Calm your panties. I'm teasing. It's legit. Four rooms on A Street for a nice family visiting from Florida for a month."

Florida. Flying-north letters. A new home. A new future.

I watch as Ira—bug-free, pancake-faced—slides into the passenger seat. Anatoly and Talia climb in behind him.

As Andréa pulls away, I lift my hand in a wave.

This thrown-together family? It might just work.

THIRTEEN

X Street

After watching Andréa leave with Ira, Anatoly, and Talia, I tell DeeDee I need to take a walk to clear my head. So much has happened. I need to make sense of it.

"Just stay out of Stone's reach," DeeDee says. "And don't go looking for trouble by mentioning Vixen or Squid to anyone. Do you hear me?"

"Loud and clear," I tell her.

I bring the key from DeeDee's block and wonder if it's all about the V too. Is this Daddy's insurance? His just-in-case back-up plan? If he couldn't get to the big blocks, he'd find a way back to DeeDee's. But what do they open? Does it even matter? Will they help save the children like I hope, or are they just Daddy's dreams gone sour?

It's a gloomy weekday in July when I head for X Street. I walk along the beach where my chances of being seen and stopped are minimal. It's low tide and beachgoers are spread out. At the ocean's edge, I pass F Street and see the carcass of the Victorian. I'm still not ready to get near it.

Suddenly, I'm ten years old, following Ivy down this same stretch of beach. My brain yanks me backward before I can stop it.

That morning, Ivy shook me awake and handed me a back-pack. "Put on your sunglasses and pull up your hood," she ordered. Ivy tightened my scarf, slung a backpack over her shoulders and whacked me. "Let's get the fuck out of here before Squid barges in."

Instead of walking the avenue, we went through the dunes onto the beach—gulls, seaweed, a man jogging at the low water mark; another staring out to sea.

"Catch up, AgLess," Ivy said, sucking on a joint, the smoke trailing behind.

I wanted to lag behind, to escape up a side street, to see the alphabet letters on the street signs. But Ivy skunk-eyed me and I knew to stay close. At the top of a dune was a green sign with white letters: X Street.

The X—butterfly wings, crossroads, two V's glued together.

We passed boxy houses and a field of sagging grasses and sick trees until we came to a fence. All I saw were a thousand X's. Ivy pulled me through an opening and we slipped past broken boats and cars without doors or tires. Seagulls slept between them, and straggly grasses grew everywhere like whiskers. A snarling dog lunged from between cars.

I stiffened, waiting for the dog to bite. But Ivy reached into her pocket, and pulled out a baggie with chunks of meat in it which she tossed to the dog. "Agnes, meet Cerberus."

The scrawny dog devoured the food.

"Cerberus? Can you spell that?"

"Damn it, Agnes, are you going to make me spell every damn word? You're a fucking pain in the ass. C-E-R-B-E-R-U-S. That's what Wizz and I call him. A junkyard dog guarding the gates of hell."

"Don't we live in Hull?"

Ivy groaned. "Welcome to the underworld. The place of departed souls."

Cerberus wagged his stringy tail and trailed after us until Ivy led us to the van tucked in a corner of the lot, surrounded by weeds. I planted my feet outside the door.

I refused to go in. All I could think of was the stink of the bucket, the suffocating hidey-hole, the sobs of little girls. And the rule: stay quiet or I'll cut out your tongue. But Ivy wasn't buying it. She tossed me inside like a rag doll and pointed to the pop-top part of the van where a mattress was molded with green and black rot. "Shut your trap and get up there."

The wraparound window was smashed, and dampness seeped into the van. Ivy pulled out a liquor bottle and a baggie, filling her palm with white pills. "Don't bother me unless you're dying." She settled into the driver's seat, lowered it all the way, and closed her eyes.

I lay on the cheesy mattress and looked at the panoramic view. The crashing ocean on one side, the calm bay on the other. Roofs stretched down the alphabet streets, and a hill of budding trees behind.

Not so bad. And I had open air.

I wrote the letters C–E–R–B–E–R–U–S on paper as I watched the dog pace the junkyard. When he stopped and his golden head jerked up to sniff the salty air, I named him Apollo—after the god in Daddy's book of myths—after playing with letters that suited him best. With my crayons, I wrote Apollo and drew a picture of him.

"Ivy, look." But she snored like a locomotive, jaw opening and closing with each snort.I opened the sliding door of the van and dangled my legs, chewing the sandwich Daddy had packed. Apollo sniffed close, and I broke off pieces for him. I patted him, and his long pink tongue licked my legs.

"Good doggie." I showed Apollo the picture. He trotted off, scaring the seagulls into the sky. I joined him, prowling the yard, poking into cars, nosing along the perimeter. When I found the hole in the fence, I hesitated only a second before slipping through.

Apollo went another way, so I shrugged and walked into the fading light, becoming an E, ready to explore. On Nantasket Avenue, I twirled with my eyes shut.

When I opened them, I was smack in the middle of the road, dizzy from spinning. A car aimed straight at me. I curled into myself, trying to disappear, but the headlights kept coming. At the last second, it swerved into an open field. A beefy man got out, yelling, "Girlie! Get off the road! You coulda been killed!"

I ran toward the bay, every nerve firing. I vaulted over a low wall—and dropped hard—into a crack between boulders. The rock scraped my shoulder raw as I slid into a deep, airless pit. I swallowed a scream.

A buzzing drilled into my skull. At first I thought it was flies, but it grew louder, like a beehive erupting inside my brain. I pressed my palms to my ears, biting my lip to keep quiet.

Rocks crunched above me. Doors slammed. I forced myself up the wall, inch by inch, hugging the stone. From the top I spotted a boat gliding toward the dock, its motor cut off and lit only by a single yellow light.

Wood creaked. A man stepped onto the dock, skinny like Daddy, shifting in and out of the shadows. Someone on the boat handed him box after box, and the man carried them to a truck that was parked near the dock. Only grunts and gravel broke the silence. The man got back in the truck and drove away.

Another motor. Louder. Closer. A police cruiser rolled in—black and white—and I couldn't breathe. The driver stepped out and for a second, all the blood in my body froze. That scar—like a butt-crack carved into his face. Sergeant Stone.

I wanted to sink deep into the ground and disappear, but I saw something that took my breath away. A girl! With long hair spilling like seaweed. Limp in Stone's arms. Being carried out of the police car toward the boat. Her head was tilted back and her chin pointed up like a broken doll.

A short round-barreled man met Stone on the dock. He laughed, like rocks crashing, like trucks rumbling, like my heart was being ripped from my chest and eaten. He touched the girl's face and unwrapped the blanket that was around her.

"¡Delicioso!" he howled. "I will get a good price for this one."

Squid!

His hands slid over her—her face, her arms, her shoulders—slow and greedy. He licked his lips. His silver teeth flashed. Like he was going to wrap her in his tentacles and crush the life out of her.

Stone shoved her into his arms. "She's an extra," he said in a rat-voice, like fingernails scraping. "No one will miss her. Mother's a junkie. The kid barely survives on scraps."

Squid took the girl, climbed into the boat, and disappeared.

The memory crashes over me. I was ten, small and helpless, watching and not able to stop anything. I ran back to the van and told Ivy what I saw, but she said I was dreaming and to shut the hell up.

I'm no longer a child, and here I am again on X Street. Squid and Stone and Vixen still roam these streets stealing children and taking them God knows where. This time, I feel hopeful—as if the answer is in the junkyard.

The X fence still surrounds the junkyard, but now there's a thick wooden backdrop. Another wall? Another trap? I throw a few rocks to see if it's electrified. Nothing buzzes, so I toehold into the X's and hoist myself up.

The second I drop in, a growl cuts through the silence. A dog—bigger than Apollo—steps forward, teeth bared. I'm prepared. I toss him bacon that I took from DeeDee's refrigerator. It gives me time to jump onto an abandoned car.

I lie back on the hood. I don't know many songs but I recall Clare's crisp voice when she sang *Rock of Ages*. I make up words but keep the tune soft and soothing.

Rock of Ages, help my plea
Take this dog far away from me.
Let him see I come in peace.
To find evidence and set us free.
Be like Apollo—stay calm
Oh please doggie do lie down.

I keep singing until the dog forgets me. I feel Clare come to me, helping me capture the dog's anger and turn it away. I move slowly off the car and onto the ground. The dog watches with one eye open, but doesn't follow. I keep humming.

In the back of the junkyard, I glimpse the shell of the shitbox van. I test the lock on the door, but neither key is a match, not that it matters because the door is unhinged. I climb inside. The stain of years slams into me—mice and spiders, ash and decay. Swollen seats. Torn rugs. Mold, soot, and sadness. The hidey-hole gapes, no longer covered by the floorboard. I feel my younger self huddling in that hole, hugging herself, whispering stories just to stay alive. I want to flee, to ignore anything that might be in there, maybe even the bones of a long forgotten child.

I hear the dog bark before I can check the bowels of the van with my flashlight.

A tow truck nears the front gate. Behind it, a squad car follows, Robocop driving. He gets out and directs the driver into the junk-yard. The front end of the towed car is smashed and the tires flat.

The driver parks close to the shitbox van. Its headlights shine in my direction. I duck out of the way. If Robocop sees me, I can't think of a lie to explain why I'm here.

Robocop's footsteps approach the tow truck. "Leave the keys in the ignition, and I'll take it from there."

I wait until the driver unhooks the smashed car, secures it and drives away. Every second drags, stretching out like a hundred alphabets. Robocop circles the car and whistles. I can almost feel his breath. I press deeper into the van's well, repeating the alphabet until Robocop drives away.

I don't stick around to see who else might show up. Crouching low, I make my way to the break in the fence, then run all the way back to DeeDee's salon.

I've found nothing. Nothing but ghosts and the rot they left behind. My throat burns. My chest tightens. And the dark thoughts slither in. Why did Ivy treat me so badly? What did I do to make my own mother hate me so much? I curl up in bed and tell DeeDee I'm not feeling well.

She leaves me alone, for now. The next day, I try again. It's twilight when I slip through the fence and throw the guard dog a bone. Instead of going to Daddy's van, I search for where he'd hide the suitcase. And then I see Gregg's white van. The place where my childhood ended. I go to the side door and try the keys but they don't fit. I go to the back door and try the key again, and to my surprise, the larger key does the trick. A rush of excitement hits me, hot and sharp. I force myself to stay quiet. Whatever Daddy hid, it has to be in this van.

I open the double doors and look inside at a place I never wanted to see again. But I'm not Agnes anymore. I'm Angel. And Angel doesn't break. I flash a light inside and see the same shelves from years ago, filled with boxes this time. I'm about to jump in when I hear the dog bark. I close the doors quickly and lie on the gray rug, which still has potato chip bags and the thermos and foil wrapping from a long ago eaten brownie. My heart races, but I keep still. The slats in the back doors of the van remind me of Daddy's handiwork. I peek through.

It's Robocop again, inspecting the vehicle that was brought in last night. As I lie there, waiting for him to leave, I think about what might be in the boxes. They weren't there when Gregg stole me away, so who put them here, and do they have anything to do with Daddy's evidence?

A commotion erupts outside, followed by the slam of a car door.

"Cowboy, what the hell? I told you—we're done with this junk-yard. Wilson and Sons is handling it now."

There was no mistaking Stone's gravel voice.

"OK, Sarge, I'll move it out, but I have to wait till tomorrow when Buster opens the yard. I gave him the keys."

An engine revs, and a vehicle pulls out of the lot. Someone's still outside Gregg's van, circling. "Damn Cowboy," I hear ButtFace say. "He's gonna fuck up the whole plan." He bangs on the side walls of the van and I jump. What if he opens the door? There's nowhere to hide! What if he sees me?

DeeDee was right. Clare was right. I could've started over, left Hull behind. But no—I'm here. And I'm about to get caught. Panic shoots through me. Stay calm. Stay invisible.

"Fuck it all," Stone says. "Now we gotta wait another day. Squid's going to be pissed. Stupid boy. Stupid, stupid boy."

I hear footsteps, the opening of a car door, and the revving of an engine. I say the alphabet again, making sure Stone is no longer in the junkyard. He's gone. For now.

I shine my light inside the first box—white powder, firmly packed. The next one—pills, stacked in layers, color-coded. The third? A dozen red sticks. Dynamite. The word is stamped right on them. This was Daddy's insurance? No. It's Squid's stash. Stone said so.

What do I do now?

FOURTEEN

Herbert

Stone's planning something. Tomorrow. But the Tribute's in two days—so these boxes must hit Squid's boat and move up and down the coast. I'm sure of it. Drugs, I get. But explosives? For what? Who do I even tell?

When I get back to the salon, DeeDee is still working. "I was worried about you, Angel. Is everything all right?"

I should tell her. But then she'd worry, and I'd never get back to X Street alone. And I have to.

Nearby, a pack of skinny kids swarms the sidewalk, yelling "HERbert! HERbert! PERvert! PERvert! Come out, come out, wherever you are!"

They're not just shouting—they're hunting.

A tall boy bolts into the salon and dives under the front counter. I can almost hear his teeth chatter. My first instinct? Face them. But I know better. Hull breeds bullies. If no one stops them young, they grow into people like Stone, Vixen, and Squid.

I hear them outside, their sneakers scraping pavement as they get closer. "Where'd you go, freak? We just wanna talk!" one of them calls out in a sing-song voice that makes my skin crawl.

I crouch beside him. "They're idiots."

He swallows hard. "Easy for you to say. You don't have to deal with them every day."

"Wish I had an easy fix. But I can help. Come on, I've got a better hiding spot for you."

His breath shudders. He nods. I take his hand, his fingers cold as ice, and guide him toward the back. He moves like someone might yank him back at any second.

DeeDee watches the whole thing from behind the counter. She arches an orange brow, then rolls her eyes. "In for a dime, in for a dollar," she mutters, shaking her head.

I turn on the overhead light in my new Reading Room. Letters explode from the walls. An S slinks like a silvery snake, curling around itself. An E scales the wall like an escalator. O's link together, stretching like a chain that could either pull you up or drag you down. Solitary O's huddle in corners, like the boy beside me. Hundreds of letters whisper their truths: some reckless and aggressive, others sweet and comforting, and a few angry and biting like the voices outside.

The boy steps inside, his gaze shifting between the letters. "Whoa," he breathes, tugging at a few stray hairs above his lip. His fingers are slender, twitchy. His wrists are narrow and bruised, like he's spent most of his life dodging blows.

"I created it. It's how I see letters." I sit cross-legged in the middle of the unfurnished room and pat the paint-splattered floor. "Come sit."

He plops down, legs splayed—too long for his body.

Not so long ago, I was his age. Kids need time to settle, so I give him a minute before I speak again. "Do any letters stand out for you?"

"That H in the center. It's bigger and heavier than the others. I like how strong it looks."

"Hmm, the H." The one he's looking at is thick and boxy with yellow shading above the crossbar, and black shading below it.

"The H has two natures. The top looks up and out. But the bottom tucks itself away, facing down. Sometimes the letter is optimistic. Sometimes it isn't."

He knots his forehead. "Letters don't have natures. That's hoohah."

I shrug. "I believe each letter carries a message. It reveals something basic about a word—or a name."

He hesitates, then says, "I'm Herbert Heath Hecht, a triple H. What does that mean?"

I hand him a piece of chalk. "Write your full name."

He scrawls Herbert Heath Hecht onto the worn floorboards.

"How many H's do you see?"

He counts. "Five. That must mean something."

"You have a lot of repeat letters, especially in Herbert." I underline the double E and R. "E's are eager for adventure, like ladders that stretch into the unknown. R's are runners and risk-takers."

He twists his lips and squints at me. "I'm betting B is for big baby."

I shake my head. "How the letter uses space is important. The B is balanced. The top mirrors the bottom, both full of pride. And the T is tall and independent. It's willing to consider both sides of an issue."

His chin lifts slightly. He's listening. "Herbert's a sissy name. The kids say so. Besides, they're just stupid letters." He scuffs the chalk with his sneaker.

The kid is hopeless, but I won't give up. I reapply the lines. "That might be, but they're your letters."

"What's that got to do with those dumb asses who tease me?"

"They go after people afraid of who they are. That makes you an easy target." I point to his chosen H. "Do you learn about metaphors in school?"

"Metaphors... like...comparing stuff?"

His words trigger a flashback—a lesson with Gregg.

"Give me three words for fall," he'd demand.

"Drop. Lower. Dive."

Instead of praise, he pushed me further. "Try plummet. Plunge. Descend. Hurtle. Falling like a thousand bricks. Tumbling into darkness." He wouldn't stop. "Use similes. Metaphors. Be creative with how you say things."

But Clare taught me something better. To look beyond the obvious. To see the larger picture. Because of her, letters are my windows into souls.

Herbert's eyes flit over the painted wall. He points to the H's. One is tall and skinny; another lies on its side with arrows at the ends. Five H's group together like a picket fence.

"I see two sticks and a bridge," he says. Then, quieter, "Or a funeral pyre."

I glance at him.

"You know," he continues, his voice distant, "where they burn the body. I read about it in a book about India." His expression darkens. "That's me. The funeral H. Ready to burn."

For a second, I want to put an arm around him. Instead, I say, "Every letter has a dark side. It can control you if you let it. But an optimistic H will get you further."

He shrugs. Then, unexpectedly, a twinkle flickers in his eye. "There's a girl I like," he says. "Two people holding hands—that's an H."

I smile. I detect his letter wheel whirring.

"What about Heath and Hecht?" he asks.

"Are those the names people call you?"

"Nope. Just Herbert. With an emphasis on HER!"

"Herbert is your name. Your bedrock. You can change it if you want. But my suggestion?" I tap his chalked name. "Be proud of your letters. The H that looks to the sky, followed by the positive energy in the rest of your name."

He smirks. "It's still hoohah. But I'll think about it." He tilts his head. "Hoohah has a lot of H's too. Maybe H is my favorite letter."

We share an easy laugh, like flowing water. Together, we walk to the front door of DeeDee's salon.

"It's kind of weird that I ducked into your store, huh?"

"We met by chance," I say. "But it's by choice that we become friends."

I hold out my hand and he shakes it in agreement.

"You and I look like an H."

On the way out, he scans the street through the window, but the boys are gone. Then his eyes land on the sign advertising my psychic skills.

"So you're Angel? I get it. You're like an A, standing high and watching over the rest of us, like me."

"Maybe you can be my assistant!"

"Yeah... Angel Baby," he says with a shy grin.

Herbert steps outside, head high, sunlight catching his face. He doesn't duck.

I hope I've given him more confidence and he doesn't care as much about those idiots. I feel good about interpreting his letters, like I've made a difference. Isn't that what I want?

If only I could change what happened to Suzanne and Jazmin and Farrah and Nadia—if only their letters could save them.

*   *   *

As Herbert walks away, Robocop pulls up. DeeDee spikes out her orange hair and swipes on green gloss.

"Just a heads-up, Auntie," Robocop says. "Sarge is on a rampage about that insect-faced pervert. He knows you and Hornet go way back. If you've got anything, now's the time to spill."

DeeDee pats his arm and plants a green-lipped kiss on his cheek. "You know I'd never keep secrets from you."

I notice her fingers crossed behind her back. X's have so many hidden corners.

Robocop nods to me. "Angel, nice to see you."

I wish I could tell him about the boxes in Gregg's van. But what would he do—run to the sergeant? Why does he admire him so much? Why can't he see through him? If only DeeDee could convince him that Stone is corrupt, maybe he'd help us.

"Any news on the girl who washed up on Gunrock Beach?"

Robocop's eyes glint, his voice suddenly charged. "You know, I sit in her hospital room and talk to her. Maybe that'll bring her back. Maybe I'll be the one to figure out who she is."

DeeDee gives his arm a squeeze. "If anyone can bring the dead to life, it's you, my sweet nephew. You have the golden touch."

Robocop blushes. "Seriously, though—I was telling her about Sarge's retirement party and how it'd be amazing if she woke up in time. And guess what? She blinked. Like she heard me." He explains how coming back from a coma is a gradual process and maybe this is the beginning of her recovery. "And when I held her hand, I swear, she squeezed back."

"Maybe she's waking up?" I say, hoping it's true—hoping she'll be able to tell us the real story.

Miss Hill comes into the shop and glides past us, chin up, lips pinched. But then she freezes, her eyes cutting toward Robocop for a beat too long.

"Afternoon, Miss Hill," Robocop says.

Her pace quickens toward the back room, her heels clicking faster. DeeDee follows, but I catch the sharp look Miss Hill throws over her shoulder—eyes cold and calculating.

"How do you know her?" I whisper.

"She works at the station a few days a week. She's been doing Sarge's paperwork for years. Never smiles. Never talks. Looks right through me."

In the private room, Miss Hill settles into the reclining chair, stone-faced as DeeDee chatters about colors and sunshine. Miss Hill grunts, more from her feet being manipulated than in conversation.

Constance Hill. Her letters float around in my head but they don't take shape the way I expect. Her C's aren't soft, comforting curves. They're hollow, half-formed circles—open but closed off.

FIFTEEN

X Street

Anatoly, Talia, and Ira have moved into their new digs on A
Street. DeeDee's shop is closed on Mondays, so we drive to the
triple decker. The stairs are steep and DeeDee wheezes her way to
the top. The apartment is spacious and bright—four rooms, high
ceilings, flowery fabric everywhere. Bread bakes in the oven, the
smell drifting through the rooms, reminding me of Clare's scones.

"I found grocery store," Anatoly says with pride. "I feed my
family."

He serves us a goulash of meat, potatoes, carrots, and celery
with the fresh-baked bread.

Ira washes the dishes while Talia sings a song she's made up
about seals and minnows. I wonder if Nadia's songs are about
stingrays and sharks.

What did I sing when I was seven? We had just moved to Hull
after the shitbox van lost its transmission. Daddy taught me *Itsy
Bitsy Spider* and *Bats and Bugs and Beetle Wax* while insects scattered
in the attic. He said it would make me less scared of the creepy
crawlers. It worked.

The memory lingers as DeeDee reapplies Ira's makeup, his

bugs vanishing. We all sit together on the back porch. Talia's red hair glows in the sunset.

Now that the family is settled, I'm itching to go back to X Street, but I'm afraid DeeDee will never approve.

"DeeDee, I'm going to take a little walk along the avenue. Get some fresh air, and all that."

"Whaddaya think I was born yesterday? Now listen here, Angel. If you're going where you're not supposed to, I want to know. All of it. I'm responsible for you and..." DeeDee takes a deep breath. "I love you like a daughter."

Can she really mean that?

L-O-V-E. The word makes my chest feel full, like someone opened a window in a room I didn't know was closed. But that V lurks within love, ready to strike.

I swallow hard and tell DeeDee what I saw at the junkyard.

"So Stone's planning something with the white van?" DeeDee asks.

"Sounds that way."

"Let's take another look. I'm coming with you."

DeeDee's hands grip the steering wheel so firmly her knuckles turn icy-white as we pull up to the junkyard on X Street. She hands me a flashlight on a rope.

"I'll circle the area," she says, her eyes glancing at me for a moment before returning to the road.

I wish I had Clare's many pockets and looped belt—something to make me feel more prepared. Clare's pockets weren't just pockets. They were proof she was always ready.

I look out the window, watching shadows stretch across the street. "It'll look suspicious if you keep driving around the block. Give me half an hour. I'll meet you at Nantasket Ave and Y Street."

DeeDee nods, but the tension in her face doesn't ease. She pulls away, the tires crunching over gravel, and I'm left standing in the growing dusk.

I climb the fence. I'd pocketed a bone earlier from Anatoly's goulash and toss it to the guard dog. I'm in too much of a hurry to name him. After making sure no one's around, I go straight to Gregg's van. My plan is to look inside the boxes—I think there were ten—to find the silver suitcase. I'm guessing here. The night Gregg assaulted me, I don't remember boxes, and the ones I saw the other night held drugs and explosives.

I open the back doors, ready to jump inside and close them, but I freeze. Half the boxes are gone. I sweep my light around—one whole side is empty.

The dog barks. A truck rumbles in. Stone's?

Heart pounding, I kill the light, shut the doors, and scramble under the van, flattening myself into the dirt. If he saw the light, I'm done.

The truck rolls past slowly. I don't move.

When it's on the opposite side of the yard, I slide out, crouching, and race to the fence.

Headlights sweep the yard. Too close, too bright. I claw my way over the fence and drop hard on the other side.

And I run.

To Y Street where DeeDee's waiting.

"Drive!" I shout, diving into the car.

As we speed away, a wood-paneled station wagon turns onto X Street.

"That's Miss Hill's car," I tell DeeDee. "She got into it after her pedicure. I'm sure of it."

As we pass, I squint to see the driver, but it's dark and DeeDee is going too fast.

"Park a few streets away," I say. "I'll sneak back and see what's going on."

"No fucking way." DeeDee's voice slams the air, using those show-stopping words.

"If we're ever going to find out the truth, we need to take chances. I'll be careful, I promise."

"No. Just plain no, Angel. I won't allow it."

DeeDee grips the wheel and drives to the salon.

I lie awake, my mind spinning so fast it feels hot.

I'm so close to learning something about Stone, maybe Miss Hill, maybe what's in Gregg's van. The thought makes my chest jumpy.

I spell my name in the dark: A–N–G–E–L. The E and L push me forward—driven, determined. I *can* do this.

Quiet as a breath, I slip past DeeDee's raspy snore and out the door.

X Street looks deserted. I climb the fence and see the dog lying on the ground, definitely breathing, but motionless like the stump of a tree. I step around him and head to the white van. I use the key to open the back doors and peer inside. Empty. Totally empty.

Stone took the boxes, all of them.

When's the drop off? Is he meeting Squid? Or is he going rogue with enough drugs to flood Massachusetts?

All I can do now is find the second suitcase. I try to think like Daddy. He was a master of what he called *trompe l'oeil*—a trick of the eye. When Gregg came to our house for my lessons, Daddy opened doors that didn't look like doors. In the shitbox van, Daddy created a hidey-hole, a false floor with an extra space beneath. He hid toeholds so I could climb to the attic. He was called Wizz for a reason.

Then I'm back in Gregg's van the night Ivy died. Gregg bragged Daddy had installed the shelves. Maybe he wanted us to live in the van for a while. Maybe he told Gregg about the hidden spaces too. I never knew Daddy's plans. But now I think I do—the suitcase was a bargaining chip. The blocks hid cash. The extra key? Another backup plan. Daddy always had one.

I study the van inch by inch, running my hand along every

seam. The panels are smooth, too smooth. Daddy wouldn't hide it where anyone would see it. He'd bury it in the bones.

I sit back on my heels. The rug wrinkles under my fingers, teasing me, hiding something just out of reach. My skin prickles.

I need something sharp—something to pry at the false layer. I have to get back to the salon.

I duck out and melt into the shadows, my pulse racing faster than my feet. The night air bites at my skin, waking me up, keeping me going.

At the apartment, the low hum of DeeDee's snore rolls through the window. Safe. Maybe. For a minute.

DeeDee doesn't keep carpentry tools, but I know what's in the drawers: knives, scissors, razors. I tiptoe in, and knock my elbow into a chair, fingers probing drawer after drawer. Combs. Clips. Finally—scissors. I tuck a pair into my sleeve and move.

Back on X Street the light from my flashlight lands on the van. I don't climb in right away. My knees wobble. Tears threaten. For a second—quick as a blink—I see Agnes, small and powerless under Gregg's assault, his weight crushing the air out of her.

But that girl has nothing to do with me. She's not Angel, not Lucille, not Angelica. She is not the girl who told Herbert to stand up for himself, or who talked Hornet into being Ira. She isn't the one who pushed DeeDee and Andréa and Vasya to act.

I don't know who I am. But there's an L inside me, a part that keeps stepping forward.

Vixen and Stone won't keep doing this.

Not if I can stop it.

* * *

I climb into the van and seal the back doors. Tonight decides everything. I can feel it.

The first place I check is the floor covering—the gray rug, stained from a leak in the roof. I grab the scissors and rip into it, tearing away a section. Nothing beneath it looks like Daddy's handiwork.

Think. Think. Think.

Be Daddy—my hero when he wasn't messing up.

Be the father he tried to be—responsible.

Be Wizz—the face he wore for the world.

He always wanted to be the center of the party, zig-zagging from one goal to the next, failing, trying again, falling flat. I can hear Clare now: "First we make our choices and then our choices make us."

I can feel how deflated he must have been that last night in the house. He and Ivy were no longer a power couple; he had no control over his business, his house, or his loyalties.

If he had evidence to elevate himself, something to hold on to, something that might give him power—where would he hide it?

I press my foot against every inch of the floor, feeling for any areas that seem different—harder, thicker. When I find one, I press the blade of the scissors into it, then cut along the rug's edge and rip it away.

And finally, there it is—the hidey-hole. Not like the secret one from my childhood. This one is a perfect wooden rectangle, buried where no one would notice.

I work the blade into the groove, feeling the strain of the wood against the blade as I lift the lid. Fear bubbles up fast. I shine my light inside, and a glint of silver catches my eye.

The color is the only thing this briefcase has in common with the one Gregg took from me. It's lightweight, made out of some sort of plastic. I lift it out, drawing it to my chest, holding it close. Whatever's inside has to matter. It just has to. Daddy knew he needed something to save himself. Something he could use if everything blew up.

I cover up what I can, but why bother? Stone and Miss Hill

already took the boxes. Who knows where Butt-face stashed them. Maybe they're on that island that I found with Ira.

The dog is still out cold as I make my way out of the junkyard with the briefcase. What did they do to him? And will they do the same to me if I'm caught? I can't risk opening the case here—no way. Not with the chance Stone might swing back around, even if the boxes are gone. I wedge my toes into the chain links, careful not to drop the briefcase, and jump down to the street. I run to the beach and rush along the dunes, counting the streets backward from X to A. I watch for shadows that might follow me. I don't stop to check out the house on the corner of F Street. I never want to go near that place again. I race straight to DeeDee's.

I find her pacing, her footsteps sharp against the floor.

"Where the hell have you been? I woke up and checked your room and saw you were gone." Instead of yelling at me like Ivy would have done, she pulls me into her full chest and hugs me. I'm happy to sink into her.

* * *

I hand DeeDee the briefcase.

"Let's see what Wizz has for us," DeeDee says, examining it from all angles.

Together, we sit at the kitchen table and check to see if the smaller key will open it, but there's no need. The suitcase latch isn't locked. We look inside and draw out a yellow envelope, large and bulky. We spread out its contents: a video tape, three black-and-white photos, and a thick spiral notepad.

Before I can look at each photo, DeeDee pulls one from the pile and holds it in her lap.

"We'll get to it," she says, her eyes not meeting mine.

A prickle moves through me. I want to ask why, to see what she's hiding, but I trust her judgment.

In one of the remaining photos, Stone practically stares into the camera—his face overexposed. His body is in silhouette, but I can see that he's carrying someone small. Her hair streams out behind her like a doll's.

I shake with the realization that I was there under the rocks while he gave this child to Squid. She was the first child that my young brain registered as being in trouble. Her letters still accuse me of neglect.

The photo is blurry and dark, except for Stone's sliced-up face. On the backside in my father's handwriting, it says: Evan Stone and Jazmin, age 5. 1982.

So Daddy was at the dock that night. He was the skinny man loading the truck with cases from the boat. I hate what this says about him: that he knew about the kidnapping and did nothing except take a damn picture.

I can hardly breathe with the next photo. My neck throbs. I feel like I'm back in the hidey-hole, about to be discovered. Stone stands beside a greasy-haired, stocky man with gold necklaces. Squid! On the back it says Evan Stone and Anthony Vasguez, 1980.

V–A–S–G–U–E–Z. All the letters describe a person hell-bent on hurting others.

"Even I know those letters are bad news," DeeDee says as she looks at the name.

She takes the last photo from where she had hidden it and stifles a cry.

"Are you sure you're ready for this?" she asks.

And there's Daddy's evidence: a naked woman posing for Stone. His tongue is hanging out. In a corner of the room is a little girl with long hair and saucer eyes. The names on the back of the photo are Suzanne, age 4, and Feisty FreeZone, 1979. She must be the dead prostitute that Ivy identified the day she left me at the playground, and Stone took her to the Cat House.

"She disappeared years ago. The little girl too. I thought nothing of it," said DeeDee with tears in her eyes. "Whores come and go. I should have paid better attention. I was too wrapped up in my own little life to give a fig."

The photos lie face up on the table as DeeDee flips through the spiral notepad. I see names, some familiar, some not: Evan Stone, Anthony Vasguez, Zachary Snow, Steven Andrews, Vincent Sienna. Z's, S's, V's, and N's. Nasty people, I'm sure of it.

"Zachary Snow? He's the former Norfolk County district attorney," DeeDee says.

Other pages contain dates and numbers with short notes beside each name. June, 79: Andrews, CEO Xytron, 2 kilos. July, 79: Sienna, VP Aztec, 10 bricks. And on and on and on.

"This must be a record of how much they bought and paid," DeeDee says. "Now for the moment of truth." She takes the video and pops it into the VCR.

The tape rolls black-and-white static at first, and then a man's face appears. His hair is slicked black; he flashes a gold-toothed smile. Squid. He sits on the edge of a bed with his G-rod at attention, thick and pointy.

DeeDee takes my hand and squeezes it. "We'll get through this together."

A girl with long blond hair staggers into the frame. She's tiny and porcelain-skinned. Her little nose and chin tilt up and her lips purse into a button.

I don't want to watch. I don't want to know.

Squid lays her onto a bed and pours lines of white powder down her bare back. He snorts them with a straw.

In the background, a woman shouts orders. "Giggle," she yells. The child chokes out a titter. A foot flies into the picture and kicks the girl. "Like this," the voice screams. There's a cackle, sharp and harsh, like a crow that the girl immediately imitates.

The video goes blank.

DeeDee and I sit open-jawed.

Then the screen comes alive again showing ButtFace standing alone, front and center, his doughy cheek sliced down the center.

"There he is. The perfect asshole," DeeDee says.

Stone is in his underwear, his G-rod bulging. In his hand is a bottle of vodka, which he swigs in large gulps. The camera pans to a bed where a sheet drapes a young girl's legs—her upper body exposed. Her straw-blond hair spreads out on a bright red pillow. Stone kneels beside her. She stirs and rolls toward him. Her blue eyes widen.

I force myself to watch.

Stone dribbles liquid onto his chest, and she licks it off, her tongue tracing its descent.

The video cuts to black.

My stomach flips like it's trying to crawl out of me. I clamp my hand over my mouth, but it doesn't stop the shake that runs through me. The room feels too small, the air thick with the sound of my pulse.

Evidence. That's what this is. Evidence.

"Damn, that's gross," DeeDee says, but her voice sounds far away.

My eyes stay fixed on the blank screen. My brain can't catch up with what I've seen. Daddy and Ivy had a real reason for hiding me when I was little. They wanted to protect me from scum like Stone, so Squid couldn't get his hands on me, so I wouldn't end up like Suzanne and Jazmin and Farrah and Nadia.

And who took the photos? My father? If he knew, why didn't he stop it? Or did he think blackmail would work against these lowlifes?

"That's Vixen in the background telling the little girl to laugh. I'm sure of it. Her cackle stops lava." I swallow hard. "DeeDee, I think Stone plans to leave Hull after the tribute Saturday, and I think Constance Hill is going with him."

"Why her?"

"Doesn't she work with him at the police station? Somehow she's involved."

DeeDee's eyes narrow and her lips purse. "Time to call in the good guys, starting with my nephew Robert."

I don't tell her Robocop isn't strong enough to face the truth about Stone. The S worms around people and tightens its grip.

I study the evidence again and wonder how we can use it. The photos are incriminating, but the video is what will convince the town that Stone is vile. But how do we show it?

DeeDee's in the living room replaying the tape over and over. Once was plenty for my stomach, so I go through the notebook figuring out Daddy's bookkeeping. Gregg taught me about kilos and grams and other measurements, and I recognize all those words. I get a pad of paper and list the recurring names.

*　*　*

A half hour later, someone knocks.

DeeDee struggles to stand. "Bobby? Is that you?" She waddles through the hallway.

"What's the emergency, Auntie? Your scissors need sharpening?"

"We have to talk."

Out of uniform, he looks like a teenager. His cut-off shorts are spattered with yellow, his t-shirt is wrinkled and stretched at the neck, and his baseball cap sits low over his forehead.

DeeDee drags her nephew by the elbow into the living room. "How much do you know about Sarge?"

"He's my rock! There's nothing he can't solve, and the town loves him for it." His face turns moony.

I shake my head. DeeDee pats the couch for me to sit beside her. She turns on the VCR. "Robert, you know I'd never hurt you."

"Auntie Dee, you're the third best person on the planet."

"The first would be your mother and the second is Sergeant Stone?"

"You got that right!"

Robocop's smile stretches like a bridge. It's about to sink.

The tape plays.

When it's over, Robocop twitches. His shoulders sag. His chin trembles. His freckles turn white and his eyes glaze.

"Get my inhaler," DeeDee shouts.

I run for the puffer on the kitchen counter. She holds it to his lips and he sucks in air.

"Breathe, baby. Take it slow."

Robocop steadies himself. He looks at us, wild-eyed. "Where'd you get that tape?"

His voice is steely and sharp.

Really? That's the question he's asking? Are we on trial? We didn't make Stone into a monster. No way will Robocop turn this around. No way will my father's evidence get buried.

I stand taller, though my legs feel like rubber. "My parents were Wizz and Ivy Hale. They were drug dealers in Hull, and they were murdered. My father had that tape to use against Stone and his boss Squid. It was supposed to protect them in case their lives were in danger."

"And you just found it? Now that Sarge is being honored by the whole town?" Robocop paces. "None of this adds up. Sarge is the most giving person I know. He's treasurer of the Hull Police Union and Hull Police Relief Association. He takes other people's shifts for them. He has the best record in town for locking up drug dealers and prostitutes. Look at how fast he's gone after that Hornet pervert. Sarge has his hand in everything that keeps this town safe."

"That's how he controls what's going on," DeeDee says. "He extorts money from me every month so the men from the Sea Mist can come here for make-overs. He gets free service from street walkers—and arrests them if they don't cooperate. The Cat Houses? He's in on them too. He's holding a child ransom. Right now. And you want to know how he got that scar?"

"In the Korean War."

"From his wife! He went too far with his stepdaughter Victoria, and his wife came after him with a butcher knife."

"That's a bold-faced lie!"

"I was ten years old and I saw it happen," DeeDee shoots back. "Ask him yourself. While you're at it, ask him what happened to his wife and daughter. Do you think they died of natural causes? I doubt it."

Robert's hand clenches into a fist. "You've got rumors, innuendo. Half-truths. You can't know the whole story."

DeeDee leans forward, her eyes hard. "How sure were you that the girl on the beach wasn't being drowned by your precious sergeant—and that other girls aren't still out there in danger?"

Her words slice through the room. I flinch.

Robert hesitates, eyes cast downward, then back at DeeDee. His jaw tightens. "I—I was never part of that," he says, his voice low, tense. "I didn't see... I didn't know..."

DeeDee leans even closer, her tone sharper, closer to a growl than a statement. "Then you better start explaining, Robert. Because right now, silence is complicity." She lets out a rough breath. "Girls disappear from Hull. You think each case is unrelated? It's child trafficking. It's been happening for years, and Stone is deeply involved."

She slams down the photos—Stone, Squid, the hooker, the child. Words rip out of me, half sob, half accusation. "Like Vasya—the immigrant woman who came for a better life and ended up prostituting herself just to keep her daughter from being sold to Squid!"

DeeDee tilts her head toward me, her gaze never leaving him. "You have to make a difference. I'm not the one in power. My mantra's always been: make no waves. Survive. Until she showed up."

Robert straightens, running a hand over his face, exhaling sharply. "You think pointing fingers will solve anything? You want answers, but what are you willing to risk?"

I swallow hard, their voices spinning around the room. Every word weighs on my chest.

"Let's say I believe you. I'm still a rookie. Sarge has been on the force for thirty-five years and has town-wide respect. What the hell do you expect me to do?"

I step fully in front of him, the marks on my neck on fire. "If we look away, this keeps happening. People like Stone will get away with taking what's precious because no one stops them. They're powerful because we allow it. With or without you, I'm stopping him, even if I have to do it alone."

Robocop wipes his forehead, slick with sweat, with the back of his hand. "We all have to calm down."

W–E. I see how the two V's unite. They lean into each other, standing together, not falling. Weird that the V can have positive power too. Clare always told me to appreciate the spaces between, to see beyond the lines and the angles. I watch how the W reaches into infinity, how the air gathers and grows and winds its way upward, and how the E reinforces the positive—branching out, seeking, and reaching for the truth.

I clasp my hands and breathe. Then I tell Robocop everything. How Gregg took the suitcase and I found the briefcase under the floorboards in his van. How he was convicted of killing my parents, even though he didn't kill Ivy and was in the hospital when Daddy was murdered. How my father's stash was hidden in Gregg's van in the junkyard, and there was one box of explosives that I saw, maybe more. How the island that Ira and I found has an underground cave and Stone definitely knows it's there. And how I suspect the girl in the hospital is Farrah, the child who went missing in 1983. She'd be thirteen now—maybe she's the child in the video? What if she found a way to escape, only Stone got to her first.

"Ira Trapper was an eyewitness to Stone's attempt to kill that child. Stone is framing him," says DeeDee, emphatically. "Hornet is innocent. Stone is the guilty one."

Like a good policeman, Robocop asks questions and jots down

notes. He watches the tape again and studies the photos. He asks more questions.

Little by little, the shy awkward man becomes the R in Robert. His head lifts, his posture straightens, and he takes the first step forward, not looking back.

Robert closes his notebook and rises. "You've given me a lot to think about," he says, nodding his head like he's making a mental list of what to do next. "My priority is the girls who were kidnapped. I'll pull Farrah Silvio's file and read up on that first. Then I'll check out Bunkny's trial documents. I have to be at Cedar Junction Prison tomorrow transferring a prisoner. While I'm there, I can clarify a few details."

"Like what?" DeeDee asks.

"Like why Wizz's briefcase was in his van and whether Bunkny knew about it? Why Vixen targeted the hiding places in the house on the corner of F Street and what Bunkny told her. And why was Bunkny accused of killing Ivy when she was already dead?"

This is my chance to face Gregg, to make peace with myself for allowing him to hurt me, or is that the victim in me talking? I know about being a victim, feeling like everything bad that's happened to me has been my fault. Like taking the blame for showing Gregg how Daddy hid money behind the panels. Like believing my actions caused the deaths of Daddy and Ivy. Like feeling guilty about Clare taking her own life because she didn't want to be a burden on me. It's time I confront Gregg and learn the truth.

T–R–U–T–H.

The H is the key here. No more hiding underneath. Everything must be exposed.

A tiny muscle in Robert's cheek jumps. He presses his thumb into the space between his eyebrows, like he's trying to hold something together—but it keeps slipping.

"I'm going with you," I say calmly.

"Impossible," Robert says. "I'll keep you informed."

SIXTEEN

South Shore Hospital

Robert comes by the salon after his shift.

"What did you find out?" DeeDee asks, her eyes bright.

"I pulled the file on Farrah Silvio. I have a scrap of information that might be relevant. She has a jagged scar on her left thumb."

"Call the nurse's station and see if the girl has the scar," says DeeDee.

"It's not that simple," says Robert. "If I start poking around, Stone finds out. And then what? I'm heading over there now to see for myself."

"What did you learn about Gregg?" I ask.

"Funny thing. Bunkny's been transferred to South Shore Hospital in a separate wing from the girl. He's on life support and his days are numbered." Robert looks directly at me. "I told my lieutenant that a relative has been informed and wants to see him before he dies."

"I didn't know he had any family in Hull," I say.

"You, Angel, are his grieving cousin. We need answers and the fewer people who know what we're doing the better," says Robert.

Finally, I'll face Gregg and get the truth. Am I scared? Yeah. But I have to do this. I need answers. "Let's go!"

I've never been in a hospital, and it's not what I expect. It's all glass, flowers, and polished floors. No vinegar smell, no women in white rushing anywhere. Music plays softly and voices are hushed.

I stay close to Robert, who's in uniform. Robert. Like the B, he's blasting into this new role, determined to right a wrong. The fact that Stone hurt him is less important than being honest with himself and the town. I'm proud to be by his side.

At the entrance to Gregg's room, a policeman nods at us. "Got the call from Lieutenant Drew. You can both go in."

I expect to see a big-bellied man with a wide face and greasy hair who eats the air in a room in one gulp. Instead, Gregg is a long lump lying on a narrow bed with covers tucked under his chin. Tubes hang everywhere: from his nose, from his arms, from the bed. His head is pea-sized, his hair stringy, and his skin a filmy yellow.

Gregg's eyes flutter open; tiny black O's lock onto mine. He's confused. I'm not a guard or a nurse, just a girl in a clean shirt and skirt. My hair is pulled back, wispy curls along my face. I tilt my neck toward him, revealing the pink lines he once pretended to pick off, savoring each one like candy. Lines I should've hidden beneath a scarf. I trusted him when I shouldn't have.

Something clicks in his eyes, like he suddenly remembers me.

"Agnes?" His voice is dim and brittle.

"I'm called Angel now."

"You look like an angel." Tears drip down his once fleshy cheeks. "Am I dreaming? Dead? In heaven? That'd be a hoot."

I lean into him. He smells me the way he used to. "I'm very real and I need to ask you some questions."

His voice bursts in watery sobs. "You're alive! I was so afraid you starved to death in the tent."

A nurse rushes into the room and bustles to his side. "You can't be agitating him. He needs his rest."

Gregg smiles at her, his tiny teeth black and pitted. "It's all right, Cara. I have to do this."

C–A–R–A. Such compassionate letters. Almost like Clare's.

She gets a needle ready and draws the curtain around him, while Robert and I wait.

"I'm going to record what he says," Robert whispers. "Death bed confessions are admissible in a court of law."

The nurse props Gregg's pillows and presses a lever which raises him on the bed. "He'll be lucid for a while." She fusses around him. "But if he's suffering, I'll kick you out immediately."

Gregg's breathing takes on an even rhythm. A smile rolls across his lips.

"You're so beautiful," he says to me. "Every day I've apologized to you in a hundred different ways. I wanted you as my wife. I wanted to protect you and teach you the world. And I blew it!" Gregg grabs my wrist, his fingers like chicken bones. "I never told anyone about you," he wheezes. "You were my treasure. Mine!"

I feel that old panic rise up, the one that makes me feel small and trapped, like the girl in the tent again.

Gregg coughs and splutters. "I'm so sorry, Agnes. I live every day regretting I was such a monster. I never meant to hurt you. Even though I didn't commit the crime that got me imprisoned, I deserve my fate. I'm a bad man."

"Then who killed Wizz and Ivy?" Robert asks.

Gregg stares at the police officer as if he hadn't noticed him before. Gregg's face grows dark and veiny. "Another asshole copper? Screwing with me even while I'm dying?"

"We're here to get your story," Robert says.

"To hear the truth," I say.

"Then damn it. Take notes! I don't have much time left."

Robert stiffens. His freckles pop. "I've got it on tape. Is that all right?"

"Rookie, aren't you? You should have asked up front. And yes, it's damn all right."

Gregg settles into his pillows. He closes his eyes and his face flattens. I feel bad for him, his wasted body, his wasted life. His body jerks around and the tubes shake. Then his eyes open wide.

"I went back to Hull to find your father, I swear. When I went to the house, a station wagon was parked on the corner of F Street. A woman comes out all dolled up. Blond hair. A short skirt, nice legs. High spiky heels. A real looker. I was hopped up on coke and pills and I felt, you know, powerful. I had that suitcase full of good shit and promise. When this bombshell woman offers herself to me, I go for it."

Gregg's eyes glaze and sweat beads on his forehead. Nurse Cara comes in. "Give the man a break," she warns.

"What's it gonna do, kill me?" Gregg laughs. "Where was I?"

"The woman came on to you," Robert says.

"Yeah. So she kicks off her shoes and we walk down the beach together. She tells me she likes watching a man walk away, so she can beg him to come back. Next thing I know my balls explode, and my body is on fire. I fall face down. Then it's all slow motion. The woman kicks me in the head. I see her feet. Blisters and scaly skin like they've been boiled. She puts the gun in my hand and I can't do anything about it. Like I'm a lump of smoldering shit."

Tears stream down his cheeks, puddling in his neck creases. "The woman laughs like a witch on crack, scatters the contents of the suitcase around me, and I sink into the sand."

"Did it occur to you that the woman was Vixen?" I ask. "Wasn't it Vixen who carved a V on your wrist? Were you part of her plan?"

Gregg shudders. "Vixen was skinny with muscles and bulging veins. She threatened me with my life if I didn't tell her what I knew about Wizz's stash. The woman on the beach was blond and had curves. How does someone do that? Change like that?"

I hold the straw to his lips and he sips slowly. His skin sags around his eyes. I hate that I'm helping him and also don't. Both feelings fight inside me.

And I feel sad for this man who once taught me clouds and currents and continents. G–R–E–G–G. His only spear now is his tongue.

"What about my parents? Why didn't you identify them at your trial? You knew they weren't Jane and John Doe. How could you let them be called homeless drifters?"

"I told the lawyer Wizz and Ivy owned the house on the corner of F Street. Only thing," he takes a few deep breaths, "I never knew their last name. There were no records of a Wizz or an Ivy anywhere near their age."

Why would Gregg have known their full names? Why would he have bothered to ask? They were Wizz and Ivy. Drug dealers. And I was Agnes. No more. No less. And Squid owned the house, not that Gregg would have known that.

Gregg moves his head side-to-side like he's shaking out memories. "And I told my lawyer about the woman on the beach. How her feet were filled with red bumps and misshaped toes, but he never checked into it." Gregg becomes blubbery. "I'm so sorry, Agnes. Truly I am. Can you forgive me?"

Robert doesn't give me a chance to answer. He closes in on Gregg with the tape recorder. "A silver briefcase was found in your van recently. Any idea why?"

Gregg's lips puff out and his eyebrows knot. "Wizz borrowed my van the week before my ...accident. He had it for three or four days. When he returned it, he had built shelves. New carpeting too. He said I shouldn't drive around in a shitbox like he did all those years, and he wanted to surprise me for being so good to his daughter."

I wonder if Daddy carved out the Z in the back lats too. Z for which-way-do-I-go. He hid his stash in Gregg's van and thought it kept him safe. It cost him his life, one finger and toe at a time.

"So you didn't know Wizz used the van to hide evidence against Vixen and Squid?" Robert asks.

I notice Robert doesn't mention Stone.

"No one told me nothing." Gregg's chin sags.

"Let's get to the bottom of this, Mr. Bunkny. Did you kill Ivy?" Robert holds the recorder close to Gregg.

"I did not. A woman named Vixen shot me and then planted Ivy's body on the beach."

"Did you kill Wizz?" Robert asks.

"No," Gregg says again, "but I wasn't witness to the crime."

"To the best of your knowledge, was Sergeant Evan Stone involved in the murders?"

Gregg tries to sit up, but a spasm seizes him. His face turns red and then drains into white.

Nurse Cara rushes in. "That's it. Out!"

I think about Gregg's words, which had been bottled up for so long, and have been flung into space. And I think about the words he has not said and what remains unknown.

Robert and I leave the room and go down the elevator in silence. He gets a cup of coffee for himself and a soda for me in the cafeteria. We sit in a corner, away from everyone, and go over the facts that Gregg revealed.

"Vixen planted a gun on both Gregg and Ivy to make it look like they dueled it out. It left Gregg paralyzed instead of dead like Ivy," I say.

"And Sarge made it all work. He can do that. He was the first one on the scene according to the newspaper article. He had access to every file and no one would suspect he'd tamper with evidence. Then he took the gun which Vixen used on your father. Easy proof that Bunkny was the murderer." Robert squints, like he's thinking. "When I'm on duty tonight, I'll dig through the files again on the case."

"If Sergeant Stone catches you, he'll sic Vixen on you when

you're sleeping, like a banshee in the night." Just saying banshee makes me recoil. The caw-crow. Daddy's eyebrows. Tom's scalp. Hornet's stomach. Gregg's wrist.

Robert's eyes narrow. "I don't understand how I could have been so wrong."

"The woman I most love in the world said we only see what we want to see. She called it selective blindness."

"A wise woman. Where is she now?"

I don't want to share Clare's story. Her walk into the water weighted down by stones seems unthinkable, but to her it was life affirming. I point to my heart. "She's here with me all the time."

Robert nods. "We have one more stop. Follow me."

Robert and I ascend the elevator to the children's ward. A police officer sits outside this room too.

"Officer Crowley," the man says. "I didn't expect you this morning."

"I was in the hospital on other business and thought I'd check on the patient."

Without looking at the guard, I trail behind Robert. He opens a curtain to a sunny room. I see a tiny body, her hair a halo of blond, two thick black pigtails falling on the pillow. Tubes and wires come out from every angle, even more than Gregg's.

"Are you Farrah Silvio?" I whisper.

There's no response. Not a blink. Not a muscle movement.

"There's no telling when she'll come out of the coma. How do you know this girl had anything to do with that psychopath Vixen?" asks Robert.

I don't know for sure until I see a delicate V below her ear. It is definitely not a birth defect, although it could be mistaken for one. "That V is Vixen's signature. She owns her. Just like she owns Nadia. I bet Stone has one too, somewhere only Vixen could put it."

Robert lifts the girl's left hand and examines it. Like the information in her file said, this child has a jagged scar on her thumb.

"She is definitely Farrah Silvio. Now I have to figure out what to do next."

Without knocking, a nurse comes into the room. "Officer Crowley, so nice to see you again." She checks the girl's vital signs. "We're detecting some movement lately. I've been in touch with your precinct to tell them the good news."

"Who did you speak with?" Robert asks.

"Why Sergeant Stone, of course. He's the contact person on file should the girl come out of the coma."

I gasp, then pretend to have a coughing fit, and leave the room abruptly. When we're outside, I cry, "Farrah needs to be moved out of this hospital! Now!"

"There's not much I can do without Sarge knowing." Robert is quiet as he gets into the squad car. Then his face brightens. "If I can find the Silvios, they can identify her, but we're racing against the clock, Angel."

I'm on overload. First I see Gregg and realize he's dying. A rush of emotions hits me—grief, relief, disbelief, even a hint of joy that he's alive long enough to tell the truth. He apologized to me. But is that enough? He told us what happened on the beach and how Vixen framed him for the murders. Does it matter that we prove it?

Then I hear Clare in my head: "When a deep injury is done to us, we never recover until we forgive."

Clare taught me about forgiveness. Without her, I'd be bitter and vengeful, taking my anger out on innocent victims. Like mother, like daughter. But Clare showed me how love and acceptance work and how to shake off Ivy's influence and carry a core of good.

SEVENTEEN

The US Coast Guard

"There's something I haven't told you," I say to Robert.

He rubs a hand over his short hair. "Haven't you told me enough?"

"Hornet and I found a secret place on an island off the coast of Gunrock."

"What are you doing with that pervert?"

"He's not a pervert. He's an eyewitness to a possible murder, and that's why your sergeant is framing him."

"Okay. Fine. Tell me about this place."

I explain about the hidey-hole in my parents' van and how my father created illusions in the landscape. "The place on the island looked like something he would've made. A secret door in the ground. It has to matter—to the drug runs, maybe the girls' kidnappings. Can I show you?"

"Hull police defer to the Coast Guard on the islands. We don't have the manpower, but they do."

"We can take a boat. I can show you."

"Angel, we already have too much going on without hunting for secret doors. I'm on my own figuring out how to nail Stone. And now you want me to row to an island where something might or might not be happening?"

I want to stomp my feet, grab his shoulders, and make him look. Make him understand. But he's right. He's drowning in work already.

*   *   *

"I need to go back to the island," I say to DeeDee at dinner.

"That's a bad idea, Angel. The police are patrolling that area—and the whole town—for Hornet. Remember?"

"But how do we get someone out there to check out the secret door?"

"I have a plan," DeeDee says, and walks me through it.

The next day, she and I drive to the Coast Guard station on Pemberton Point. We ask for the officer in charge.

A man in a navy-blue uniform comes to the desk. His name plate says L. Matthew. Knowing he has an L for a first letter makes me feel like we've made the right decision.

"Ladies, can I help you?"

DeeDee puts a chubby hand at the small of my back for support.

I gather my courage. "Drugs are hidden on a small island off the coast of Hull near Gunrock Beach."

Officer Matthew's eyes are steely-blue and steady, but his fingers are fast. He grabs a small map of the area and zeroes in on a dot of land. He taps it with square, clean fingernails.

His eyebrows arch. "Is this the area of concern? Why do you suspect this?"

DeeDee nods at me in a tell-your-story-he's-listening way.

I swallow hard and let out a deep breath.

"My parents were drug dealers in Hull from the late seventies until they were murdered three years ago by a woman called Vixen. She took over their trade and stashes her goods in an underground cave. I saw the door. I know what's under there. My parents showed me the hiding place when I was little."

This is a lie. Their drops were at X Street, but the Coast Guard has no jurisdiction on Hull land, only on the water and the scattered islands.

"Why not go to the local police?"

Damn. He'll never believe me, but I have to try. "We have evidence that Sergeant Evan Stone of the Hull police is involved in the drug interactions."

DeeDee clamps her lips together and nods with quick chin drops.

I bring out Daddy's logbook with the list of names—who bought what and for how much. "Sergeant Stone took bribe money from my parents every month so they could deal drugs in Hull. See his name, right there?"

Officer Matthew studies the list. "This is incriminating, but it's not proof of guilt. Besides, Sergeant Stone is a respected officer. We'll need to verify this before taking any action."

DeeDee and I exchange a glance, a flash of frustration passing between us.

"I own a beauty salon on Nantasket Avenue," she says. "Stone takes money from me each month so prostitutes and drag performers can come into my shop without fear of harassment. I will testify to that in court."

Quickly, I set down the picture of Squid from the photos that Daddy and Ivy stashed. I hate looking at his face, but Matthew needs to see it. I say his real name aloud: Anthony Vasguez.

Officer Matthew's eyes light up, his eyebrows shooting high. "I'll be right back."

His voice is sharp, the letters hard and enunciated; the K bites into DeeDee and me.

We watch through an open door as Officer Matthew places the

picture of Squid on a machine that whirrs and clicks. The phone rings and he answers. "Yes, sir. Yes, sir. Right away, sir."

He rushes out and slaps the counter. "You say you know where we can find this man?"

"He makes regular trips to Hull. In fact, the house at the corner of F and Beach Street is owned by him. There's a retirement tribute to Sergeant Stone on Saturday. I suspect he'll be in the vicinity for the festivities. He probably moors his ship on the other side of the island we're talking about. We can take you there."

He shows me a larger map of the Atlantic with every island measured and labeled. I pinpoint the place for him. He takes notes as I describe the covered path that leads to the iron hatchway and its concealment of a door.

"The United States Coast Guard thanks you for the information. How can we get in touch with you?"

"But we want to help!" DeeDee's eyes widen, her eyelashes speaking for her.

"You've done more than enough." He walks us to the door.

I turn to him, full on. "But we need to find the missing girls!"

Officer Matthew resumes his steel-blue stance. "Are there girls on Gunrock Island as well?"

"I can't say for sure, but children have been kidnapped, and they're somewhere in Hull. I can feel it."

"My team will investigate and will establish a connection with the local police. I'll keep our conversation about Sergeant Stone confidential when I speak with the Chief. We'll get to the bottom of this."

What if this man doesn't follow up? If he thinks we're looney and tells Stone what I said. "What does the L in your name stand for?"

"Chief Warrant Officer Liam Matthew, at your service."

L-I-A-M. Commanding letters. Listening. Active. Strong.

I have faith in him.

EIGHTEEN

Discovery

We're getting ready to visit Andréa, Ira, Anatoly, and Talia for an early dinner. I'm putting together a salad, thinking about how Clare grabbed her ingredients straight from the dirt, when I hear a gasp.

"Angel! Hurry. Ya gotta see this!"

I run into the den and see the video paused at the spot where the foot kicks the little girl and Vixen forces her to laugh.

"See those bunions and warts and the fat knuckle over the toe? I've been massaging those feet for ten years. Constance Hill is Vixen. I'm sure of it."

Constance Hill? That snotty woman with the bun in her hair, the thick glasses, the button-down sweater no matter the weather, the one who works with Stone. She's Vixen? I remember what Gregg said about the woman on the beach with deformed feet. She's been under our noses the whole time.

My stomach flips. The letters in her name rattle around in my head like they're laughing at me. No wonder I could never make sense of them—none lined up right.

My voice shakes with a mix of fear and triumph. "Now we have to prove it."

DeeDee calls Robert and tells him what we've discovered. She puts the phone's receiver between us so I can hear what he says.

"It's beginning to make sense," Robert says. "Constance Hill types and files Stone's reports. She's his go-to. She has nothing to do with anyone else at the station—like she's better than all of us."

"Is she working today?" DeeDee asks.

"She's in Sarge's office right now. I'm going to put my ear to the wall and see what I hear."

"Be careful, Robbie. You don't want a V tattooed on that beautiful body of yours," says DeeDee.

I try not to laugh.

While Robert might discover more about her and Stone at the station, DeeDee and I toss around ideas, ways to make ButtFace admit what he's done.

"What if Talia confronts Stone at the tribute? She could say 'Do you know who I am?' He'd think she was Nadia and he'd freak out," said DeeDee.

"Wouldn't that be dangerous?" I ask.

"What's he gonna do with a shitload of people watching?"

I like the idea of ButtFace losing control, but what would that prove? Part of me wants to see him freak out. The other part wants Nadia safe more than anything.

"It's just one idea, but it's a good start. Let's see what the family thinks," says DeeDee.

We find them on the porch watching the sun's rays sparkle on the bay. Vasya is there too, her hair pulled into a ponytail, her face radiant.

Ira's gotten really good with the makeup DeeDee left for him. Except for a few random bugs, his face and body are covered in bronze like he has a summer tan. Andréa gave him chunky-heeled shoes from the Sea Mist's costume closet so he stands taller.

We sit in the spacious kitchen, a pot of chicken soup on the stove. The room smells like rosemary and thyme, reminding me of Brewer Island.

"The Tribute is the perfect place to nail Stone." DeeDee's voice is strong and steady. "There will be contests and prizes and fun kiddie activities all afternoon. At some point he'll strut around the fair grounds. Imagine his reaction if Talia speaks to him."

Vasya rushes toward DeeDee, stabbing the air with long red fingernails. "I lost one daughter. I won't lose this one."

I stand between them and speak quietly to Vasya. "You want to save Nadia, don't you?"

Tears pool in her eyes.

"Stone is involved in her kidnapping."

Vasya nods.

"If Talia goes up to him..."

"No!" Vasya wails. "He'll take her too."

"We won't let that happen. She'll be surrounded by other children, Officer Crowley and all of us," I tell her.

"You're putting Talia and Nadia in danger and I won't have it."

Anatoly steps in. "I kill that man if he touches her. You leave it to me." Anatoly's face hardens. His lips clamp and his shoulders pull back.

Ira steps forward behind Anatoly, standing tall. "On my honor as an American soldier, I will allow no harm to come to Talia. I might not be able to show my face, but I've practiced being invisible. I'll be there when you need me."

I believe him. He's come a long way from being Hornet.

Vasya crumples into me and I stroke her hair. She feels like the Barbie Doll I never had. And just like that, I'm back in that hidey-hole, seeing that cloth doll staring at me in the dark. Vasya feels my breath catch and holds me tight.

"We'll get through this," I tell her. "Nadia will be returned to you, I can feel it—she's strong. The letters show it. She had a rough start, okay, but she's smart and resourceful. She'll find a way out. Trust me."

I say it, but a tiny voice whispers: What if I'm wrong?

NINETEEN

Farrah

"The Silvios live on Prince Edward Island in Canada," Robert tells me when he calls that evening.

I go quiet and listen to the letters.

P-R-I-N-C-E E-D-W-A-R-D I-S-L-A-N-D.

The E's, the D's, the C and the W show comfort and open arms.

The N's and the S express loss and sadness.

But I see healing in the P and the I's.

No wonder they went to PEI. They've found peace there, but imagine how much their lives will improve once their daughter is back in their arms.

Robert keeps talking. "I sent them photos of the girl we hope is Farrah and told them how she had been found on Gunrock Beach. I zoomed in on the scar on her thumb in one of the pictures. I don't want them getting their hopes up, but if you're right, Angel, they'll be united with their daughter as soon as they make arrangements for their other children and complete the ten-hour drive."

"What if Stone acts on the news that Farrah is waking up? Did Miss Hill overhear our conversation at the salon? They'll want to silence her."

"I'm working on a plan. I'll call you with updates," says Robert.

I worry about keeping Farrah safe until her parents show up. She has police protection, but that's not enough. Vixen could disguise herself as a nurse and smother her. How can we make sure Farrah stays in the spotlight until her parents arrive?

I go into my letter room and sit in its center.

The letter A reaches out first, of course, and then an E. Other letters pop up, slowly gathering into a word. M–E–D–I–A. We need to put the information out there for all to see.

"DeeDee, what if we call *The Boston Globe*? Tip them off—how Sarah went missing in '83 and might be the girl who washed up on the beach a few months ago. We can say the Silvios have been told and are coming from Canada to see their daughter. That would bring reporters and cameras. The publicity alone could mean more security. Maybe even around-the-clock protection."

"Let me call Robbie. If the story comes from him, it'll be more credible," DeeDee says as she dials.

Robert swings by the salon around lunchtime. "The press is on it. They'll be swarming the hospital like flies. You're a genius, Auntie."

"The idea was Angel's."

I fill him in on the plan for Talia to confront Stone at the tribute.

"You've been a busy woman," he says, nodding at me.

W–O–M–A–N. I'm uncomfortable with the word.

The open arms.

The rolling potential.

Shoulders that carry a burden.

The towering A.

But the final N? It drags me low, disappointed and frustrated, forcing me to try harder for every success.

"Miss Hill's been working for Sarge for years. So I examined other documents unrelated to Bunkny. Guess what I found? Felony cases with convictions based on Sarge's testimony. Crimes written up by Miss Hill, stuff I know never went down."

"Sarge has been a shit for a long time," DeeDee says. "Time to clean out the cesspool."

Robert shakes his head. "I've been so blind."

"Clare always said, 'Every man can see things far off, but they're blind to what's close by.'"

Clare seemed to know so much about my parents and their faults. She understood my hatred for Stone and never tried to tell me that all policemen swore an oath and lived by it. She worried that I would come to Hull and try to find the girls on my own. *Cockamamy*, she called it. But she never questioned my need to save the vanished children. "Pay attention!" she said. "Don't leave your children to chance." She blamed herself every day for her sister Lucy's death.

"An odd thing happened at the station. A Coast Guard captain showed up," Robert says.

DeeDee and I exchange a glance.

"He talked privately with Lieutenant Drew, the commanding officer on duty. When the captain left, Drew tore into Sarge's office, and there I was with files scattered around me. I thought he would discipline me, but he wanted to know what I found.

"I told him about the suspicious documents and Bunkny's deathbed confession. He didn't name Stone directly, but I'm hoping there's enough to warrant an investigation. I thought the lieutenant was going to cry. Stone's fooled us all."

"So let's call off this sham of a tribute and put the asshole in jail," DeeDee says.

"It's not that easy, Auntie. Turns out some of the guys at the station have been whispering for years about Stone's shady deals. I didn't know a thing about it till now. But there's no real evidence— just rumors. Drew can't go to the chief with that. The lieutenant wants me to find facts, and fast."

Stone's a bully, intimidating others, tricking them and making himself out to be the star. The S feels superior to others, like it's above the law. I'm hoping Stone's S will finally kick him in the ass.

"Keep digging, but be careful," DeeDee warns. "Stone's dangerous."

"I'm following a few leads. I'll come by later."

Andréa drops by the salon after Robert leaves.

"Lacy LaRue's got a plan. He and his friends hate Stone, so they're planning a little entertainment at the tribute in his honor."

I want to know the details, but Andréa snaps her gum and tells me to get her coffee. I hear DeeDee and her whispering and laughing.

"What's the big surprise?" I ask when I bring her the mug.

The women giggle. It's fun to see a side that's not heavy with regret, anger, or streaks of black mascara.

"Suffice it to say," Andréa titters, snapping her gum with a wicked grin. "Stone will get his due."

"And the good people of Hull will have a great laugh," DeeDee chuckles.

If it nails Stone for harassing Lacy LaRue and his friends and lets them have fun at his expense, I'm all for it. I don't mind being surprised. It's one less thing for me to worry about.

I escape to my letter room.

Once I settle in, questions zip through the air: How can we flush Vixen out? What's inside the bunker on the cliff? Is that where Nadia's being held? What will happen to Farrah? Has the Coast Guard searched the island and found Squid's stash?

Then there's Stone's video. DeeDee says we'll pop it in while he's on the podium giving his speech. "Drama, babydoll, and timing. It'll bring down the house."

"What about kids seeing it? Won't it traumatize them and do more harm than good?" I ask.

"We have to believe that what we're doing is in the best interest of the town—and its children. I don't know what the fallout will be, but the public needs proof that Stone is evil."

I want to hug DeeDee and thank her for doing what's right, but she bustles away, leaving a trail of E's.

Robert calls in the early evening. "I'm heading to the hospital for the night shift. No one's going to hurt that child."

I'm proud of him—how he's stepped up. Maybe he really can turn things around. For once, Hull might stand a chance.

The next day, DeeDee and I wake early and drive to the hospital, but we can't get close to Farrah's room; the press has swarmed the area. We can't find Robert to ask him, but we feel so much better knowing that Farrah is being watched and cared for. Vixen and Stone have no way of getting to her. If only the Silvios would hurry and get here.

Talia and I spend the day combing the beach for treasures. Then we create letters out of feathers and shells, kelp and pebbles. Some are sayings that we glue onto driftwood: Life's a Beach, Happy Tides, Make Waves. And others are names: Sarge and Farrah and Jazmin and Nadia.

I think back to my days with Clare, sitting outside the cabin, making dreamcatchers, bamboo chimes and cattail baskets, reading books and talking about them. I scoop up a large white shell and write CLARE in bold red letters. What I've learned is the world changes from year to year, and day to day, but the love and memories I have of Clare will never fade.

I fall asleep that night, hoping the tribute tomorrow will honor the right people and keep everyone safe.

TWENTY

The Tribute

The morning of the tribute arrives. I'm jittery and say the alphabet over and over until my nerves settle.

In front of the salon, a white stretch limo pulls up. Half a dozen men pile out, draped in pink boas and turquoise feathers. They strut through the door in high-heeled boots, each carrying a wig under his arm.

"We're ready for our makeovers. Aren't we, ladies?" says Lacy LaRue.

A chorus of deep voices yells "You bet your ass!" "Bring it on!"

With cheers and applause, the air inside swirls with perfume and hairspray.

On the sidewalk, a young boy on a bike brakes to a stop, staring through the glass. His mother hurries after him, grocery bags bumping against her knees. I can't hear her words, but I see the sharp tilt of her head, her fingers trembling on the handlebars. Fear radiates from her, clear even through the glass.

The boy doesn't move, eyes wide, captivated by the color, the sparkle, the energy spilling out of the salon. His mother tugs gently, nudging him forward. He resists, still watching. She leans closer, pressing a hand to his shoulder, and finally he pedals on.

I watch them drift down the sidewalk, the mother keeping pace with the boy. She's scared for him—afraid of the world outside, of the unknowns that could spin out of control. And just like her, I can't stop thinking about what might happen later today. Too many people, too many unknowns.

Inside, DeeDee and Andréa work on the men's hair and makeup—laughter and brushes flying. But their joy feels fragile, like it could shatter any moment.

I retreat to my letter room and shut the door, settling before my wall. My heart thuds too fast, and my breath chugs like an old steam train. I try to steady my thoughts, to imagine how the day will play out—and fearing all might fail.

I hear a rap at the door. When I open it, Ira stands proud in a cowboy outfit, a ten-gallon hat and boots.

"Come on in."

He sits beside me on the floor, his bees humming and whir-ring with small electric sounds. His makeup has softened him, concealing his facial tattoos and turning him into someone almost unrecognizable—calmer, more confident, easier in his own skin.

"Why so sad? Farrah is safe, and in a few hours, we'll expose Stone. You should be happy."

I shift, unease crawling up my spine. A knot contracts my stomach—what could go wrong, what might fall apart. If Stone catches even a glimpse of our plans, all of us would pay the price, including Robert.

I sigh. "Clare always told me to look twice when opportunity knocks. 'Gain one thing, lose another.' But what if we lose too much? When the day ends, what if I don't even know who I am anymore?"

I can't explain to Ira that I've been Agnes, Angel, Lucille, and Angelica. In Hull, I came with a mission: find the girls, uncover Daddy and Ivy's truth, punish Stone and Vixen. But will it make me stronger, wiser, any closer to where my E's and L's will lead?

Ira tilts his head as if he can hear my thoughts. "I may not be the smartest guy, but I know this: Hull will rise out of the sea and take its place in the sun...because of you.'"

My port-wine stains deepen.

"Because of us," I say.

I try to hold onto his confidence, but the thought of everything that could unravel at the tribute sticks with me. I'm glad he's stronger now, finally embracing his birth name. But the pit in my stomach stays. Stone still prowls, and we're one wrong move from disaster.

At least Farrah has a second chance. When her parents arrived yesterday, they identified her by the scar on her thumb, though they said they would know her anywhere. She even fluttered her eyelids and squeezed their hands when they talked to her. The press went crazy.

The cheers from the front room jolt me back to now. I take one last look at my letter wall, and draw in a deep breath.

Showtime.

I emerge from my room to see all the men from the Sea Mist with black veils covering their faces. They sing "Hi ho, hi ho, it's off to work we go," as they march out the door. Their spirit is infectious. We crowd together in the waiting limo. Ira sits beside me. His bugs are shaded in sunburnt browns.

We drive up the hill to Fort Revere toward the tip of the peninsula, park and bustle out. I've never been here. Hull spreads below us like a postcard. Flags and balloons everywhere, beach chairs dotting the hillside, concessions circling the fort. Banners brag about Stone.

My Letter Reading booth is on the hillside closest to the stage. I want him to stop and squirm.

Talia sits on Anatoly's lap at the corner of our booth. His eyes stay sharp, tracking anyone who comes near his granddaughter. Sweet on the surface, but ready to pounce.

Herbert Heath Hecht shouts a howdy and introduces me to Rebecca, his crush. I tell her the B in her name shows she's ready to be kissed.

"People I'd helped stop by—Morie, CeCe, even Grace—each lighter than before."

DeeDee and Vasya cruise the craft tables, oohing and aahing over hand-made earrings and bracelets.

On the steps behind the stage, Andréa waits with her Ladies of the Night. Toward the back of the amphitheater, a VCR on a cement wall loops: Stone posing with Massachusetts big-wigs—Attorney General Brooke, Governor Dukakis, Commissioner Taylor.

Dusk settles in, the tide whitening at its edges like lace. Then sirens wail, cutting through the festival laughter.

I wipe my sweaty palms on my jeans as the procession moves up the hill, slow and deliberate. Stone steps out in his medal-studded blue jacket, grinning like he owns the world. Three yellow V's blaze on his sleeve.

The crowd hoots and claps like he's royalty. Stone quiets them with Nixon's victory pose. The crowd holds up two fingers in imitation. V's are everywhere—on the banners, the signs, on Stone's damn sleeve. V, the vicious letter, aggressive and vengeful. Stone stands there, smug. The S. All about self. He thinks he's untouchable.

He works the tables and booths as he nears the stage. The crowd swoons and cheers.

Are you all blind? He steals kids. Sells them. Takes bribes and buries the truth. He let my parents rot as Jane and John Doe. He fed Ivy's addiction and let her think she mattered. He could have made a difference, brought her up on charges, imprisoned her, set her straight. Instead he encouraged the drug trade, let her believe she was important to the town, and even if he didn't commit the murders, he sure as hell let her and Daddy die. And then he pinned it on Gregg.

I hear Ivy's voice again: He's a fucking piece of shit.

When Stone walks close to my table, I want to scratch an S into his skin so everyone knows him for what he is—a sneaky, slimy snake.

But today to the town of Hull, Stone is the H, the Hero. His shoulders are back and his head is high as he passes.

"Come by DeeDee's Salon for a reading," I say soft and inviting. I want him to stop and see the signs Talia and I made. I want to watch him squirm.

Stone turns to me. "Like in seances and voodoo?"

"Like in revealing your future through your letters."

"I already know my future."

"And what would that be?"

"Retirement. Leave the force and rest my weary bones on the beach."

Or under it like my parents.

I signal Talia. She hands him the sarge sign. He doesn't even look. She runs her fingers through her red hair.

"The letter S means danger," she hisses.

The sign drops. Stone squeaks, his putty face gone pale. Anatoly whisks Talia off before Stone can touch her. Then Miss Hill swoops in—black skirt, white blouse, thick glasses—linking her arm through his and whispering something we can't hear.

A uniformed officer approaches them. "Sarge, we're starting now. We need you and Miss Hill onstage."

Vixen shakes her head, like she wants Stone to go up there alone, but the officer takes her arm and guides her up the stairs. "You're his right hand."

And his killing partner.

She turns to my booth and gives me the skunk-eye, like she knows who I am and can't do a thing about it. I watch as she takes a seat beside Stone. If this goes sideways, there's no place to hide. I'm roadkill.

I see Ira near the trash barrels at the back of the arena, but I don't see Robert anywhere. I'm counting on him to be here, to bring Nadia, and to make this right.

The Captain of the Hull Police Department takes the stage and welcomes the crowd. Everyone stands for the Star Spangled Banner, which is sung by a trio of boys with high-pitched voices, all blond, all eager-eyed, never in danger of Squid stealing their childhood.

Next up is Hull's Chief of Police who introduces Stone and lists his accomplishments. He even gives Miss Hill a compliment, saying she's kept Evan on his toes for the six years she's been by his side.

My teeth feel like they're ground to stumps. A roar of applause invades my thoughts as Stone is welcomed to the microphone.

"Ladies, Gentlemen and Little Germs," he begins, "thank you for honoring me. I've been here for you through thin and thick"; he pauses to pat his belly and the crowd laughs. "Serving you honestly and ably. . ."

Bullshit!

"I've worked hard to keep the people of Hull safe."

Safe? No one is safe with you slinking through town.

I cough loudly and with deep rasps.

Stone's scar twitches, like I've interrupted his speech on purpose. He recovers and continues. "I've tried to make the sad happy and the weak strong through kindness and compassion. You, my good friends, will have to decide whether or not I've done my job."

The crowd claps and whistles, glad to be witness to his day of glory.

While Stone chatters about his wonderful deeds, Robert finally shows up at my booth. "Get ready," he says.

He takes Vasya and Talia by the hand to the back of the arena where I see a tall officer in a formal uniform carrying a child wearing a baseball cap. I see Ira in full make up, cowboy boots and a ten-gallon hat slip the damning video tape into the VCR. I breathe with relief.

A bare chest bursts onto the screen. No big deal—it's a beach town. The crowd barely stirs.

The camera zooms in. Stone's bloated face. A dumb, drooling grin.

A bed. A child. Stone's fingers reaching.

At the podium, Stone entertains the audience with feel-good stories about his career and has no idea what the onlookers see on the screen. Vixen swivels to look, but the image is so close, it's hard for her to tell what she's viewing.

The camera angle changes and suddenly Stone is in his underwear. In his hand is a bottle of liquor, which he swigs. Then the film pans to a child with long blond hair lying on a bed before him. The child's eyes go wide as Stone comes toward her.

Vixen doesn't wait for the next part. She runs down the steps and into the dark. I see Lacy LaRue and Hedda Lettuce chase her, grab hold of her arms in a vice-like grip, and force her to the ground. She bites and kicks, but the men are iron strong.

The crowd, meanwhile, watches the larger-than-life image of their hero. Maybe they believe Stone will save the child, snatch her up from the bad guys and bring her to her family. But Stone's fat fingers caress her body as she licks his chest and then his belly and descends lower.

Murmurs roll like waves as Stone turns around to see the screen. "What kind of sick joke is this?" he roars.

The Ladies of the Night—glamorous, towering, unstoppable—march onto the stage. With one synchronized motion, they rip off their veils.

Gasps. A few shrieks. Someone drops their drink.

And there it is. The scar. The proof. The butt-crack imitation painted onto their left cheeks. A mirror image of the one on Stone's face.

Stone finally gets it. His hands go to his own scar, like he can erase it. He hesitates, uncertain, caught between outrage and disbelief.

Lacy LaRue and Hedda hurl Vixen into the center of the men, who have formed an unbroken circle. Heels clicking like drumbeats, the circle snaps closed around her, leaving no escape. Vixen struggles, but the Ladies are unyielding, each holding her position like living walls of strength. Vixen is trapped, and there's no breaking through their circle.

Stone watches, frozen. His moment of hesitation is all they need. In an instant, hands clamp on him, pulling him into the circle alongside Vixen. He struggles, but there's no escaping.The crowd is on their feet—some fists in the air, some rushing toward the stage, others leaving the fort with their children. I stand on the table at my booth, watching as policemen descend en masse, arms outstretched, demanding calm.

"Settle down, everyone," booms the tall officer—I think he's Lieutenant Drew. His voice is strong and in command. "Quiet, please. Let me explain what's going on." Robert is on stage too, along with Vasya, Talia, and Nadia.

I wish Clare were here. She'd look at the mocking faces of the men, standing like soldiers, and Stone and Vixen pushing and shoving at legs and arms and beefy bodies, getting nowhere, and the frozen picture of Stone on the screen in full predator mode, and she'd harrumph. "This time, like all times, is a very good time, if only we knew what to do with it." The audience stills. Even Stone and Vixen stand at attention and wait to hear what's next.

Drew begins. "Let me start with Vasya Jones, who came here from Ukraine with one daughter, hoping for a better life. Vasya was financially desperate, so with limited education and no employment opportunities, she turned to prostitution. Sergeant Evan

Stone encouraged her trade, setting her up with clients. But there was a problem. Vasya Jones had a young daughter who got in the way of business."

The crowd is silent, listening to every word.

"Vasya, with your permission, may we hear from your daughter Nadia?"

Vasya nods and Nadia approaches the podium. Drew lifts up the child so she can speak into the microphone. The Ladies of the Night kneel slightly so Stone and Vixen have a view.

"I was riding the merry-go-round and having a fun day with my *mamushka*. She strapped me onto the painted horse and went off to get coffee. All of a sudden, a policeman unbuckled me and told me my mother had an accident and he would take me to her. But he didn't. He took me to a cave where a woman with white hair and black lips locked me up."

I watch Nadia, a tiny eight-year-old speak up for herself. She's strong-voiced and unafraid, everything I wish I had been at her age. Anatoly stands beside me, tears streaming down his cheeks. I lean my head on his shoulder. We listen as Nadia talks to the crowd like she's in their living room.

"That woman," Nadia points behind her at Vixen, "took pictures of me and I knew it was wrong. But if I posed real cute and was good and kissed her on the lips and called her mommy, she'd feed me and let me play the piano and pat her cats. But if I cried or made a face, she chained me to a wall and left me for hours."

The lieutenant brings the child to Talia and Vasya. They hug her and fold her inside their arms.

Robert steps to the microphone. "Special teams found Nadia Jones a few hours ago in a bunker inside a bluff on Gunrock Hill. To our shock and horror, she wasn't the only child in the underground."

Everyone leans forward, like their ears have been tuned to this one channel and no one is going to miss a word. The local police force, scattered throughout the fort, looks as surprised as the audience.

"Let me tell you about these children whom we just saved from a life of degradation and neglect." Robert turns toward Stone. "One little girl said Sergeant Stone rescued her when a wave thundered toward her. Instead of delivering her to her parents, he brought her to a cave where she was enslaved, made to do unnatural acts, and cater to the whims of Constance Hill. The third child we found said Sergeant Stone found her wandering the streets and told her he'd bring her home. Instead he locked her in a basement where Hill abused her, took photos of her, and starved her whenever Hill didn't get her way."

Heat bubbles inside me. I see Ivy pulling my hair, sealing my lips with tape. Daddy watching, doing nothing—never interfering until Ivy passed out.

I will never let this happen to any other child. This is my moment. The moment I've wanted ever since I saw Suzanne carried from the basement of our house. My L rises. My legs move—stiff, but Clare pushes me forward. I take full strides and find a strength I didn't know I had.

I meet a sea of bewildered faces. Ira. DeeDee. Andréa.

Robert and Lieutenant Drew step aside. I grip the mic.

"Sergeant Evan Stone and Vixen Constance Hill, I accuse you of murdering my parents, William and Ivy Hale. I accuse you of kidnapping innocent children. I watched as my parents gave Stone a child they had stolen. Her name was Suzanne. With my own eyes, I saw Stone at the X Street pier hand off a little girl named Jazmin to Anthony Squid Vasquez, a drug lord and child trafficker. I don't even know Suzanne or Jazmin's full names. They were invisible. Daughters of prostitutes and drug addicts. Worthless."

Stay calm. Tell my story.

"And every month like clockwork, Sergeant Stone appeared at my parents' house on the corner of F Street and Beach Avenue. He took thousands in bribes so they could sell drugs. Stone warned my parents not to traffic in children. Trafficking in children was Stone's job. Then a woman named Vixen joined up with him to terrorize the people of Hull. It was Vixen who kidnapped Farrah Silvio, the girl who washed up on Gunrock beach a few months ago and whose parents identified her yesterday to the delight of the press."

Stone and Vixen bang and push into the tower of men, but the Ladies stand solid.

"And Vixen? She's Constance Hill, Stone's secretary at the police station. She fakes reports and buries the truth—anyone who gets in her way pays with their lives.

"You might remember Gregg Bunkny, a Hull resident. He was convicted two years ago of selling drugs and murdering my parents. But Vixen and Sergeant Stone were the murderers. And most recently, my friend Ira 'Hornet' Trapper was accused of molesting a child, a ruse to get rid of an eyewitness to Stone's cruelties."

I catch a glimpse of Vixen through the barrier. Her face is chalk-white, her neck veins purple. Her chin is jutted out and her nose is pointy—a banshee-witch in every detail.

"All the other children were younger than six years old when they went missing from Hull. The sergeant approved of their kidnappings. For what reason, you may ask?"

I stop and take in the crowd. Every eye is on me. The only sound is the ocean in the distance, roaring and crashing, announcing high tide.

"The wisest person I have ever known said, 'The measure of a man is what he does with power.' Those were Plato's words, but my friend Clare Brewer interpreted them. She said men like Stone need others to look up to them, to idolize them, no matter the consequences. They care only for themselves, like a happy tick sucking blood off its victim. You believed in him. We all did. And the whole time, he was laughing at us."

The crowd sits forward in their seats, on the edge of my truth.

I want to tell them about the letters in Hull, how the H rises into the sky or sinks into the ground. I want to tell them how it's a ladder to their future, how the secrets of the U tip into the double L and that will propel the town forward. But they need direct words, not the letters that shout to me, that tell me Hull will be doomed unless they listen.

"Healthy children need stable adults who watch out for them, who protect them, who never allow abuse or trafficking or pornography or neglect."

I hear Herbert Heath Hecht's voice shout from the audience. "Angel, you're right. We believe you. Stone has to be stopped."

Members of the audience take up a chant: "Stone Stone." They rise and yell louder. Police rush to surround the stage. Mob justice. Like in *The Lottery.* Clare's voice rings through me: "We're measured by the wrong we do to others."

"Stop!" I shout, as loud as thunder, as loud as the ocean. "Today is the time to end Stone's rule, not to become like him. He's evil, but we aren't. Don't chant *Stone Stone.* Chant *Children First.*"

Herbert takes up the call: "Children First!" and the audience repeats it.

The Ladies of the Night move as one across the pavilion with Stone and Vixen dragged along inside. The crowd surges. "Children First! Children First!" they roar until Robert and Lieutenant Drew shove Stone and Vixen into a squad car and drive away.

DeeDee, Andréa, Ira, Vasya and the twins hurry to my side, cheering, calling me their hero. I don't want to be a hero. I want Hull to be heroic, to stand up for kids, to stop people like Stone and Vixen, and anyone else who forgets what really matters.

But I can't quiet the storm inside me. Relief, disbelief—and something sharp—twist together, impossible to untangle. I should feel triumphant. I should feel light, victorious. But the feeling never comes. It slips right through me, leaving only tired bones and a shaky kind of quiet. I'm too worn out to celebrate. Too used up to stand tall.

All I can think is, *What now? What happens to me? To this town?*

TWENTY-ONE

Fall-Out

The front page of *The Boston Globe* blazes with stacked headlines:

Hull Cop Arrested for Sex Crimes

Sergeant Evan Stone was arrested at his own retirement party for sex crimes, child trafficking, and bribery. Once respected, he was exposed by multiple witnesses.

I hoot and flip to another shocker:

Drug Cartel Infiltrated in Hull

The U.S. Coast Guard arrested Venezuelan drug lord Anthony "Squid" Vasguez on Gunrock Island with 1.5 kilos of cocaine and 1,000 kilos of marijuana. On the FBI's Most Wanted list for years, he finally slipped up when a Hull resident tipped authorities three days ago.

Finally, justice! But the letters V–I–X–E–N leap off the page. "DeeDee! You've got to see this!"

Mystery Woman's Double Life Exposed

Notorious in Hull as Vixen, Victoria Stone—also known as Constance Hill—was arrested for murder, child trafficking, and drug trafficking.

She is the stepdaughter of Sergeant Stone, also arrested for sex crimes, child trafficking, and bribery.

Charges include the murders of William and Ivy Hale (for which Gregg Bunkny is serving life) and the kidnapping of three girls: eleven-year-old Farrah Silvio, seven-year-old Nadia Jones, and another motherless seven-year-old who was likely homeless.

Victoria returned to Hull in 1980 after her mother died. By day, she worked for her stepfather at the police station; by night, she prowled Hull as Vixen, selling drugs and terrorizing residents.

Victoria attended Hull schools until ten, then Essex Academy in New Haven. As a senior, she filed suit against the headmistress and dean for child endangerment, but they died before the case went to trial.

DeeDee devours the article. Her eyes widen. Her face flushes as she scratches at her neck until purple lines appear, resembling mine!

"Son of a bitch. Vixen is Victoria? Damn. She sat here every Thursday for six years, and I had no clue—but she knew me the whole time."

Ira comes into the kitchen. Most of his bees have returned, buzzing happily.

"Even as a kid, she was one mean fucker," Ira says. "Practicing with knives in the yard, waiting to skewer anything—a squirrel, a bird, even me."

DeeDee's skin settles back into pink. "I carried her in my head since I was ten, thinking she was at the bottom of the ocean and

Stone had killed her. To find out she's been here, abusing children—that's worse than anything I could imagine. Why my salon? What made her feel safe here?"

Safe. That sneaky word. Pretending to be high and mighty, all the while playing with lives like they were puppets.

I think about Victoria being abused, and that boarding school where the headmistress and her husband died. What did they do to her? What did she do to them? Why do grown-ups need power over kids? How does a child ever stand up to that?

I could never confront Ivy and win. Ever. And Ivy couldn't stand up to her parents either. If I ever have kids, I'll be a kind, loving mother who marries a man who isn't selfish. That's what breaks the cycle. Putting kids first.

"Angel, I should have confronted Stone years ago. I was a coward. I closed my eyes to Ivy. I was blind," says DeeDee, her voice quivering.

I take her hand gently. I don't need to soothe her with words. DeeDee knows my heart. Ira settles beside us, taking my other hand, and the three of us sit quietly together like a family.

"What's next? Will there be a trial?" I ask.

"This'll drag on for years," DeeDee says. "Our job is to make sure Hull doesn't forget."

"So I should stay in Hull and see it through?"

"Sure, Lovey, you have a home with me for as long as you'd like," DeeDee says.

I could stay here with DeeDee. I could be Angel—read names, or volunteer as a big sister. I'm sixteen now—I can imagine tomorrow filled with knowledge, good people, and children. I even think about teaching. But that means an education, and how do I even begin?

As if reading my mind, DeeDee says, "You know, Angel, you should get your GED, then go to college."

"What's a GED?"

"It's a Graduate Equivalent Degree—a high school equivalency test in language arts, math, science and history."

G–E–D.

The G is no longer Gregg's weapon. It's a C that hugs itself.

The E is always seeking.

 The D will be filled with knowledge.

"How do I go about getting a GED?" I ask.

"I know you have a huge vocabulary, but you'll need more than that. Tell ya what—I'll buy some GED workbooks, see what we need to work on."

An education would be a dream. In the books I've read, kids go to school—but not me. Maybe the GED won't fix everything, but it gives me choices.

"Thanks, DeeDee, I'd like that."

I retreat to Clare's journals, searching for clues about myself. It's my time to figure out what matters for my future.

One passage hits me: "She's a beautiful young woman, thoughtful and bright. This is the time she can choose to make everything new."

Clare believed in me, more than I believe in myself.

Maybe a walk will clear my head. I don't wear my hood or a scarf. I don't cover my birthmarks. Who's going to care now that Stone, Vixen and Squid are in custody, and Daddy and Ivy are dead?

The beach draws me, but F Street pulls harder, like a magnet.

I stop in front of the house. The portal in the roofline is still intact. I see myself there—pressed against the louvres, looking out at the ocean, at the stars, at children running along the edge of the water, at dogs, at swimmers, at families.

Everyone lived out there while I was trapped in the eaves.

Today, I'm free. I twirl on the sand and shake my finger at the house. You don't own me anymore.

I get closer. I consider going inside. Ira holed up there in bad weather, but I can't climb those stairs. Not to that place. Not where death and ugliness reigned.

Instead, I do what Clare taught me. I walk around the outside of the house.

First Round: Measure what I have to do against what I've done.
I reunited Nadia and Farrah with their families.
I saved a homeless child, Beatrice, from a life of exploitation.
I exposed Stone and Vixen and stopped Squid from taking more children.
I forced Hull to face its underbelly.
I can walk proud.

Second Round: Open my mind to what feels impossible.
I feel Daddy and Ivy in the roots of this place, their shadow across the dirt.
This was their hunting ground.
They lured drug addicts here, fed them marijuana, cocaine, quaaludes.
I think about Daddy's secrets, his hiding places.
Did he ever really show himself to me?
Do I care?
Do I even want to?

Third Round: Body and spirit come together.
Inside and outside become one.
I listen—to the urge to keep going, and the wisdom of letting go.
Clare always said, "A good night's sleep is more than rest. It resets our bodies and our minds."
Time to go home and reset.

Clare's Journal

As I lie in bed, I'm restless, like something important is missing. I toss and turn trying to understand Clare's words about merging body and spirit. I want to move toward what is valuable and strong and true. That feels possible—but how do I actually do it?

When I wake, I look through *The Letter Bible*. Maybe it has answers. I think about the name Angel and reread what Clare and I discovered.

"A's reach the apex of success at a young age because they analyze a situation and make accurate decisions." Okay. That sounds like me. But does apex mean I've already peaked? I hope not.

"N's are bold and aggressive. Never afraid of failure. Always rising again after falling low." I've focused so much on the negative N in Sergeant Stone that I never considered its strengths. I was bold when I stood before the whole town and told my story. But I still don't trust the N.

"G's get the most enjoyment from reading, researching and asking questions. They don't like guess-work and prefer to ground themselves in facts." Gregg's G was a weapon. My G is my inner life. I love reading and researching. I love asking questions. I just haven't had the chance.

"E's exist to explore. They don't accept boundaries. They explode with energy." This describes DeeDee more than me. But maybe, as I get older, I'll understand how the E moves me forward.

"L's lust for life. They follow their dreams. They value loyalty." Even in death, I'm loyal to Clare. But Daddy? I don't know if he deserves my loyalty.

I set the book aside and lie back, thinking about my future. But something gnaws at me.

The house on F Street.

It keeps crawling into my nightmares.

I reach for Clare's journal, flipping through pages, looking for what she wrote about that hulking house.

> *It was an angry house, charred and still smoking. Its skin sagged.*
> *Its body festered. I got the feeling ghosts spiraled around inside.*

It's not smoking anymore, but its body is burned and blistered. It smells like vinegar.

> *I circled the pitted yard, searching for that kernel of truth. I*
> *stared up at the attic where Angel had lived. It gaped and yawed*
> *and gave me no answers.*

Yesterday, I stared at the attic and heard it say—*Never ever return here.* I thought of my miniature blocks—probably rotting in the waterlogged floorboards. Are they still crying out for me? Is the K chomping at me? Is the B blasting me with Ivy-swears?

And then Clare wrote something I missed.

> *At the back of the property was a rock wall—misshapen stones,*
> *bricks, boulders, and sticks, all glued haphazardly together like*
> *a story told backwards and inside out. Did Angel's father start*
> *this messy border and never finish it?*

Daddy's hiding places were planned and well crafted. Precise, built with purpose. Drugs. Money. That's what he hid.

I have to go back.

I return to the house by way of Nantasket Ave, heading straight for the backyard. Most of the bushes died in the fire, but the rock wall remains, crumbling into rubble.

I dig at the rocks. I scrape away dirt. Beneath it all, I find a hollowed-out pit—like a shallow well.

And inside?

A door.

Just like the one on the island.

Just like the one inside the cabinets.

Just like the one under the floorboards.

Daddy's stash.

My skin prickles. I *have* to see what's inside.

But I don't have the tools to pry it open.

I push to my feet, brushing dirt off my hands.

At DeeDee's, I find a flat bar in her trunk. That should work. But I can't get back to the yard until twilight. DeeDee keeps me busy—sweeping, making coffee, doing a few readings. I race through them, trying not to look suspicious. Finally, I get out on my own, saying I need a walk.

I don't waste a second. I head straight for the yard and drop to my knees, shining my flashlight into the hole. Inch by inch, I work the flat bar around the edges, making space between the door and the earth.

It isn't easy.

I think of Daddy's blocks—how I pried them open to find the money hidden inside. I work the same way now, slow and deliberate.

Finally, the tension releases.

The trapdoor opens.

A metal box sits there, half-buried in dirt and splintered wood.

I dig around it with both hands, clawing out the packed earth, prying it loose. When it finally comes free, the weight of it yanks me backward. I hit the ground hard, the box slamming into my chest. For a second, I can't breathe. I shove it off and sit up, shaking.

I pull the box into my lap.

Is there more evidence inside? What could possibly be left?

The video and pictures already damned Stone and Squid.

The black book is under investigation. Higher-ups will be exposed. Maybe even punished.

Vixen is in custody.

Gregg is dying.

Examining the box, I realize it's locked. My hand flies to DeeDee's key. I unclasp it, slide it in, and turn.

The lid creaks open—and what's inside hits me harder than the box ever could. I tip back on my elbows, gasping.

Daddy's deepest secrets. The things he hid from me.

Laminated pages, folders, photos jammed tight, like the box had been sealed for years. One folder lies on top. Thick black letters on the cover: *REST IN PEACE.*

My heart pounds against my ribs. I tear into the pages.

> *Child vanishes in plain sight.*
> *Abduction spree in Richmond.*
> *Vigil for missing toddler.*

Photos of sweet faces and crying parents. Search teams. Beaches. Woods. Streets. Page after page.

Daddy kept files on the missing children?

Like trophies?

I move to another page—and freeze. My hands go cold.

Taped neatly in a row are locks of blonde hair. Under each one, names in Daddy's handwriting:

Rosalyn Sayle, age 3, Myrtle Beach, 1976.
Whitney Savage, age 2, Rye, 1977.
Suzanne Arquette, age 4, Hull, 1980.
Jazmin Bernhardt, age 4, 1981.

The letters cry up at me.
S's and Z's. N's and Y's.
So much challenged these girls right from the start.
I cry so hard the pages slip from my hands.
My heart slips too.
My head pounds with certainty.
Daddy was involved.
Not just involved—
As evil as Ivy. As Squid. As Vixen.
How did I not know this?
How did I love him?
At the end of the file, there's a pocket. An article pokes out.

New York Times, April 16, 1975

I pull it free.

Millionaire's Daughter Disappears on Her Third Birthday

Ariel Blythe, 3, daughter of New York City philanthropist Conrad Blythe and his wife Cheryl, was last seen playing on a Savannah, Georgia beach.

Ariel is 3'2" tall, weighs 35 pounds, has brown eyes, dark brown curly hair and a series of port wine stains along the left side of her neck.

Port wine stains.
My port wine stains.

My hands shake.

I want to bury the pages. Shove them back underground. Pretend I never saw them.

But this—this is my truth.

The thing I've been searching for.

Ever since the S in Agnes felt wrong in my ears, even as the L sounded familiar.

I swallow hard. Sit up. Breathe through my nose.

I can do this.

I can read the rest.

> *The family's au pair said the child was curious and had a habit of wandering. "I had my eye on her one minute and the next she was gone. This time she didn't come back."*
>
> *Beach goers said they saw the child near the edge of the water, where she might have been swallowed by the heavy surf. A search and rescue team was organized with no results.*

My vision swims.

Wizz and Ivy stole me from the beach. Stuffed me in the van. Kept me as their own.

I think back to Ivy slapping duct tape over my mouth. I ripped it off and screamed so loud Daddy flew up the ladder. "Ivy, what the hell?" Blood seeped from my pores. "Leave the kid alone. I'm warning you."

"She's a goddamn pain," Ivy snapped. "We should have dumped her at the side of the road. Now's the time to ransom the kid and leave Hull."

I was too young to understand.

But now? It's all too clear.

I turn over the article. A photo stares back: a handsome man, a beautiful woman, and a toddler between them. Pudgy fingers hooked to her parents' hands. Pink cheeks. Saucer eyes. And the purple birthmarks on her neck.

I know for certain I am Ariel Blythe.

The letters swell before me.

Ariel.

Ariel.

Ariel.

My beloved A.

The ready-to-run R.

The independent I.

The explorer E.

And my look-forward-to-the-future L.

No N.

No G.

No S.

Not Agnes. Not Angel. Just A–R–I–E–L.

My true letters.

My real name.

Ariel.

The original me.

TWENTY-THREE

Confusion

I clutch the folder, but my fingers are numb. My legs carry me like they belong to someone else. By the time I reach the apartment, I crawl into bed, pressing the folder into my chest. I tell no one. Barely even myself.

My new name, my new letters—where do I go from here? What must I do to become Ariel?

My breath is unsteady, but I need to make sense of this. I turn to a blank page at the end of Clare's journal and write:

> *Dear Clare,*
>
> *I'm so confused. I need to understand who I am. Please help me.*
>
> *A*

Where do I turn? To DeeDee? To Robert? To Tom? To my birth parents? Do I tell them where I've been, how I was stolen? Will they see me as damaged beyond repair? How did they move on without me? Do I have brothers, sisters? Are my parents wealthy?

Do they give their money to charity? Would they welcome me as their own?

What if I hadn't been stolen? I wouldn't be living downstairs from a hair salon and reading people's letters for profit. I'd be in a swanky apartment, going to school, hanging out with classmates, having dinner with my parents. I'd be a normal girl.

But then I never would have met DeeDee and Clare and Max, my guardians.

Guardian. The letters are strong together. They protect, surround, hold. But maybe the answer isn't in the letters. Maybe people are more than names.

Still, I believe in them. They reveal truths. They predict. They expose what's good and what's not. A name is powerful. The way someone reacts to it, the way it fits—or doesn't. But to think individual letters hold power on their own. . .is that crazy?

Maybe now's my time to find out.

I'm not a child. Not an adult. Just an in-between. I can make mistakes. I can learn from them. I can be independent, but I can still lean on others.

Who? Who will guide me?

I need to calm down. I need to think. I'll pretend Clare is writing to me, like she wrote to her sister. Maybe that will sort this out.

July 1989
Dear Angel,

You've learned something earth-shattering and don't know what to do. Let yourself sit with it. Take in what you've found. Look at it from all angles.

Ariel is a beautiful name. There's no rush to make it yours. Let it seep into you. Taste it. Become it, if it works. Go slow. Go slow.

I think you already know that the N and the G in Agnes

and Angel were never yours. They were given to you, but they never felt right. Even so, they're part of your history.

Don't dwell on the past. What happened to you, to the other children, happened. You cannot change it. But you can understand and move forward.

You might be sixteen, but you don't have to do this alone. Finding your birth parents is too big to take on by yourself. You need help. Decide if DeeDee is someone you can trust. If she is, confide in her.

Love, Clare

DeeDee calls from the other room, "Dinner." I put the journal away, but I'm not ready to face DeeDee or Ira, not yet. I tell her I'm tired and need to sleep. I have to process what I've learned. Process. Oh damn. Maybe process isn't the right word. Those S's will sink me. Maybe accept is. Accept. Yes. That's better, I guess. The C's will comfort me and send me in a better direction.

DeeDee checks on me in the morning, but she seems to understand that I can't be with her or anyone or come out to the sunshine or face the world today. She thinks it's because I exhausted myself at the tribute and all the publicity I received after it. Radio stations, newspapers asking for interviews. It was all too much, she thinks, and it has been, but there's so much more. I'm not ready to tell her what I found. What I know. I curl into myself and concentrate on breathing.

My new letters ease themselves into my body: Ariel. The I for independence. Standing alone. Figuring out who I am. That's my next step, right? The letters are not so different. Not so foreign. Just unknown. Agnes. Angel. Lucille. Angelica. Ariel. My letters have always been within me, except the R, and I like what that letter means: ready to take a risk.

I take up the journal again and answer Clare.

Dear Clare,

I've thought about the Emerson quote you mentioned over and over again: "This time, like all times, is a very good one, if we but know what to do with it."

I get it now. I don't have to go through this alone. I can trust DeeDee. She loves me, not because she loved Ivy, but because she sees me for who I am: good and strong and smart and capable.

Thank you for listening.

Love, A

I shower and dress. My first day up in three. DeeDee is working upstairs, but notes are pasted around the kitchen. *Have breakfast. Put a smile on your face. You're the town's hero. Join the living.*

When I go through the archway into the salon, DeeDee rushes toward me full steam. "Angel, I thought I lost you. I thought you went somewhere in your head and would never come back to me. Angel, what's going on? How can I help you?"

I don't look at her, but I feel her eyes on me, waiting. Expecting. I start small.

"DeeDee, I've decided to take a trip to New York. Would you come with me?"

DeeDee's orange hair lights up from the roots outward. Her yellow liner forms a ring of sunshine around her eyes. "Hot damn. Broadway!"

I give her the article about me from *The New York Times*. She reads in silence.

I can't tell what DeeDee's thinking from the blank look on her face. I'm so used to smiles and frowns and crinkled lines around her eyes. Now she just looks up from the paper and stares at me. I scratch at my neck, the purple marks deepening.

"So you're not Wizz and Ivy's kid? I never did see a resemblance. The longer you've been here, the more I believed Ivy was a bad woman and I should have seen it. Blind. Isn't that what you called Robert? That's me too. I'm so sorry, Angel. Or should I call you Ariel?" DeeDee strokes my hair. "We'll make this right. Together. Let me see what Robbie can do to help us."

DeeDee and I cuddle for a long time. Then she calls Robert, who comes immediately, but I'm too tired to talk. I go back to sleep while DeeDee explains the contents of the folder.

He promises to investigate.

TWENTY-FOUR

New York

Robert calls early the next morning. He's spoken with the detective who worked the Ariel Blythe case thirteen years ago. "He was new to the force then," Robert says, "and it's always gnawed at him that he couldn't solve it. He said he'll speak with the Blythe family and let them know the new development."

He pauses.

"But before I ended the call, I asked a few questions."

I stop breathing.

"You have a fourteen-year-old brother Carl, and a twelve-year-old sister Charlotte. Conrad, your father, owns a real estate development company. Your mother Cheryl chairs several charities."

All those C's—the listening letter—make my heart glow. They must be compassionate and open-hearted. But maybe the C shows an emptiness that needs to be filled to make the family whole again. Maybe I'm the missing link to close the circle.

I can hope.

Midday, Robert rushes into the salon with more news.

"The Blythes responded right away," he says, breathless. "They're sending an overnight courier with airline tickets for two to New York."

"They acted fast," DeeDee says, "like they've been waiting thirteen years for this chance."

"You can leave tomorrow if you want. They know you've been living with DeeDee, and they don't want you to rush into anything. They just...they really want to see you. They understand your history and...they won't pressure you to live with them if you're not ready. They'll do everything they can to welcome you back, if that's okay."

My whole body shakes—my bones vibrate like they might rattle apart.

"What else? What else can you tell me?" I blurt, the words spilling out too fast, too loud. I need more. I need to know everything.

Robert shakes his head. "That's all for now. The detective is faxing more information to the police station, but it hasn't come through yet."

The rest of the day stretches on like elastic, pulling tighter with every hour. My thoughts spin into each other—faces I've never seen, voices I've never heard, names that should belong to me but don't feel real yet. Letters vibrate like signals I can't quite decode—bright, insistent, but out of reach.

So I go for a walk, hoping the air might help, but as I leave the salon, I spot the mail carrier sliding several envelopes into DeeDee's box. The one on top is addressed to me.

It's from Tom.

I tear it open.

Dear Angel,

    I finally have good news. My lawyer says the court will rule in my favor. It's a bunch of gibberish and legalese, but the bottom line is that my dad's money belongs to ME and Penny has no claim to it.

I'm still committed to working in Alaska for a few more
weeks, but when I return, we'll sit down together and figure it
all out. Between Clare's savings and your father's contribution,
there's enough money to secure your future.
    I won't be your dad, but I can be your favorite uncle!
    Rest easy knowing that I won't let you down.

                                                        Tom

I reread the letter, letting it sink in, assuring myself that Tom is being truthful. It almost sounds too good. Too neat. Too perfect to trust.

Regardless, I'll be okay on my own, if it comes to that. Maybe my birth parents won't want me after all. Maybe DeeDee might find that I'm a burden. But Clare won't let me fail.

She'll make sure I don't just survive—she'll make sure I thrive.

And for the first time in a long time, I sleep easy knowing I'll be all right. Maybe even better than all right.

In the morning, Robert comes by earlier than expected to drive DeeDee and me to the airport.

"There's something I need to show you before we head out," he says.

"Do you need me too? Or can I wrap it up here?" asks DeeDee.

"We'll be back in an hour. Be ready," says Robert.

He drives me past the roller coaster and Ferris Wheel toward Gunrock Beach. At a fork, he turns inland, climbs a short hill, then veers right onto Tower Road. Another rise leads to a tin-green water tower, fenced in by wire.

From this height, I see Hull's outline in its smallest details: the sheer cliff at the end of Z Street; the breach way; the silhouettes of houses and boat moorings. The carousel's cap and the lattice of the roller coaster. The rush of the tide and the stillness of the bay. Even the variation in water's color, from shallow browns to deeper greens. Like Clare's transparent eyeball, I experience the town—its L shape, its collective breath.

I imagine how Stone held court down there while Vixen sharpened her knives. Somewhere below, kids were trapped—too young to fight back, too scared to run. Maybe they looked through narrow window slats and befriended clouds, just to feel like they had something of their own.

I fold my arms around myself, grateful for Clare and Max, DeeDee and Robert, Andréa and Ira, who showed me that good exists. The Stones, Vixens, Squids, and Bunknys aren't the majority.

Robert parks the cruiser. "Follow me."

He opens an iron gate, rusted by the wind and years of neglect. We walk around the tower along a gravel path to a quiet plot where several granite stones huddle, each with its own engraving. On two narrow strips, I see their names: Jane Doe and John Doe. And the date, 1986.

I place a foot on each grave that covers Daddy and Ivy's bodies. I wait. I close my eyes. I shout at them from every fiber of my being. Why didn't you let me be Ariel Blythe? Why did you take me from my birth parents and steal my spirit?

I expect feeble cries and excuses. A powerful tremor presses into my soles, up my legs, through my gut, inside my chest, past my port wine stains and into my brain, knowing, without a doubt, that they feel me here.

I breathe in the last thirteen years and exhale fear, abandonment and lies. I am not the daughter of kidnappers. I may be a child of abuse, but I will not carry it with me. I take back what they stole from me: my name, my life, me.

The headstones glare at me. Should I change the names to William Perry Hale and Ina Vee Yunis Hale? But John Doe and Jane Doe are who they are.

The letter J anchors them to the ground and keeps them there;

the N speaks of their downward slide throughout life, their inability to rise and seek out anything positive.

"Forgive us," I hear them say.

The girls I've been—Agnes and Angel, Lucille and Angelica—are not ready to forgive them.

Maybe one day, Ariel Blythe will.

But not today.

The Letter Bible

The commentary reflects the author's interpretation of Angel's point of view.

The Achiever

Traits:
- **Positive:** Analytical, adaptable, and highly aware, Positive A's excel at reaching success early. They analyze situations with precision and adapt to change seamlessly, often rising to challenges others fear.
- **Negative:** Arrogant and aloof, Negative A's believe their answers are the only correct ones, often alienating others.

Associations:
- **Professions:** Advisor, Psychic, Educator, Stockbroker, Addict
- **Body Part:** Brain
- **Symbol:** Mountains

Angel's View:
Angel interprets the letter A as a positive symbol, towering confidently into the sky. It offers a safe perch midway, standing alone with independence and power, unaffected by the letters around it. Having an A at the beginning of her name gives her confidence.

The Brave

Traits:

- **Positive:** Balanced and bold, Positive B's excel at managing both family and business. They make confident leaders and bond easily, building friendships through reliability and even temperaments—until provoked, when they defend themselves fiercely.
- **Negative:** Negative B's are bullies—boastful, brash, and constantly belittling others. They dominate conversations with self-centered talk.

Associations:

- **Professions:** CEO, Orator, Politician, Lobbyist
- **Body Part:** Lips
- **Symbol:** Balloon

Angel's View:

Angel appreciates this letter but feels distant from it. To her, it symbolizes kissing—a gesture she has rarely experienced.

The Caregiver

Traits:

- **Positive:** Compassionate and caring, Positive C's listen intently and offer advice with sincerity. They act as an open cup—receiving and sharing with others. C's are diplomatic, delivering criticism gently and effectively.

- **Negative:** Negative C's struggle with societal norms, retreating into isolation and living covertly.

Associations:

- **Professions:** Psychiatrist, Psychologist, Therapist, Diplomat, Swindler
- **Body Part:** Ear
- **Symbol:** Waning Moon

Angel's View:

Angel loves the C, associating it with Clare, a comforting, enveloping spirit who provides her with both warmth and space to breathe.

The Defender

Traits:

- **Positive:** Dedicated and dependable, Positive D's are fiercely loyal to friends and family, forming unbreakable bonds. They boldly express their tastes—whether in hair color, clothing, or decor—and confidently voice their opinions. Physically, they are durable and strong.
- **Negative:** Negative D's lack self-discipline, indulging in luxuries and denying themselves nothing.

Associations:

- **Professions:** Politician, Salesperson, Lawyer, Doctor, Tyrant
- **Body Part:** Stomach
- **Symbol:** Waxing Moon

Angel's View:

Angel laughs at the D, seeing it as a playful letter with a big belly. It bumps into others in a friendly way and risks toppling over if it gets too heavy.

The Extrovert

Traits:
- **Positive:** Energetic and enthusiastic, Positive E's embrace exploration and refuse to accept boundaries. They shine as entertainers, captivating audiences with singing, dancing, jokes, and charm—ideal for any emcee role.
- **Negative:** Negative E's are like earthquakes—unpredictable and disruptive, leaving chaos and damage in their wake.

Associations:
- **Professions:** Hairdresser, Artist, Musician, Explosives Expert
- **Body Part:** Hands
- **Symbol:** Stairs, Ladders

Angel's View:

Angel admires the E as a letter of forward momentum, nudging others into action. When standing alone at the end of a word, it symbolizes hope and the promise of good things to come.

The Friend

Traits:
- **Positive:** Carefree and spirited, Positive F's live for fun and festivity. They forge ahead confidently, sometimes forcefully, and embrace life without regret.
- **Negative:** Negative F's act impulsively, failing to think before they leap, often leading to mistakes.

Associations:
- **Professions:** Football Player, Pitcher, Musician, Clown
- **Body Part:** Fingers
- **Symbol:** Brain, Open-Air Stadium

Angel's View:
Angel feels frustrated with the F, seeing it as a letter with its head in the air, oblivious to how it has exposed itself. It teeters precariously, always on the verge of falling.

The Giver

Traits:
- **Positive:** Gregarious and curious, Positive G's thrive in social settings and enjoy gathering knowledge through reading, research, and conversation. They dislike guesswork and prefer to ground themselves in facts.

- **Negative:** Negative G's weaponize their knowledge, humiliating others to boost their own egos.

Associations:
- **Professions:** Social Director, Researcher, Blackmailer, Male Escort
- **Body Part:** Groin
- **Symbol:** Sword

Angel's View:

Angel initially thought the G resembled the C, but after experiencing the sting of its sword, she realized it was dangerous and untrustworthy.

The Helper

Traits:
- **Positive:** Positive H's are humanitarians, healing hearts without distinction and offering help wherever it's needed. They bring hope, downplay hardship, and excel as mediators in times of conflict.
- **Negative:** Negative H's avoid challenges, hiding their heads in the sand and hindering healthy relationships.

Associations:
- **Professions:** Clergy, Contractor, Architect, Warlord
- **Body Part:** Torso
- **Symbol:** Heaven, Hell

Angel's View:

Angel appreciates the H for its balance and the resting place it offers in the middle. However, she finds it deceptive, as it holds the potential to ascend to heaven or descend to hell.

The Individual

Traits:

- **Positive:** Positive I's are independent, intelligent, and inspiring. They include others in their strength while maintaining their towering independence. Though self-reliant, they willingly support those beside them.
- **Negative:** Negative I's isolate themselves, remaining aloof, impenetrable, and alone, unable to connect with others.

Associations:

- **Professions:** Salesperson, Conductor, Director, Songwriter, Spy
- **Body Part:** Spine
- **Symbol:** Backbone

Angel's View:

Angel respects the independence of the I but remains wary of its selfish streak, shaped by her experiences with Ivy, Wizz, Squid and Vixen—all of whom bear this letter.

The Jurist

Traits:

- **Positive:** Positive J's are joyful, just, and non-judgmental, making them trustworthy and uplifting friends. They juggle multiple responsibilities with confidence and are steadfast anchors in any situation.
- **Negative:** Negative J's justify illegal actions, believing themselves above the law. Their path often veers off course early in life and struggles to recover.

Associations:

- **Professions:** Farmer, Fisherman, Environmentalist, Warden, Traitor
- **Body Part:** Nose
- **Symbol:** Anchor, Hook

Angel's View:

Angel appreciates the hook of the J for its ability to carry items securely without spilling them. It also represents plants and vegetables, their roots below and their beauty above.

The Knower

Traits:

- **Positive:** Positive K's are knowledgeable, kind-hearted, and self-aware. Though reserved, they know when to seek connection and excel at making others feel at ease. They thrive with adventurous and risk-taking individuals.

- **Negative:** Negative K's are ruthless and immoral, metaphorically "knifing" into their prey and stopping only when their objectives are achieved.

Associations:
- **Professions:** Talk-show Host, Comedian, Fitness Instructor, Bodybuilder, Conman
- **Body Part:** Mouth
- **Symbol:** Scissors

Angel's View:

Angel feels uneasy about the K, perceiving it as a letter poised to bite her.

The Leader

Traits:
- **Positive:** Positive L's live with passion, pursuing dreams and valuing loyalty above all. They love to learn, driven by an insatiable curiosity about people and the world.
- **Negative:** Negative L's are deceptive and manipulative, spreading lewd tales and lies to elevate themselves at others' expense.

Associations:
- **Professions:** Professor, Dancer, Boxer, Actor, Con Artist
- **Body Part:** Legs, Feet
- **Symbol:** Boot

Angel's View:

Angel treasures the L in her name, seeing it as a symbol of progress and the future—a step forward.

The Master

Traits:
- **Positive:** Positive M's are strong, mature, and self-motivated. They seize every moment, measure success by their achievements, and dedicate themselves to noble causes, whether climbing mountains or running races to support others.
- **Negative:** Negative M's can be overpowering and manipulative, treating others like marionettes under their control.

Associations:
- **Professions:** Manager, CEO, Police Officer, Mercenary
- **Body Part:** Shoulders
- **Symbol:** Peaks and Valleys

Angel's View:

Angel worries about the M because of its sinking V in the center, but she admires its sturdiness and ability to resist negative influences.

The Nay-Sayer

Traits:
- **Positive:** Positive N's are bold, noticeable, and unafraid of

failure. They nurture their own needs and rise again, no matter how low they may fall.

- **Negative:** Negative N's are narcissistic and domineering, believing no one can compete with them. They bulldoze anyone who limits their options, convinced they alone have all the answers.

Associations:
- **Professions:** Entrepreneur, Soldier, Guard, Gambler
- **Body Part:** Legs
- **Symbol:** Slide

Angel's View:

Angel despises the N and sees it as a source of inner turmoil she cannot escape. She connects the N to her nemesis, Sergeant Stone, whose troubled and evil nature embodies everything she fears about the letter.

The Observer

Traits:
- **Positive:** Positive O's are open-minded and adventurous, eager to embrace challenges. They surround others with warmth and trust, using their observant nature to understand emotions and navigate problems.
- **Negative:** Negative O's overindulge in luxuries and take up excessive space, often excluding others in the process.

Associations:
- **Professions:** Optometrist, Poet, Editor, Photographer, Thief

- **Body Part**: Eyes
- **Symbol**: Circle

Angel's View:
Angel trusts the O, seeing it as a protective and dependable circle that surrounds her with safety.

The Power Broker

Traits:
- **Positive**: Positive P's are practical and powerful, skilled at making strategic moves to maximize success. They tackle problems head-on with purpose and an enterprising mindset, ensuring results.
- **Negative**: Negative P's are pompous and overbearing, projecting false confidence. Beneath the facade, they can become paranoid, delusional, and self-destructive.

Associations:
- **Professions**: Politician, Actor, Lawyer, Pilot, Salesperson, Scam Artist
- **Body Part**: Head
- **Symbol**: Flag

Angel's View:
Angel admires the P for its boldness and directness but worries that it lacks the stability to uphold its convictions and achieve lasting influence.

The Questioner

Traits:

- **Positive:** Positive Q's are quick-minded and confident, subtly influencing others with their wit and insight. They seek knowledge with determination, trusting in their ability to succeed.
- **Negative:** Negative Q's are quarrelsome and combative, quick to provoke arguments and agitate those around them.

Associations:

- **Professions:** Orator, Politician, Talk-Show Host, Prostitute, Demagogue
- **Body Part:** Tongue
- **Symbol:** Worm

Angel's View:

Angel appreciates the protective circle of the Q but remains wary of its vulnerability to infiltration and compromise.

The Realizer

Traits:

- **Positive:** Positive R's are responsible and forward-thinking, standing firmly behind their decisions. They set realistic goals and carefully consider the consequences of their actions. Respected for their can-do attitude, R's blend mental acuity with physical determination.

- **Negative:** Negative R's are ruthlessly vindictive. They harbor grudges and pursue revenge with calculated precision until their enemies are defeated.

Associations:

- **Professions:** Physical Therapist, Athlete, Fencer, Dancer, Embezzler
- **Body Parts:** Head and Foot
- **Symbol:** Finish Line

Angel's View:

Angel admires the R for its forward momentum and willingness to take risks when needed to achieve progress. She sees it as an integral part of her own future.

The Sidewinder

Traits:

- **Positive:** Positive S's exude charisma, attracting attention with their seductive charm. They're quick to act, offering steadfast support to friends and presenting a formidable challenge to foes.
- **Negative:** Negative S's are sly and untrustworthy, maneuvering through situations with sneaky, underhanded tactics.

Associations:

- **Professions:** Detective, Police Officer, Salesperson, Bank Robber

- **Body Part:** Hips
- **Symbol:** Snake

Angel's View:

Angel fears the S, sensing its serpentine ability to infiltrate and manipulate the souls of others.

The Triumphant

Traits:
- **Positive:** Positive T's are trustworthy and truthful, reliable keepers of secrets who approach conflicts with fairness and empathy. They stand tall as protective figures and loyal friends.
- **Negative:** Negative T's are turbulent and disconnected, often lost in their own world, failing to ground themselves or follow through.

Associations:
- **Professions:** Judge, Utility Worker, Lumberjack, Fortune Teller
- **Body Part:** Top of the Head
- **Symbol:** Tower

Angel's View:

Angel admires the T for its potential, imagining it as a whirly-bird ready to soar but balanced by its towering strength.

The Useful

Traits:

- **Positive:** Positive U's are upright and reliable, using their strength to safeguard life's secrets and keep information confidential. They balance a unique ability to either share or conceal, depending on what's needed.
- **Negative:** Negative U's hoard secrets, withdrawing into themselves. Silent and solitary, they become unwilling to compromise or connect with others.

Associations:

- **Professions:** Undertaker, Tax Collector, Antiques Dealer, Banker, Lender
- **Body Part:** Throat
- **Symbol:** Urn

Angel's View:

Angel is uneasy about the U, perceiving it as a vessel for too many hidden secrets.

The Victor

Traits:

- **Positive:** Positive V's are valiant and determined, valuing victory above all else. They persevere relentlessly and prove to be invaluable members of any team striving for success.

Unwavering in their resolve, V's are natural leaders who take charge and inspire confidence.

- **Negative:** Negative V's channel their aggression destructively, becoming vindictive and vicious. They vilify opponents, acting with a sharp edge of revenge.

Associations:
- **Professions:** Conductor, Drug Dealer, Magician, Assassin
- **Body Part:** Jaw
- **Symbol:** Triangle

Angel's View:

Angel fears the V for its sharp, piercing nature, like a blade ready to wound. She feels it hides too many secrets beneath its angular precision.

The Wizard

Traits:
- **Positive:** Positive W's win love and affection from all. Their wise advice is worthy of respect and trust. They are warm and welcoming, their arms open and ready. They have a wholesome regard for life, and they speak with wit and confidence.
- **Negative:** Negative W's weave a web of wrath and wickedness. W's watch for weakness and wreak havoc when they find it, their damage doubled by the sharp points at both ends.

Associations:
- **Professions:** Greeter, Teacher, Nanny, Drug Dealer
- **Body Part:** Arms
- **Symbol:** Wings

Angel's View:
Angel sees the W as double-trouble, like two V's ganging up. In her father's name, she hopes it will mean "welcome." It doesn't. The W disappoints her.

The Extremist

Traits:
- **Positive:** Positive X's thrive on growth and discovery. With extraordinary energy and boundless curiosity, they expand through every experience. X's explore all possibilities, embracing adventure and forging friendships with openness and inclusion.
- **Negative:** Negative X's veer into extremes, prone to mood swings and exaggeration. They compartmentalize their emotions, keeping their deepest feelings hidden from others.

Associations:
- **Professions:** Chemist, Mathematician, Critic, Exhibitionist
- **Body Part:** Torso
- **Symbol:** Jumping Jack

Angel's View:
Angel perceives the X as a crossroads—some paths lead to soaring heights, while others plunge into dark depths.

The Yearner

Traits:
- **Positive:** Positive Y's embody youthful optimism and adaptability. They carefully weigh options, balancing perspectives to choose the most promising path. Once a decision is made, they remain steadfast in their commitment.
- **Negative:** Negative Y's hesitate, caught between choices. Their indecision leaves them in limbo, avoiding action and responsibility.

Associations:
- **Professions:** Coach, Judge, Therapist, Drifter
- **Body Part:** Pelvis
- **Symbol:** Tree

Angel's View:
Angel finds Y unreliable, its sturdy base masking deceptive branches that mislead and falter in critical moments.

The Zealot

Traits
- **Positive:** Positive Z's are energetic and determined in their pursuits, resilient in the face of disappointment, and capable of bouncing back quickly. They are focused problem-solvers who approach challenges with enthusiasm and

persistence, striving toward their goals even when success isn't immediate.

- **Negative:** Negative Z's, on the other hand, tend to meander aimlessly, moving through life in a zigzag path. They often struggle to regain control when they veer off course and usually recognize their missteps only after it is too late.

Associations:
- **Occupation:** Fisherman, Hunter, Politician, Football Player, Addict
- **Body Part:** Haunches
- **Symbol:** Fire Escape

Angel's Interpretation:

The Z represents life's zigzag journey, uncertain of its ultimate destination but always in motion.